TO THOSE WILLING TO DROWN

by

Mark Matthews

A Torch Lake Souls Novel

Wicked Run Press
"The wicked run when no one is chasing them"
Proverbs 28:1

To Those Willing to Drown is a work of fiction. Names, characters, corporations, institutions, organizations, events or locales in this novel are either the product of the author's imagination or, if real, used fictitiously. Any resemblance to actual persons (living or dead) is entirely coincidental.

For more information or media rights, contact: WickedRunPress@gmail.com

Cover Art by Ben Baldwin
Edited by Julie Hutchings

ISBN Digital: 978-1-7377021-1-5
ISBN Paperback: 978-1-7377021-3-9

Also from Wicked Run Press

GARDEN OF FIENDS
"What fertile ground for horror. Every story comes from a dark, personal place."
—*Josh Malerman, New York Times Best Selling Author of Bird Box*

LULLABIES FOR SUFFERING
"Chilling and thought-provoking"
—*The Library Journal (Starred Review)*

ORPHANS OF BLISS
"A powerhouse anthology"
—*Publishers Weekly*

Table of Contents

"And it's peaceful in the deep,
Cathedral where you cannot breathe,
No need to pray, no need to speak."

~*Never Let Me Go*, Florence + the Machine

<u>**INTRODUCTION**</u>

I SPENT 30 YEARS of my life vacationing at Torch Lake, the deepest inland lake in the state of Michigan. In a sense, this novel, despite its darkness, is a love story to the lake and the area. There is truly something magical about the cold, crisp waters. The lake is alive, the lake gives life, and it dazzles with a rainbow of blues every sunset. Torch was reportedly ranked as the third most beautiful lake in the world by *National Geographic*.

Much of what you will hear about Torch Lake lore in this novel is true, including the story of how it got its name, and the mysterious wooden cribs on the lake's bottom (give "Torch Lake Cribs" a Google).

Beyond my lived-experiences on the lake (thank you, Mom and Dad), I did hours of research into various elements of the book such as Native American history, facets of Hinduism and Civil War facts. I learned about the Mishipeshu, an Ojibwe water creature and true legend of Northern Michigan, though more often associated with Lake Superior. The Pishachi referenced in the novel is a Vampire-Like creature of Hindu mythology said to haunt cremation grounds. The names of civil war doctors mentioned, other than Lucas Lamia, are also true surgeons of the era.

While some elements are either historical fact or drawn from mythology, others are creative license. I found no evidence any society cremated the deceased over Torch Lake, but the story of Native Americans holding torches to the water to summon fish to the surface is well documented history.

I'm saddened to report that a few months after finishing this novel, my dad passed away after 84 years of a very full life. During the funeral home visitation, shortly before he was cremated, a family friend brought a jar of bona fide Torch Lake Water and placed this inside his casket. He was cremated with this jar full of the cold, blue water, and now the lake is forever part of his remains.

It only seems right. Life imitates fiction.

If you know the lake, you'll note that the location of Camp WaakWing in the novel is in the same location as a current well-known camp on Torch Lake, Camp Hayo-Went-Ha. Due to the geography of the lake and current development, this is the only area that made sense. Nothing about the camp is meant to depict the current YMCA camp in structure, in staff, in history, so please do not confuse the two.

That said, I did correspond with Camp Hayo-Went-Ha staff member Dave Foley, who is credited with telling campfire stories of the Torch Lake Monster. In his story, as in the song by staff camper Bob Thurston, he describes the monster with the lyrics: "One eye is brown, one eye is blue / His body covered all in icky green goo." As you will find in every lake and in every camp, there are stories told around the fire at night about mysterious things in the water and in the forest. In the case of Camp Hayo-Went-Ha, Foley used the legends of mysterious monsters, both within the lake and the surrounding woodlands, as reason Hayo-Went-Ha could afford to be lakeside in an area with property values so high.

Of course, just as mysterious as what lurks in the lake, is what lurks within the depths of our own heart. There are deep recesses of Torch lake and even deeper ones in our souls. This is my story of both.

PART ONE

CHAPTER ONE:
OF SURGEON LUCAS LAMIA, 100TH INFANTRY UNION ARMY

JUST AS MANY SOLDIERS HAD, I packed up my wounds and went north after the war. I aimed to distance myself from the horrors I'd seen, and leave the bloody battlefields behind.

What I found was a land of rolling green fields and majestic blue waters. God had clearly stretched the heavens over northern Michigan. The air was so fresh and beautiful, the town would soon be named *Bell-Aire* for the magic you inhaled in your lungs, where logging and farming and trade blossomed and soon the rails would follow.

But I brought the war with me.

To understand this, you must have stood as I have, witnessed the effect of shells, explosions, the incessant discharge of musketry, men falling dead, some without a groan, yielding up their life with their chest imploded. Others hurt in battle and covered in dirt, blackened by their own powder, cries of agony, a language understood as the prayer of a wounded soldier. These prayers go unanswered and weaken as their eyes grow dim.

You must have smelled the putrid scent of exposed wounds as I have, begging for an amputation, as if the very limb could speak. If you heard this you would know true horror. Aye, you may not believe me if I describe what I saw, all that I felt, during that awful conflict, caring for the wounded and bringing them back to life as a surgeon practicing in battle. I observed soldiers who were superhuman in their bravery, anointed by God, infused with His spirit. That was the only explanation for their courage, staring at Death's face with piercing gaze and piercing bayonets. If I ever felt my constitution fade, I remembered those men, and I'd fight on.

So I matched their intensity and waged my own battles to

comfort the dying and heal the wounded. Under intense heat, sweat and blood beading on my brow, soldier after soldier was placed on the scaffold and put under chloroform while surgeons performed the operation. Separating the inflicted body part so that the spirit could live on—an empty sleeve but a patriot's heart.

Enemies were everywhere, invisible invaders of smallpox, typhoid fever, yellow fever. All attacking the body, and so the cleansing and closing of the wound was critical to have any defense. I mastered the art of leaving a good flap of flesh above the amputation site, folded down to ensure a cushion of skin around the severed bone. It took the care of an artist to make a fine stump.

I carried with me the visions of my mistakes, born of hesitancy and caution, when urgency and action were required.

Once such man, George Alexander Hanna, who, feverish from malaria and the burden of a soldier's heart, fired (by accident, he insists) his own gun into his leg. The ball passed between tibia and fibula, severing both main arteries. We waited to amputate after I conferred with the revered Dr. Robert Liston. He urged my patience, so I ended my protests and agreed to delay. When we finally amputated the infected leg, it was too late. He died a day later, having endured the operation and many days of pain, when acting sooner may have saved his life. Dr. Liston and I changed our approach from that moment on and began to take pride in how quickly we severed a limb.

The question I did not share with any surgeon nor any man of God was this: *Did I also sever part of a man's soul by performing an amputation? If they die with their body disconnected, are souls also split forever, the way our country seemed split, North and South, Rebel and Yank?*

I thought of the limbs left on the battlefield, of the mothers who received bodies not fully complete. Fractured hearts, fractured souls, scattered pieces trying to find their match. I prayed that God would find the grace to unite these desecrated bodies in Heaven, for I'd seen too many torn asunder.

So if you stood where I stood, you would have traveled as I traveled. Far, far north, to flee these horrors, with my love Lilith by my side, grateful I wasn't one of the many parents who buried less than a full child.

We settled here not far from the *Lake of the Torches*, a name given to this remarkable body of water with an expanse so long surveyors could not yet measure. It was the savages, the heathens, who ruled this lake. You could see them from our hilltop at night, floating in their canoes, holding their flames to the water.

Those who were here before me speak of the bounty they summon with their flames, luring fish to the top to be speared for sustenance. But others whisper the flames are meant to work their sorcery in the dark of night. The flames summon demons, the flames burn their young. And the torches they hold are fueled by the oil of a witch.

#

With my inquisitive and curious mind, I preferred to make my own informed judgements on the local natives, so I traveled to the water one night for a better look. I moved silently through the lakeside foliage, crouching in the brush, spying on them in their canoes.

They worked in pairs, one with flame held to the water, the other with spears ready to stab. When the time came, they struck with a splash, then raised their spear out of the water with long trout flapping on the end. The fish got clubbed with one smack, ending their protest, falling dead into the canoe. One after another they pulled fish from the water, and I imagined myself coming here for my fill.

But then I heard a splash in the water, and saw a large body swimming near the surface. I held my breath, remained still, trying not to gasp out loud at this creature, at this *behemoth*, gliding slowly just below the surface. It seemed like a gigantic squid, or a sea dragon, or a monstrous eel, or all of these things at once. Sailors blown off course to uncharted oceans speak about such creatures, but their words fell short compared to this vision.

The heathens held their spears. They didn't feel threatened. They left this creature be. It was clear the behemoth was ancient and had been through many battles. I saw large wounds on its flesh as it slipped in and out of the water, sinister and seductive. The beast finally dove back into the lake for good, returning into the depths, leaving behind a deafening quiet.

This demon of the lake is their god, was all I could think, for the reverence they paid.

The fishing appeared over, the spears set aside, but one savage held up what at first seemed a doll. In the light of the flame, I saw it wasn't a doll, but a human child. Deceased. I could tell. Its limbs hung lifeless.

I watched with a mix of wonder and fear as this child was set upon a bed of twine and twigs inside an empty canoe. It was then set adrift, but not before the funeral pyre was set aflame with torches on all sides. I watched as the carcass of this child burned, along with the canoe, until the flesh and twine and canoe of ash fell into the depths.

This was their burial ritual, cremating their children on this lake. Or perhaps a sacrifice the dark devils demanded.

With the child's remains in the lake, the savages began to paddle away, and I realized I'd stayed there too long. The vessels were coming right towards me, so close I feared they could hear my heartbeat and smell my scent.

They floated so near I could see their flesh, their skin of leather, their muscles svelte, their eyes piercing. With my back hunched in the brush, my long black hair, my green eyes that sparkled like a feline in the dark, I may have been confused as one of them, but I did not take that risk. I rushed out from my spot, beyond the foliage, away from the lake, my senses electrified from terror.

I knew these natives could track like a lion, so I weaved my way through the brush, trying to lose my tail. I could still feel their presence no matter how far away I ran, heart pounding in my chest, lungs gasping for air. Farther and farther away from the lake, up a hill where I could hold an advantage, I finally turned to face them.

They had not given chase.

I was free.

Or at least I thought. Something from the lake had attached to my heart that night, the way a mollusk would to the hull of a ship. I did not return to visit the waters at dark anymore. I bathed in the lake during the daytime only, so refreshing I felt my pre-war vigor return. But at night, I stayed away from the natives and their flames.

Was it smart to build a home so close to the heathens?

I thought about abandoning this land, going somewhere safer, but I felt a calling, a voice beckoning me, confirming that my God was greater than these devils. I would make my home on this hilltop, and keep my faith that God would provide.

But men of faith are often misled. Godly men like myself who believe in the Lord are the Devil's favorite prey. I survived the Civil War, escaped to the north — but a more sinister battle awaited me.

Chapter Two:
Of Sharon Murphy at Camp WaakWing – Day One

CAMPFIRE FLAMES ROSE into the sky, glowing in the lakeside darkness. Logs that at first resisted fire were now burning bright, casting a circle of light against a starless sky. The water itself was quiet and calm, as if it, too, wanted to hear the campfire story.

Standing before them was camp director, Paxton Transou. He moved like a spiritual sorcerer, carrying a crooked stick as a magic staff while he circled the fire. The wind seemed at his command, smoke always drifting in the opposite direction. The glow of the flames turned his deep eye sockets into cavernous shadows.

Sharon sat on the bench, ten-year-old Dylan nestled into her side. He'd been clinging to her like a baby chimp to his mother since drop-off that morning. After Dylan scanned Sharon for safety, he became attached to her on the spot.

"He's quiet," Dylan's mother had explained, "but we don't say *shy*, we say *quiet*. And he likes the insides more than the outsides."

"Inside it is, then. Inside our camp, inside the lake, inside our group. He'll never be outside, always in, I promise."

"I like that," said his mom. "*He'll* like that. But if he needs me, call anytime. I can be here in a few hours. For anything."

With his mom a few hours away, Dylan's first campfire story began. Sharon sat on one side, veteran counselor Kai Jordan on the other.

"My friends," said Paxton, "some think it was named Torch Lake because of its shape. Well, we know differently. It was from the Anishinabek, the first humans, who lived on this lake for hundreds of years."

Paxton pointed the long, crooked tree branch he was holding towards the lake. Dylan and Sharon turned their heads, expecting to see something in the water — but all they saw was the brightness of the flames making the lake a dark, infinite shadow.

"The first humans knew this lake was alive with an abundance of riches within its waters. A lake so deep that creatures on the bottom never came to the surface. The only way to make them rise was to summon them with flames, same as I have summoned you all here with this firelight glow. The first humans rowed their canoes out at night, holding torches to the water. The lake creatures below couldn't resist being drawn to the light.

"I cannot tell you all that appeared, because some are so rare, we don't have names, but among the lake creatures were fifty-pound muskie, long, meaty whitefish, and tasty trout. The first humans speared the fish they needed and cooked them over fires, same way we cook our s'mores right here."

Paxton tapped his stick into the fire, three times — tap, tap, tap, sending sparks rising.

"When the first European adventurer, a Frenchman, stumbled upon this lake and saw the torches he dubbed it 'the lake of the torches,' or as the Ojibwe said, *'Waswaaganing,'* meaning 'Lake of Flames.'

"And when this French expedition began bathing in the shallows of this water, a liquid so rich with nutrients, so pure of essence, a color of blue only seen in the oceans of the Caribbean, the leader sent a message back to his king:

'We've found the magical waters. The rumors are true. The waters here give life. There is something godly in the lake, in the land, in the canals and waterways. There is an invigoration, a baptism in this lake of flames.'

"The Frenchman made camp, but as they fished at night, mimicking the first humans, they began disappearing into the water. One by one, something from the shadows snatched the fishermen into the lake. The group returned to the shore, one body less each night. And that body, or what was left of it, would wash ashore days later."

The audience was quiet, even the crickets seemed to pause. Dylan was holding his breath next to Sharon, both of them hearing this for the first time.

"Yes, there are creatures in this lake, my friends, some who may look a bit human, but are more of the lake than they are of the human race. They long to leave these waters, but cannot. If you catch a glimpse, consider yourself chosen.

"Not all are friendly, and not all were ever human. Some with fangs of a tiger, some with tentacles of a squid, one with jaws big enough to swallow this fire."

Paxton once again made a circle with his stick as if tracing an outline of the twenty-two campers. Each of them followed the circle with their eyes, their faces bathed in the orange glow of firelight.

Dylan's tremor betrayed his fear. Sharon glanced at Kai, and they moved in tighter, protecting Dylan on either side.

"There is one who is the queen of the lake creatures. Most believe she's a sea panther, with the head of a lion and a magnificent black mane. You'd swear she could roar if you see her. She's got a giant lizard body, flesh smooth and slippery as an eel, with antlers of an elk. Some say she's a *Bakunawa*. Others say *Makara*. Those who know her best, and are native to this land, know her as the *Mishipeshu*.

"Mishi spends most of her time gliding across the bottom, exploring the deep fissures and tunnels and caverns. Legend says she is the product of a sea witch who gathered dead parts from the bottom of the sea, put them together, and brought them to life in this lake. The witch gave Mishi tentacles to capture her prey, and great jaws to eat them in one bite. She even has powers to communicate. Now this sea witch watches over the lake as if it were her baby's very crib.

"Well, Mishi developed a taste for these humans, these French adventurers. Bewildered after losing so many men, the lead adventurer, Jean-Pierre Renault planned to abandon the lake and travel south instead. He wrote a final message to his king:

'These waters that give new life also take it. We've lost a score of good men, and buried what body parts we've found. The savages have learned how to live and hunt and raise children on this lake and whatever monstrosity swims inside does not hunt them back. Our efforts to match their industry have failed. We are abandoning this area in the morning.'

"But the message he wrote was never delivered, for on their last night, the remaining men, so happy to be leaving and having survived, began to celebrate. Singing, dancing, drinking whiskey, banging and yelling on the beach into the dark night.

"Well, Mishi doesn't take kindly to loud celebrations after dark, and my friends please believe me when I say she can swim into shallow water, look her enemy in the eye, and snatch them with long tentacles that reach from her side. When they spotted Mishi just off the shore, face to face, the Frenchmen mocked and jeered her, thinking themselves safe. Instead, all of them were snatched by their necks, pulled out to sea, screaming into the underwater void and eaten alive. Their belongings, their journal, the final message, were found many years later, not far from this spot."

Paxton stared into the fire as if translating the flames and burning embers. A log shifted just then, followed by a firework display of red sparks. Dylan clawed at Sharon's side. Like every child in this circle, he'd been hooked by this story. The lake nearby gave watch, as if waiting for the fire to die.

"So, please, my friends, do not venture into the lake at night. We will swim during the day in these sacred and pure waters. We respect the lake and we respect the creatures and we respect Mishi in all her shapes and forms. But we do *not* swim past the buoys, we do *not* swim in the dark. When it's bedtime, you must be quiet and not cause mischief. During the day, we will sing all day and wake the angels, but at night, we stay quiet and sleep. We shall not wake the devils. For we do not want to anger Mishi. Her reach is far. Stay in your cabins, stay in your sleep, unless...well...just please believe me."

Paxton bowed his head and started poking the fire with his stick, stabbing logs until sparks lifted up into the air, twisting in the wind, before burning to dust. Dylan was burrowing behind Sharon by then, peeking from behind her waist. He couldn't resist hearing the end of this fairy tale meant to scare them into good behavior.

Don't stay up all night – we don't want cranky children.

And don't sneak into the lake at night – we don't want to risk a drowning.

All of this told by counselor Paxton, or *Pax*, as she heard Kai call him. A man who seemed as old as his mythic Mishi.

"My friends," said Paxton, in his story conclusion voice, "your parents were given full disclosure. They're aware of what lives in this lake, and should you choose not to respect these rules, your parents agreed not to hold us responsible. Such is the waiver they have signed."

Dylan hid behind Sharon's shoulder after that closing bit, so she decided to undo some of the story's dark magic. She cupped her hands and whispered into his ear, '*your parents signed no such thing.*' Kai also reached over and put a hand on his shoulder.

Paxton stepped back from the campfire, as if contemplating a painting to see if it was done. He held the stick in the air, and this time, rather than poke the fire, he laid it at his feet. A painter satisfied with his canvas.

"Now go to your cabins and prepare for a week of adventure and song! Sleep well. Your dreams after breathing the Torch Lake air will be like none other."

Paxton spread his arms, a preacher dismissing his choir. Sharon tapped Dylan on the shoulder. The boy looked up at her, looked over at Kai, and then popped up to his feet to join all the other campers scattering off to their cabins, leaving the campfire behind. As Dylan walked away, each step a bit slower than the one before, he kept glancing back over his shoulder.

Was he expecting her to follow?

So cute with his little hiking boots, cargo shorts and blue sweatshirt, Sharon wanted him to be confident on his own. These moments at camp could change him. To be away from Mom, whose presence was his comfort, was like losing a limb, maybe two. Now, without her, he could learn to do things on his own.

But then Sharon realized it wasn't her he was turning to look at—it was the lake. Dylan was worried he was being followed, turning back every few strides, staring down the water, as if a sea panther named Mishi was waiting to snatch him with a tentacle. Each step he was falling farther behind the group of boys, barely looking forward at all but facing down the lake, as though if he took his eyes off it, the monster would take that chance to appear.

And just then Kai's instinct kicked in that he was missing part of his flock, and like a sheepdog herding, he walked back to scoop Dylan right up, pulling him up through the air to sit the boy on his shoulders.

Dylan towered above them all now, bouncing around on Kai's shoulders, and though she could no longer see his face, Sharon could feel his smile. Kai had him, and he was okay. Inside the camp. Nothing to fear.

#

The campers had cleared, and Sharon stayed with Paxton to help put out the fire. She separated the logs until they were flat on the ground. Paxton was in the water, just a dozen yards away, dipping a bucket into the lake.

"Most shark attacks happen in a foot of water, isn't that how it works?" Sharon said from the shore. "Your Mishi might be right next to your leg."

"Ah yes. But Mishi has a taste for newcomers. She's no doubt waiting for your next swim," he said, walking from lake to campfire with a bucket of water, looking himself like a swamp thing of sorts.

"I'm sure I'm safe," Sharon said. "I'm just doing that thing where you feel pressure to humor the boss with witty small talk."

He smirked, pouring water over the smoldering logs, targeting the embers. The logs hissed their last gasp, grey smoke coming up in big puffs.

"That kind of honesty will get you far around here. Kids will know if you're faking it."

But I'm not being honest, she thought, worried she couldn't keep her truths hidden from this campfire wizard.

With the fire out, Sharon could see across the lake. Cottage lights from two miles across the water seemed like stars of another galaxy. One seemed to be moving…not a cottage, but a small boat. A fishing boat, trolling up and down the nineteen miles north and south, perhaps.

"Mesmerizing, isn't it?" said Paxton, standing alongside. "Sometimes we stop somewhere and it latches onto us and we can't move on. It will latch onto you, and latch onto that boy Dylan who won't leave your side. He's the kind of kid who comes back years later to join our staff because of you, because of the lake. You'll be part of this place for life. If not, we've failed you."

Sharon wasn't sure if that was an invitation or a challenge. She'd let him believe she was going to stay in Michigan, but the truth was, stopping here was an accident. She planned to go to the upper peninsula for the summer, but after driving by Torch Lake and seeing the sun sparkle upon the magnificent blue water, something pulled her in. She rented a room for a week, then two, then read the camp WaakWing website and applied on a whim. Working for her had always meant travel, moving about the country with her grandmother, art fair to art fair. Her gramma's death couldn't stop this inertia, and Gramma had more art to sell. After fairs in Ann Arbor, then Traverse City, the plan was St. Ignace and Escanaba. But now they'd have to wait.

After three weeks of training, dress rehearsal was over. She now had kids to take care of.

She said goodnight to Paxton, quietly, of course, for they were lakeside at night and Mishi did not take kindly to loud noises.

Back to her cabin, and her first night with her kids. Fortunately most of them were veterans of this camp, so they knew the routine. They competed to tell her stories of what happens at WaakWing Camp. The 8 a.m. Polar Bear Club. Capture the flag. The cook, Sandy, and how her buttered toast is so perfect. They whispered to each other about Mishi and the other lake creatures, '*Do you believe?*'

The volume and frequency faded over time. Sharon curled up, snug under her own covers. The walls of the cabin were screens without the lining zipped up, and cooler air was coming in off the lake. Air so fresh and beautiful, and her body tucked away in the sleeping bag. The nighttime orchestra of crickets chirping a soft lullaby. Traveling with her grandmother, she'd camped in cars, Walmart parking lots, rest areas—few campsites as pleasant as this.

Sleep soon took her, and a dream swept in. Insects buzzed at her cheek, a mosquito ready to land on her flesh and drink fresh blood. The little flying vampire whispered in her ear, *Psstt...Sharon. Pssst. You awake?*

Her eyes snapped open. It took a bit to remember where she was.

There was a shadow of a man standing just outside her cabin, looking at her for who knows how long through the screen. Her internal alarms rang out and she got up ready to fight.

"Sharon, Sorry. Sorry. It's me."

It was Kai.

"Is Dylan with you?" he asked, and she felt such panic, like she lost him.

"Is Dylan with you?" he asked again.

She looked about her bed, patting the places around her, as if expecting to find a boy who crawled into his parents' bed after a bad dream.

"No. No he's not here. What's going on?"

"I lost him. Dylan's gone."

CHAPTER THREE
OF LUCAS LAMIA, SETTLING IN NORTHERN MICHIGAN

YOU CAN LEAVE the battlefield, but stay stuck in the war.

Gone were the screams in the air, the scent of blood dripping off each sound, the agony of death. But a war remained inside my skull, my thoughts, my brain, constantly reminding me that this world is such a hurtful place.

I had hoped this land would bring peace, that I could sign a treaty with the world and forget the horrors I'd seen. The place was so beautiful, I could smell its purity, feel it on my flesh, and even hear it speak to me in words and whispers. I did not share with my wife that I heard these voices, for such celestial messages lose meaning when conveyed with human language.

The land we found had briefly been claimed but then abandoned, and had already been cleared. We built our home with the help of a proud, pious community of post-war settlers. It was a beautiful hilltop, a quarter mile from Torch Lake and in between two small towns, Bellaire the closest at just a quarter's day walk.

The land even included a working well. The marksmanship that made this well was not of a civilized land. If built by the heathens, whose influence was shrinking in Northern Michigan, then I owed them more respect before their kind was vanquished from here forever. The stone mason had perfectly shaped the stones to fit the curvature of the well shaft, truly a jeweler's work fit for royalty, for each stone seemed precious, each one seemed alive, cells of the larger being. It certainly was part of that land more than I had yet become. I thanked the Lord for the well which brought forth water and wisdom. An ancient wisdom inside each rock that seemed to infiltrate my own desire for beauty.

As I slept, I felt the stones outside our home shifting in their spots. Rearranging. Then put together in different shapes, refitting as I dreamed.

In the morning, as the golden light shined just above the eastern horizon, I often walked the circle around the well, one finger lightly tracing its outline. The feeling was sensual, even erotic (though I'd confess that to nobody). Standing in its presence was calming, as if a harp was being strummed somewhere deep in the earth.

So giving, so benevolent, as was the land itself.

But when the land bit back to those forging their home here, it was I, the doctor, who provided aid. For more than once I came upon loggers whose bones were crushed from an accident, who certainly would not have healed. Not have *lived*. One arm dangling from their shoulder, just a limp piece of flesh with shattered pieces inside. Left untreated, it would turn black from infection and slowly kill its host if I didn't lob it off.

The amputation was most successful if I didn't delay.

And more loggers meant more limbs. They traveled here by the score to make their fortune, and if the mammoth stocks of wood crushed a limb, I used the weight of my body and a sharp edge against bone to take off the damage and let them live on.

Do not believe those who allege I was too fast to amputate, who say I only knew one course of treatment and would not heed patience or calls for delay, for I know the risk of hesitancy. It's a terrible mistake to fall prey to false sympathies if the patients begged for another way. My stumps became a work of art.

And I did not leave them in pain, for the morphine I offered was the hidden grace of how I delivered God's gifts.

The new science of injecting morphine by syringe into the pain was not just for soldiers. My medicinal supply was becoming well known. I drew on my studies with Doctor Alexander Wood, who had perfected the art of medicine straight into human flesh and veins. He explained that "a more direct application of the narcotic to the affected nerve, or to its immediate neighborhood, would be attended with corresponding advantage — like a bee sting."

They came for the aid of my needle's *bee sting*. These syringes I used improved with each sunrise it seemed, and a critical weapon of war against pain. I soon learned the morphine in a syringe can relieve absolutely anything, though cure nothing.

Farming became a smaller part of our world. Summoning the sick to offer healing and grace was our primary purpose. One can miss hearing the screams, one can miss the battlefield, so I continued with my new war. There's a heightened sense of life surrounded by death, so I invited those who had the pain to my quarters, this glorious house on the hill, near the well, by the lake, where my family grew roots.

I sought the comfort of the morphine needle myself at times, seeking the relief only a bee sting could offer, my wife looking on as if studying the art of medicine herself.

Indeed, it was my sweet wife who got me through the horrors of the war between North and South. I could finally be by her side and lay with her as God intended rather than just sending letters as we did during the war, the bloody fingerprint stains on the sheet speaking more than the very words.

Only such northern waters could cleanse the stain of blood, and only such waters could deliver us life.

We conceived during a morning of amorous congress in the Torch Lake waters, I am sure of it, for the gift sparked a cry of joy in my heart unlike any other. The heavens that God pulled over that northern land gifted us a child.

We named him Benjamin, and just moments after he breathed air on his own, sitting next to our fire, the nearby community heard of the news and brought gifts. Like wisemen to their newborn king, they delivered food and supplies. Small sweaters, socks, and trousers for his first years.

Lilith nursed the infant, and held that child so close, no less attached to her at one year old than when he was inside her womb, so that by the time she first set him down onto the earth he was already at the age to walk away. He never ventured far. Even on her walks at all hours, Benjamin was beside her.

Lilith was an amazing specimen, with a height that matched my own and the iron constitution of any soldier. Her long brown hair at times wrapped in tails, other times set free like a bustle of snakes across her back. She greeted new patients with the warmth of an angel, and they often stayed in our extra bed when too fragile to travel or if the weather was harsh.

And when my boy began to talk, not long after he said *Daddy*, he began to ask about these visits: "Will the patient be okay? Is the patient going to live?"

"Aye, they will." God's grace let me reply in the affirmative quite often, but not always, for some died in that home and had to be carried out to family, rather than walk out on their own.

But more lived than died. The land was bountiful. The rails came. The well filled our life with water and wisdom, the ornamental stones clearly made with an ancient love that fit this sacred land.

We lived through the scorching summers of boiling heat, where you could hear the temperature rise from the greenery, and the winters, when snow piled to my waist, and we learned to hibernate nearly as deep as the bears who inhabited those woods.

We gazed at the lake of the torches from the perch on the hill, the magnificent colors that shined from its surface during sunsets, the flames of savages on boats that dotted its darkness at night. We watched rain storms coming off the lake, clouds gathering like an army in the heavens ready to battle, fresh and mystic waters replenished the lake with the Lord's blessing.

God indeed spread heaven over this northern land, but every door on every home is an invitation for a stranger to knock, and so it was with ours. Beware of being inhospitable to strangers, for they could be angels in disguise. Or they may just as well be devils. I would soon learn such a lesson when I heard the stranger outside my window, and saw his dark shadow by our precious well.

CHAPTER FOUR:
OF SHARON MURPHY, FIRST NIGHT AT CAMP WAAKWING

"I LOST HIM, Dylan's gone."

Gone?

Kai was a dark shadow looming outside Sharon's screen window, his words a shrieking fire alarm making her senses burn.

The drop-off scene with Dylan's mom flashed across her mind, when Dylan was so scared, his mom so anxious. She promised to care for him. She promised his *safety*.

Sharon kicked out of her sleeping bag and rushed outside, joining Kai outside her cabin.

"Never even heard him leave the cabin," Kai whispered with urgency. "I just woke up and something felt wrong. Sure enough, I checked his bed and he was gone. I checked the bathroom, and nope, not there. Thought he might have come to find you. Sorry to wake you up."

"I'm glad you did."

"We have to check the lake first. That scares me most. Either that, or across Torch Lake Drive, where the woods are much deeper."

Kai knew this place. He'd been a camp counselor for years. She agreed with his instinct. The water held the most potential danger.

But that's why Paxton scared them away.

Just thirty yards to the small beach, they approached at a sprint. The dock, the benches, the now ashy campfire, barely visible under the stars and a crescent moon. Sharon looked into the lake, scanning for evidence of a young boy fighting to stay on the surface. Flailing, gurgles, splashing, but there was nothing, just tiny dark laps of water coming to shore, then receding.

This means he's safe, right?

Or he's already gone under.

Kai tapped Sharon on the shoulder, interrupting her dark conclusion, and pointed to a shadow hunched over in a ball.

Is that him?

They rushed over and found the boy curled up, legs pulled to his chest, arms hugging them, facing the lake. He barely noticed the adults, just staring into the water. Kai sat on one side of him, Sharon on the other.

"Dylan, we were terrified. What's going on, why are you here?"

They waited patiently. This seemed an important moment, and any wrong move could topple it over. Dylan started rocking before answering.

"My heart was beating so scared, I wondered if Mishi could hear it and might snatch me with her tentacles. I thought about those Frenchmen. They never went home again. What if I never go home from here?"

"Dylan, you will not only go home from here, but you'll be a better person," Sharon answered, probably faster than she should have and before Kai had a chance. "That's what we do here. Fun and friends. You *will* go home from here, I promise. Every single person goes home from here. I know this new place can be scary. I'd be a little scared too, so next time, please come to talk to us first. We need you to follow some rules, or talk to us, okay? Talk to us about what you're feeling."

Dylan looked up at Sharon, then Kai. His eyes pleading: *Can I trust you?*

"What I'm feeling is if the monster comes out of the water and I can see her coming at me, at least I'll know. I can face her. If I'm asleep, I won't know to run. I want to see what I'm scared of, because then it's less scary."

"Dylan, there are a few things Mr. Paxton didn't tell you," Kai said, leaning back as if he had a lot to say, so better get comfy. "This camp was built on the safest area of the lake, a sanctuary. Ask anybody. There's something in the lake, almost like a mermaid, who lives not far off this patch. She speaks to the lake creatures, she watches over the kids here, so please do not fear, for there is a goddess in the seaweed. I know, I've seen her, talked to her. She won't let you get hurt."

Dylan kept his thousand-yard stare at the lake, as if waiting for it to confirm it was okay to look away. *Did he believe the story?* At that hour of the night, the way the air tasted, stars out, the lake listening before us, everything was possible. Dylan stood up, brushed some grass off his pajamas, and seemed ready to go.

They walked back to his cabin in silence. Dylan hesitated before walking through the open cabin door.

"Can someone stay here, like stand by the door? Just in case it followed us?"

"We'll both wait here," Sharon answered.

Dylan slipped into the cabin, burrowed into the sleeping bag, a little larva in his cocoon, and Sharon and Kai stood guard outside.

Like gargoyles they protected the entrance, making good on their promise, until the silence felt awkward. Sharon hated silence, so she did that thing she does where she'd ask a question she already knew the answer to, hoping she'd get to a fuller truth.

"So you really live here? Must be nice."

Must be nice? That sounded snotty, she thought.

"Yep, fell into it, really. My grandparents bought a house just south of Dockside. My family tends to die young, it seems, so when you're the last heir, it's part of the inheritance."

"I inherited that Jeep Cherokee and a large inventory of hand-crafted jewelry when my gramma died," Sharon said, her head motioning towards the road where her car was parked, even though it was out of sight. The night was a darker shade with no city lights, but the clouds had cleared and the stars burned bright and abundant. Standing outside the cabin door, they were shadows to each other. The brightest light one single bulb from the latrine twenty yards away.

"My gramma was basically my family. She was my mom, my queen, my guide."

"Sounds like my Paxton. He's my family now."

"Good choice," Sharon said. "I like talking with him. Drop some Paxton lore."

"Oh, the lore. A mysterious man. Even after that scary story about the lake, he'll be up at sunrise going for a swim. You've seen him in the morning, I'm sure. He'll share his Paxton-isms with you soon."

"There are Paxton-isms?"

"Yes, 'Be like water' he tells me. 'Fluid, soft, and yielding. To yield is to also win the fight, like water to rock. Be patient, flow to where the gaps are, and nothing can defeat you.'"

"The Tao of Pax," Sharon said.

"And I'm sure there were Gramma-Murphy-isms."

"Oh yes."

"Let's hear."

"First to last, or last to first?"

"First you remember."

It was so easy to share this in the dark with a face she could barely see, with whispers that could hardly be heard. She realized every bit she put out there was like an anchor that would chain her to this place. *Do I want that?*

"'Your parts are damaged — good for a lifeboat, not good for life,' was one she repeated to me quite often. Not sure if it was the stroke talking, because half her face was paralyzed and droopy and she muttered in a language only I could grasp. But for her last years, she said it often. Either her way of cursing me or thanking me for saving her. I was just thirteen years old and she stroked out on me on the road. I had to get her to safety, driving her car with my arms and legs too short. 'Damaged parts. Good for a lifeboat, not good for life.'"

"But good in a lifeboat *is* good at life," said Kai.

That was fire, that was brilliant, Sharon thought, and as if in agreement, the crickets chirped their approval, the stars glittered with more brilliance. If Sharon could respond back to Gramma, that's what she would say. *Good in a lifeboat is good at life. Doesn't matter my damaged parts.*

"You've traveled all over then?" Kai asked.

"'*Go where your art goes,*' another Gramma-ism. That one I love, and it explains why you stayed by Torch Lake. This is your art. This lake speaks to you, *sings* to you. You can feel it breathe, hear its music. And *that* is what I *really* meant when I said *must be nice.*" That seemed a good way to end her night.

"I think Dylan's good now," she said.

"Yep. No monsters invited inside on this night."

Sharon returned to her cabin, full faith that Kai wouldn't let any monsters in.

She was falling in love with Kai right then, the man who yielded like water when she was rigid, the man she spent her first night at camp acting as a surrogate co-parent, standing guard over this brave child who would look fears in the face.

That wouldn't be the last time Sharon and Kai would be faced with monsters. The monsters kept coming, and coming, and Sharon would soon have to keep another truth hidden:

She was the one who invited them in.

Chapter Five:
Of Doctor Lucas Lamia and the Stranger Outside his Door

THOUGH IT WAS NIGHT, I felt a shadow over the house. I heard movement outside my doors. I felt the invasion. All of this before I saw the figure outside.

I found the stranger beside the well, huddled against its stones, shivering as if trying to chisel them free. It was autumn, the temperature at night dropping, and it was clear he'd been out in the elements for much of the night. The color of his skin was changing to the shades of hypothermia.

"You must help. Must help us. Must help us, please."

His body shook, his words shook. Beyond the malady of his body, I feared he had madness of the brain that no medicine could reach. I could hear it in his voice, the sound of a soldier who had seen too much and ventured to a hell where angels feared to tread.

"You must help us."

I could not see in the dark if he was human or savage. His flesh so dirty and worn, it would not betray deeper truths, especially with the poor light and his ragged clothes. I reached down, slowly, making it clear I was not a threat. He allowed me to place a finger on his neck, right at the jugular. Blood was racing rapidly through his veins, and his flesh seemed to change from ice to fire back to ice again.

I helped him to his feet, and brought him inside. What else was I to do?

"You must help us."

"Will you heal him, Daddy?" Benjamin asked. "Will the patient survive?"

He was not a patient yet, but with my son bearing witness, he had to be.

Soon after, his clothes were drying in front of the fire and in their place he wore my clothes—my trousers, my shirt, and lay in our extra bed.

I asked little of him, for I knew any answers given in his shock would be unclear, so waited until the heat from the fire penetrated his cold flesh.

He lay in bed, eyes darting about the room, head spinning side to side, as if he feared being attacked from the flank. Rather than being comforted by the warmth, his shivering continued, his face changing colors as we watched. Something inside him was boiling, pressuring him to ask questions:

"Does she talk to you? Can you hear her? Is she talking? But of course she's talking, but can you *hear*? Do you listen? Ask her, she'll tell you. I owe but I can't pay. I can't pay."

I had no answers, certain he was addressing someone else, but then he looked at me straight in the eye. "You and me are the same, you see, I'm just like you," he assured me, leaning forward such that I feared he may need to be forced back to bed. "I'm of moral character. I persuade men to forsake evil and embrace truth. But she's slippery. She's *slippery*. She slips."

He stopped talking. His movements slowed. The room seemed to change colors as he fell to sleep and his dreams were exhaled into the air. The confusion in his soul filled the room like rotten incense.

I felt a duty — I always feel a duty — to help him. I'm just a vessel, I let the healing come through me, giving what I could. I used the herbs and plants I'd gathered, fungi from tree stumps where the sun could not penetrate, mushrooms that preferred the moon. They would help ward off this deep, dark sickness that was killing him.

"Can you heal the sick patient? Can you make him better?" Benjamin asked.

I had no answer, and I could smell death approaching. It slowly fills up a body, the scent at first far away, but then seeps out one's pores when it's close at hand.

Was this the smallpox? The yellow fever? The typhoon fever? This seemed a mix of them all, his body both shivering from chills and hot from fever. At times, he stopped flopping about and remained quiet and still. I was certain the Lord had taken him at these moments, but after a long pause he groaned again and thrashed on, a fish's last moments on land. The still periods got longer, the thrashing more desperate, and the lucid moments seemingly gone. Every sane thought was burned alive by his fever.

"I don't think I can save this one," I answered my son Benjamin, "but I can make him rest easy."

I was going to give him morphine, enough to make his last

moments more tolerable. "I don't think I can save this one," I repeated as I prepared the syringe, ready to bee sting his vein.

And as if the soul of the man heard me and wasn't ready to surrender to this war, his eyes popped open, and he spoke.

"Please. Ask it. Ask it for help. She'll answer you. Please."

His voice was faint, so I put my ear up to his mouth. I felt his hot steaming breath in my ear as he spoke.

"Ask the Well for help. Ask the WELL for help."

I will not ask the Well, I thought, or said out loud, and suddenly wondered if I would ever be able to wear the clothes of mine I'd let him borrow again, since they were full of such death and madness.

"Your God, your Jesus. You pray to them for help. Ask the WELL just the same."

I've heard men mutter words of epiphany under their last breath, messages from the other world. Stonewall Jackson himself reported a vision of traversing to Heaven with his last words: "Let us cross over the river and rest under the shade of the trees."

Something in me felt a truth in these words, pleading with me to ask the Well.

I walked out the front door then, Benjamin and Lilith with no awareness of what the man had asked. Perhaps they didn't hear. Perhaps only I could. The moon was on its way to be full—not tonight, tomorrow or the next, but the glow gave a blue-ish hue to the sky. The air was chilly and brisk, but refreshing. The insects were quiet as if they stopped whatever chorus they were singing when I interrupted.

I walked to the Well, each rock glowing in the blue. Dazzling, diamonds sparkling. I got on my knees beside the stones, fearful a passing villager might witness my acts. I'd certainly be called a witch, and was that not true?

No, it was not true. This was a Godly moment.

I filled my heart with humility, and softly asked for help. "Please, help me save this man. Help me save this man." I paused a moment, same as I do when praying to the Lord, silent reflection, not disturbing the air.

Then I heard a voice.

"You must return them."

I spun, looking all around me, searching for the source of the voice, and was not done looking when the voice of the mystical woman spoke again.

"You must return them to the Well. Squeeze them out, bring back the blood."

I must have gone feverish, devilish fevers, same as my patient, because I soon believed this was the voice of an angel, or of Mary herself. Somehow within the depth of this Well, a message from God, was whispering to me as if from a burning bush…

"You will do this. Return them and squeeze the blood from the leeches back into the Well. Squeeze them out, bring back the blood."

"I will do this," I muttered under my breath, and then repeated it. "I will do this. And then I will return and squeeze them into the Well." I was mesmerized into obedience and paid little heed to what I was promising.

I could hear them, I swear I could, when the leeches began marching towards the lip of the Well, climbing up the walls, the tiny noises only heard by human ears because they gathered by the score, because the entire Well was surrounded. I remember how the air tasted, so fresh at that moment, so full of promise.

I knew what the Well was suggesting. I was no stranger to bloodletting. I had used it often, and seen the evil sucked into these creatures who have an appetite for it. I had heard stories of Confederate surgeon Dr. Zacharias and how an army of maggots can suck the gangrene out of a limb and bring the seemingly dead back to life.

I plucked the leeches safely from the walls of the Well, gathered them together, and transported them to the patient's bedside. After I applied them, one at a time, to his temples, neck, forehead—a dozen hungry leeches placed at the source of his distress—it was clear they brought instant relief. The shade of his skin changed color as the sickness faded. His breath grew regular, and his sleep grew deeper. As I joined Lilith in bed, I could hear the leeches slurp, growing larger, sucking the disease from this man's body.

This bloodletting by dark magic continued for the next three days.

I gathered the leeches in the dark of night, when the moist ones clung to the sides of the Well, moving up the slick rocks as if summoned by the moon. I plucked them off in the cover of darkness.

A ritual that should not be done in the light of day.

The stench in our modest shelter made me wince. They were sucking some dark evil, some exotic disease, from his veins. They had a thirst, a hunger, and they grew fat, sucking harder the more that they consumed with an appetite that could not be quenched.

"You've taken a turn," Lilith said to me. "You need to stop this." She cautioned me with vague warnings that I swatted away like a horse's tail to a fly.

"Can you heal the sick patient, Daddy?" Benjamin kept asking. "Will the patient live?"

"Yes," I could finally answer. "I can heal him."

And I did, because when I woke the next morning just before sunrise, I found him standing over Benjamin's bed, looking over him for who knows how long. Gone was the stench of sickness. I waited to make sure it was not a dream, and soon enough, he turned to face me. His eyes locked on mine for just a moment, and then he dashed out the front door, fleeing as if a thief, but his hands empty. Nothing was stolen except my clothes on his back. He left dressed as me.

I went to the door to watch him off, and was shocked at what I saw.

Am I hallucinating this vision in the predawn darkness?

For the man didn't make it to the road with his new health as I expected. Instead, he was dragged, taken, by a long, giant arm, like the tentacle of a squid, that had whipped out of the Well and wrapped around his foot, the way some ocean behemoth of the deep might. He barely had time to scream before he was dragged into the Well, clawing and scratching at the earth.

I'd heard stories of ships being wrapped in the embrace of such creatures and pulled under the sea, and I knew of the whale that swallowed Jonah. I believed in both. But I had little faith in what I saw just outside my door.

But the Devil plays tricks, and shadows have backstories.

I rushed over to see, and again heard the voice I mistook as the Virgin Mary, but I realized it was not, but was some demon goddess who spoke to me.

"You did not squeeze them out. You did not return the blood. I have it all now."

I felt myself grow dizzy, the earth rotating in contrary fashion, the sun was about to rise on a day that I wish I could stop.

What is happening? We need to leave. This is witchery, there are devils afoot. Pack up and go. That was it. Leave town.

The voice of the Well spoke to me again.

"You did not squeeze them out as you promised. You did not return the blood. I have it all now."

My heart was beating too loud to think straight. With one thought, I imagined gathering the discarded leeches and dropping them down the Well, paying penance for my broken promise. The next moment I thought of destroying this Well, smashing it to pieces, or better, filling it with dirt to the rim, packing it solid, silencing the voice.

No, I may need it. I may still need the Well.

I returned to where my son slept, eager to be back with those I loved, looking for safety and sanity. Instead, I found more madness.

My son was in bed, spinning about as if internal devils were wrestling in his soul. His skin was radiating heat like a small fire, and his skin just as red, his flesh trembling and sweaty. He had a foul stench, an odor of sickness, even though the stranger was long out the door and taken into the depths of the Well.

The man had passed on his disease to my child. My Benjamin was sick.

My son! Now my son has the sickness. Why has God cursed me so? What more can be demanded of me?

CHAPTER SIX:
OF KAI JORDAN, DAY TWO OF SUMMER CAMP AT WAAKWING

KAI STOOD TALL on the swim raft as nine-year-old Tasha announced her cannonball with a scream mid-air. She kerplunked into the lake, splashing water onto Kai's shoulders. The drops landed with a chill but the hot sun soon sizzled it right off.

A slight breeze from the north blew the raft south, stretching the chain link anchored to the bottom with a cinder block. The bottom was ten feet under, but the water clear enough to see straight down, the light slightly fractured. The bottom was rippled with sand, a few rocks, and just a trace of seaweed to hide a few crayfish.

In the shallows of this lake, the water was an aqua blue, but the shade grew darker by degrees towards the deep middle, moving from turquoise, azure, to navy blue at the center. In the distance, a speed boat was pulling tubers, water spraying, the boat spinning. The tube bounced in the air and the kids went careening off. The boat stopped and circled back to collect the children who waited, bobbing up and down in the water.

Boats didn't get too close to that part of the lake, and if they did, a buoy floating fifty yards out warned them this was a swimming area.

There were fewer cottages near those campgrounds, a quarter mile either way was undeveloped, though the word *cottage* didn't fit anymore. Nearly every cottage on the east shore had given way to million-dollar homes. Sprawling mansions that made boaters' eyes pop out with envy. Kai's place was of the smallest one left in this area. He had inherited a true lake house, and working as a counselor in the summer, plowing snow in the winter, paid the property tax.

It was the first full day of the camp, and the campers had been split up. Half hiking, half swimming, then reversing it after lunch. Kai was glad to be teamed with Sharon's group. She brought a complexity to this camp, carrying with her traces of faraway states; Montana, North Dakota, Oregon. An air of mystery, and with such kindness. She gave such full attention to everyone she spoke to, like she couldn't possibly have that much for everyone, but she did, and when it was on you, you felt the light of heaven shining down.

She let him inside her world last night—for a bit, at least. To be let inside and allowed to stay would seem a gift, but he was certain he'd have to pass a series of tests first. He had to earn it. Same as every kid on the raft had to pass a swim test that morning with a counselor standing guard.

"Dylan seems completely fine this morning. Not scared, not worried. Well played last night," Sharon said to him.

"Yes," he answered. "Losing a kid on the first night takes special skills."

"No, the way you took the campfire story farther. Dylan wouldn't have believed you if you just said the Mishi story was a lie, but that whole part about the sanctuary and the mermaid… Stories have power. Art has power. The truths in the lie."

Dylan certainly was happy that morning, swimming close to the raft, never far, climbing up the ladder and then jumping off. Sitting on the edge and splashing his feet with enthusiasm. He didn't say much, but as he sat on the raft his lips were moving, as if talking to his private self.

"Those are no lies," Kai said. "That part of the story is true — this part of the lake was considered a paradise, a heaven underwater. The mermaid stuff, well, that position is open. In fact, I think you were hired to fill that role."

"Right, who wants to be the catcher in the rye, when you can be a mermaid in the weeds, lifting kids off the bottom?"

"I get the reference, I do," said Kai, "but you're no phony. That's why Paxton hired you."

Sharon already had the allure of a mermaid, like she was part of nature, part of the sea, and could seduce or slaughter any sailor as needed. Impossible to share how beautiful and mysterious the waters could be, but Sharon was starting to witness for herself. She was slowly immersing herself into this lake life.

Kai didn't want to share the things he's seen from the shore, always in the corner of his eye, but when he turned to look, that *thing* was gone. Or the shadows he'd seen deep in the lake, moving against the current. Or the feeling during camp that something was in the water. *'The Master doesn't worry about such things,'* Paxton would say, quoting the Tao, usually with a tinge of sarcasm. *'The Master just observes. She knows nothing can hurt water, so be like water and flow like the water.'*

A low-toned bell went off from the shore and got everyone's

attention.

"Five minutes!" Kai announced, and they'd have to go in soon. Nine-year-old Tasha looked up at him, troubled by something, water dripping from her long hair.

"We didn't race," she said. "We need to race. A race!"

"A race, a race!" the kids all mimicked, as if it was a code word for something bigger than that, and a delay tactic. *We don't want to go in just yet.*

Kai hesitated, teasing as if he were deciding, knowing he was going to agree.

"We race from here to the buoy and back," Kai explained to Sharon, "three of yours against three of mine. Camp counselors are always the anchor. Loser serves lunch, winner eats first."

"Why just four and not the whole group?" Sharon asked.

"Like the Olympics," Tasha interrupted.

Sharon picked Tasha and two others, and they lined up in front of her, unable to stand still, bobbing up and down on their tippy toes, the rest of the group behind ready to watch and cheer.

Kai tapped Dylan, but Dylan bowed his head to decline and looked away, out into the lake. He kept mumbling, his lips moving in near silence, and then finally spoke louder, "I'll be the alternate."

"Well, the alternate is the one who goes next time, so please, watch closely," Sharon said. *Keep those not involved in an activity engaged* – something counselors always aim to do. Some were born counselors, and Sharon was one of them.

Four swimmers lined up on each side. "On your mark, get set, Go!" Kai shouted, and the first swimmers dove in. One clearly left too early, but who cares, this was fun.

The race had started, Sharon and Kai shouting cheers to the first swimmer. Their strokes were full of vigor, because who wants to let their team down? Who wants the public shame? And everyone was excited, this little sanctuary on fire with the joy and cheers of kids swimming the fifteen yards and back. The white plastic buoy bobbed up and down in the water after being tagged.

The first swimmer returned, touched the raft, and the next swimmer dove in. "Let's go!" yelled Sharon with a *whoop whoop.*

Kai mocked her. "You're gonna need that lead."

Sharon cheered each swimmer when they arrived, fumbling, climbing onto the raft, hair dripping and chest heaving for air. She took them by the hand, held it in the air to an imaginary audience watching the event, like a championship boxer who just won their heavyweight fight.

Kai's turn to dive in, his team with a slight lead, the girls' team just moments behind. He swam like he was drowning—not very skilled at this. You'd think it was Sharon, not him, who spent their life on a lake. When he tilted his head for air, it felt like he was faking that he knew how to swim.

Faking this, faking that, faking everything. *I am one big fake.*

But swimming in this lake with Sharon by his side, he felt so alive and the sun was shining and the lake was happy for him to be inside it. *Just be like water and flow like water.*

Sharon caught him and they both tapped the buoy at the same time, her hand landing on top of his. They paused, their eyes meeting, the kids cheering so loud and her face with a smile she couldn't hide. They had the same length to go, but she was better at swimming. He knew it, she knew it, but while swimming back, she waited for him.

She wants to be by my side, that's why, he convinced himself, his grin nearly letting the lake water rush into his mouth, bubbles coming from his lips, breathing hard. At the last minute she pulled away and swam like a submarine missile back to the raft, and she was already up on top and celebrating victory when Kai pulled himself onto the raft. He couldn't help but admire her strength.

His mermaid already had a swimmer's body, toned muscles, and with an elfin look that spoke of such mysteries. Soon, he'd be ashore, serving her group a lunch of grilled cheese, melty American, bread lightly browned and sizzled with butter.

But first, head count before they went in.

12, plus the counselors, right?

Nope, just 11

Wait, recount

Yep, just 11!

Just 11?

Wait, where's Dylan?

He did a double-take. *Count must be off, he must be sitting on the edge, last place we saw him.*

Nope, no Dylan.

It's happening. Again.

But don't worry, we'll find him super quick, again.

"Who saw him?"

Nobody answered, everybody quiet, so they both bent down to each camper's face, one at a time, Sharon asking each girl, Kai asking each boy. "Did you see Dylan jump off the raft?"

Nobody did.

Don't worry. This will get fixed again soon.

This was different. They were on the lake, not on land. On water.

Oh my God.

Looking at the shoreline, was he there? Just empty benches around the campfire, the sailboat on the dock slightly swaying. Cabins showed no sign of life. Nobody there.

Kai walked along the sides of the raft, peering down at the lake bottom. Sharon doing the same.

We were having fun, we weren't paying attention.

They all agreed, last time they saw him, Dylan was sitting on the edge, kicking his feet, talking to himself.

Sharon was the first to dive in, head first, nearly to the bottom in an instant. He could see her in reflective waves on the bottom. Back arched, legs kicking to keep her submerged, hands scouring the sand, her head glancing left and right.

Kai stood on the raft, heart pumping with fear. He could see the bottom fairly clearly, like a mirage with details wavy, but if Dylan was down there, they would be able to see him. Right?

If a body was down there, they would be able to see.

If a body was down there…

The current would push a body from northwest to southeast, the wind driving it towards shore.

And nobody saw him, nobody. The poor boy, the invisible boy.

No, Mishi didn't get him. But that story. The lies we tell our kids.

Kai kept looking to shore, that was the only acceptable option, that Dylan had swam in. It was easy to swim in, light waves pushing you, nearly body surfing, and it certainly happened while they were racing.

But he saw nobody. Nothing on the shore. Just the rocks in a circle round the campfire pit, burnt-out logs from the fire the night before.

Kai again asked each child:

'Did you see him? What was he doing last? Was he in the water? Did you see him during the race?'

Now Michael...
Now Drew...
Now Tasha...
Now Chloe...
Nobody could answer.

Sharon had been up and down twice, gasping for air, dutifully resubmerging. Everybody was breathing so hard, the lake itself breathing so hard.

Kai ordered each child not to move, to stay in the center of the raft, and then he started to dive with her, his brain whispering, fighting off words of doom and death.

If he was this long without a breath? It's already been too long

How long did they dive, up and down? Hard to say. Time changes when your brain is full of fear. It can't be measured by seconds and minutes, but beats of the heart, and they dove for an eternity, bouncing up and down.

We have to find him, have to. In his mind's eye, Kai saw Dylan's body lying cold, lifeless, his eyes open. Kai felt himself drowning, the air he took in wasn't working anymore, the world not safe, the lake not safe.

And Sharon was not going to survive this. She called out orders as she submerged, directing Kai to search certain areas, asking kids to hold hands as they went down. Each time he dove, he came back up and did another quick head count, waiting to hear that Dylan was found, but there was no relief to this crisis. No Dylan. So, he took in more air and went down again. He could only swim so far of a radius from the raft. When Sharon dove, she could stay longer, go farther.

Should I go to the shore?

Lungs on fire from diving, he was running out of places to check, each dive closer to shore. He knew from years on this beach how the water subtly but surely pushes you. *But would the current blow Dylan this far? No, of course not, because he's not down here. He was taken. Snatched. Or drowned.*

Confusion. Terror. Alarm. The camp was in crisis when they all came ashore, the other half of the campers all back from their hike.

There were protocols for this. The kids were gathered around the camp. The same questions repeated.

'Did you see him jump in?'

Nobody could answer.

'Did you see him swim to shore?'

Nobody could answer.

Sharon spoke in short spurts to Paxton, who stood at the center. Pax was the God of this camp for generations. Now that he knew, Kai wanted to believe he'd make everything okay.

Paxton was on the phone for the sheriff on the lake. The Coast Guard was coming.

Off the phone, Paxton talked with Sharon. "I can't. I won't. I can't. His mom… I can't let… I can't let this happen..." With every word, Sharon got louder, especially when Paxton asked her to calm down. They began shouting over each other, their words tangling, their pitch thundering, rolling together in a cloud of chaos. The whole camp was abuzz in crisis.

Suddenly she stopped, and whatever Paxton said, Sharon took off in tears, walking briskly up the driveway towards the road. Kai was torn between following her and comforting the kids.

Dylan's mom was coming. The sheriff was coming. Maybe the Coast Guard. He couldn't handle any more victims so he managed the kids and lassoed them into a single group telling them lies about how it was all going to be okay. Those who knew heartbreak were not convinced, others were naïve and remained hopeful.

Kai then searched places around the camp. Somewhere inside him he knew he was hiding too. Hiding from the truth, from facing anyone. He had let them down. *So much for your paradise, for your sanctuary, a child eaten by the lake, right?* Because all fairy tales are true, the monster in them is real. We give it a heart and mouth and fangs but that's just putting a face on the forces that kill us.

Check the cabin.

He sprang to the cabin, the solid footing of land propelling him with renewed hope. He yanked on the screen door, yelled Dylan's name.

No sign he was there.

Of course, they'd checked here before. *You're fooling yourself, You're a fake.*

He pulled off the covers off Dylan's bed, like some magician yanking a tablecloth, *Ta-daaa!* And expected him to magically appear, all would go back to normal, but nothing. Just a plastic mattress.

He peeked under each bed and each corner, aching to see him

huddled in the corner, afraid of making friends, afraid of monsters in lakes, afraid of being away from his parents.

Back out the cabin door, he walked up to the road to check on Sharon. He saw her walking off, just a dot, moving fast, until the dot disappeared, and he was left on the road.

Soon, Dylan's mother would be driving down that road, and would arrive to hear the message of her child's death.

CHAPTER SEVEN:
OF LUCAS LAMIA AND HIS SICK SON BENJAMIN

CURSES! MY CHILD has the sickness. Brought in by the stranger.

The Lord is testing me. I thought of the Civil War soldiers and the battles they fought to preserve this country. They did not surrender. They did not quit fighting. I would do the same.

I brought Benjamin the best herbs I could find, and we made soups, but he barely had the energy to slurp. Lilith held him, I fed him, and our love surrounded him.

But overnight as we slept, the pocks on his skin multiplied, red wounds rising, first one, then two, then a dozen red bumps, turning to scabs on his flesh. As soon as I saw them, I inoculated him in the old ways, peeling off scabs and exposing his blood, then making a cut in the meat of my own thumb and rubbing my bloody cut deep into his wound.

This is how we did it in the war.

But the goodness had been sucked out of me.

Benjamin became delirious, shaking and sweating, sickened by the same devils brought in by the stranger. I barely slept. My wife wailed, holding her child, no concern of catching the same sickness, for if he passed on, she'd want to go with him.

I soon learned there was a wave of sick children in nearby towns after parents began traveling to my home and knocking on my door, frantically begging, "You must come, my child is sick!"

"No, I cannot come," I told them, "for my child is the sickest of them all."

So I turned them away. But this disease, this demon brew of fevers, was quite deadly, because days later the same families returned, weeping at my door. Their children hung limp in their arms, caked in scars and pocks, hideously disfigured.

None of these children would live.

All of them died.

And my child, with frigid skin and sweaty flesh, would join these children soon if I could not save the patient.

I decided to return to the Well to speak to the underground spirit, but this time, I would pay my debt if offered the chance. Before I could even walk out the door, Lilith stopped me, as if sensing my plan. "Do not give those demons any more reverence. You let them in, and they will stay. They will not save his soul—they will consume it."

I stood accused. I feigned ignorance but the look on my face betrayed my guilt. I looked about the room, it was unrecognizable and offered no comfort. The walls were coated with such sickness that would make the battlefield jealous. A husband leads, a wife commands.

I lifted my heated, desperate gaze into hers.

"What do you know of the Well? What do you know about it?" I asked her.

"You fool," she spat. "I hear her daily. I hear her but do not listen. I do not comply with the witch in the Well."

"What? When, how long? What does she say?"

"From day one I heard her, like you, you're just a fool. She asked for our family! She wanted all our children. She wants Benjamin! She asked me for him many times. When I let my mind wander and covet what I do not have, when I dream to live as a queen with riches, the Well whispers back that she can answer my prayers, if only I make a trade. I do not make that trade."

"What if the Well is the only cure?"

"You must not ask the Well."

"Do you not believe the Well is but a vessel of God?"

"These are not our gods!" she said, her voice thunderous, her hands in the air, waving about.

So I heeded her warning, and did not go to the Well.

#

The hours passed in a misty reality. The air felt thick. Benjamin was no longer responding to us, sucked into his internal world of sickness, lying in bed, his head shaking side to side as if saying no a thousand times to the death that beckoned him.

I could not wait.

My wife's anger at me for disobeying her request would be nothing compared to her anguish at a dead child. So I acted, as a father, a doctor, and a man of the Lord should.

I walked out into the night when Lilith was asleep. No moon to light my path, but I knew my way to the Well in the dark. Hands clasped in prayer, I fell to my knees by the Well, as though at the steps of a great, sacred cathedral.

"Please. I beg of you. Send your leeches and I will bring them back and squeeze them dry. I shall return his blood. Please."

There was a pause, as if making me pay a penance, and then the Well answered.

"You will do as you are asked this time?"

"Anything, I shall do anything."

"We shall send the leeches, and you may keep the leeches."

"Thank you for the blessing," I cried in gratitude,

"But then you shall return with blood. And flesh. And bone. And marrow."

"How? How do I do this? Tell me and it will be done."

"His limb. You will return with his limb. You must promise this. Cut off a limb as you've done hundreds of times, cut it off when his sickness is gone, and bring it to us."

Do not hesitate. Hesitating costs lives.

"I promise."

"You promised last time."

She knew I would promise anything at this moment.

"I will bring back a limb. I promise."

"Which limb?"

An arm? A leg? I thought of Benjamin's legs running up the hills. I thought of his arms throwing rocks into the lake. Then I imagined him buried under the earth.

"I will offer a leg."

"That shall suffice, but know this before you make this deal. If you do not bring back his leg to us, and if he returns to health and walks with arms and legs intact, his flesh will burn in the sunlight. Bring us a limb, or the sunlight will burn him to ash where his soul will remain, and then we shall consume the soul in his ashes."

"I will bring you a leg. I will. I will obey. I will return a limb in exchange for his life."

A light fog started to rise, a rich scent within the moisture, something deep within, full of soil and earthworms and darkness where no light has ever graced.

Then the squishing sound of the leeches.

Slowly they emerged from the Well, tiny creatures marching, like an army, a concentric army rising to me, ready to do battle. I gathered them with my fingers, not letting them take root, and soon they were on my son, on his temples, on the nape of his neck, his chest, and three near his spleen, where I feared the poison truly lived.

His eyes stayed closed as they fed, and I felt a peace come over his soul.

This was going to work. I could see health returning to his flesh before my eyes, the pox fading, the cauldron of heat coming from his skin a fire soon to die out.

For three days I gathered the leeches, then stood over him, placing my hand on his cheek to feel the fever retreat. Such a tender thing, such a perfect creation, it was the right thing to do to save him, by any means, by any sacrifice.

I wrapped my fingers around his tiny calf, just below the knee. If I pushed the skin in tight enough, my index finger and thumb could meet, circling the bone and flesh of his shin. A quick procedure beckoned, and the Well that yearned for this sacrifice would not be denied.

Who could deny this was a fair trade?

My son's eyes opened just then.

"The patient will live, Daddy. He will survive," he said, then smirked. Proud of himself for his wit, for surviving. His moves so gentle, the air so beautiful, loving and graceful. I imagined him playing outside again and the sound of laughter.

I thought of running from that land right then, going back south instead of cutting my child's leg off. But the visions of the tentacles and the reach of those demons stopped me from going. I could feel them burrowing inside me, right into my chest, my thoughts growing dark. They had a hold of me, and the voices echoed: *Do not try to leave. Our waters are cold and deep.*

A village of families are burying their children today, but not us.

The bargain was worth it. His leg bone was tiny, the procedure would be fast and mostly painless with chlorophyll over his mouth. I could do this. Even if Benjamin screamed, I'd learned to ignore such terror to save a life.

And if he ever expected to see the sunlight, I had no choice.

\#

My plan was to put Lilith in a deep sleep with the right dose of morphine. She'd be oblivious to me sawing through Benjamin's bone, and I'd sew the flap of flesh over the stub before she woke. It would be an immoral act not to perform this deed. The Well had delivered on its promise, and I had to deliver on mine. Benjamin had enough love from us to heal and prosper. The missing limb would serve as a testimony to his father's love, and the new prosthetics being developed were nothing less than a work of art. I would send for one soon.

Yes, I would comply with the Well's command the way Abraham did as God asked, without question. Just as he bound Isaac to the altar, I would bind my son and make the sacrifice.

I began to look forward to the morning's amputation. A husband leads, and when he makes these hard choices, they are done with love. One does not hesitate. I needed to do this before the sun rose, and before Benjamin walked out the front door.

Next to me, Lilith in her dreams, sleeping better since Benjamin's health returned. I would be awake all night, unable to sleep, I was certain of it. I would start this procedure on my son in the darkest hour of this saddest night. I'd give Lilith a dose of morphine, then carry my son to the side of the Well, far from earshot of his dear mother, close to the presence who demanded the limb sacrifice.

I laid in bed and awaited, but with this newfound sense of peace, sleep snuck up on me. Like a traitorous spy in the dark, it grabbed my thoughts, and sucked me down into a sleep deeper than I've had in months.

Vivid dreams awaited me. Feverish dreams.

The heat of the summer sun blazed through our front door. Flesh was turning to flames, then to ash. Leeches rose from the Well, tentacles grabbed my foot, arms pinned me down. A series of bee stings punctured into my veins, injecting poison into my blood. Though I tried my hardest to wake, I was weighed down by a leaden poison in my flesh. I heard a scream, one quick scream full of pain, that came and went quick as a lightning bolt.

I had to wake from this dream, I had to do this, I was being beckoned.

Finally, I could open my eyes, the thin veil of my eyelids lifting, slowly, and the reality it revealed was stranger than the one in my dreams. Such brightness that it hurt, and my wife standing above me. Her face was strewn with tears, standing there like she was looking over my corpse.

A check of my senses—they all worked, but still leaden and soft. I could move, but only slightly—for I was tied down to my bed. Literally tied down by ropes, surrounding me like tentacles.

What devil...?

I tilted my head best I could to see a set of syringes bedside. She'd been mixing the morphine in my syringes. She'd been awake, that was clear.

I spun my head to and fro, looking towards Benjamin's bed. His bed was empty.

"Where is he?" I asked. "Where's our son? Where is he?"

"He's not here; he has risen. He woke, got out of bed, opened the door, and the sun hit him. He's gone. I watched it happen."

"You...he's gone?"

"What a miracle to see him rise from his bed," she said. "It was like watching a newborn babe walk. The pock marks all gone from his skin, the smile back on his face. He was going to gather eggs before we woke, I figure, out into a morning we thought he'd never see again. He moved with remarkable grace."

She spoke with a mix of tragic stoicism but also complete madness.

"The sun greeted him at the door. You didn't even stir when he started burning, and I screamed. He burned fast as a blink. I'm quite sure I hurt inside more than he did, all my love watching him turned into pain."

She stopped talking and paced across the room, eyes darting about as if searching, and I imagined it might be for a weapon to kill me, or kill herself, some mighty climax awaited. Then she returned bedside, words her sharpest weapon.

"You think you are smarter than the rest, and you think me a fool. As soon as I saw the pile of ash, I knew. I knew it was you who did this. I didn't need to go to the Well to ask, but I did, and she told me. You made a deal. I warned you the Well wanted him all along. Still wants him and expects his ashes. You don't know the difference between God and the devil, 'cause you think yourself a God."

No! I screamed inside, *no,* I demanded, *this can't be true. A dream. I woke from one nightmare into another. I'll wake from this too.* The dream had me, just as the ropes had me.

"Yes, I kept his ashes, see?" She held up a bowl, and my stomach turned into rotten meat. I retched at the sight of the pile of black and grey soot.

"This is all of him. The Well is asking for them back. His soul is so strong, I can still hear him calling to me from Heaven. Benjamin is screaming from Heaven into my ear. The Well wants his ashes, and she will have them — but the ashes will be inside you first. Then the Well can't avoid but sucking *you* down if it wants *him.* I will do my best to live on, but until my soul meets Benjamin's in Heaven, I'll make sure you'll be in Hell."

I realized I'd been poked with the sting of the morphine as I slept, who knows how many times, and she injected me again with more just then. Strange to admit I admired how efficient she was — the injection, the aim, and then she began fixing up more, boiling the water ready to make the mixture and then pull into the syringe.

But wait, what is this? The morphine had made me mad, for it wasn't morphine in the mix anymore.

She was adding the ashes.

First, she put a small bit of water into a pot above the fire, as if fixing soup, but instead of bones and vegetables, she poured the tiny bits of flaky greys and blacks. The remains of my son in the concoction. Soon after, she began filling syringes up with the mixture.

Bee sting after bee sting as I laid there in delirium, Jesus crucified on the cross, and transfigured just as much, for my skin was changing with each injection into my flesh. The pain itself was turning delicious, desired, for a strange sensation swept over me.

I was becoming a child again.

The ashes coursed through my veins. They pumped through my heart a thousand times over. I couldn't fight back from this twisted reality of the absurd. My old self, my old life, my old body, all were gone.

My Lilith was stout and strong, and she dragged me off from the bed like a wrapped-up package, my legs stumbling as she pulled me. My ability to withstand was gone, my desire to fight vanished. I was resigned to this fate, to the pull of the Well I was about to be dashed into. Whatever the descent that awaited, I accepted my doom.

I'd been in bed all day. The sun was gone. Outside, the dark, crisp air with a tint of blue from a tiny slice of a waxing moon, hung like a scythe in the distance. From the top of this hill, I saw the torches dotted about on the lake, so many gathered now, as if they were part of this madness, of this offering my wife was making.

We approached the circle of stones. The light of the moon could not penetrate the darkness below, and my wife spoke to it like one does a drunk, uncertain if the drink had filled them with joy or rage.

"We are here. You can have him now, all of him. My son's soul is in Heaven, but his ashes are yours to keep. His ashes are now in his father's blood and yours to retrieve."

No voice answered, but a tremble shook the earth. Out on the lake, the torches moved in unison, fireflies in sync. In the forest that surrounded us, the deer lifted their heads, their nostrils alert at the strange scent.

I waited to be pulled into Hell.

I felt something breathing, making the ground expand and shrink, expand and shrink, like I was standing on lungs. Stars above sparkling, devils' fire burning in the lake, and before us, something rose from the Well.

The tentacle, moving slow but certain, snakelike, surveying the Well's circumference as if each round sucker on its belly was an eye for what lived below. It slithered to within inches of my face, a lover full of desire, that moment before a lover's kiss. The suction cups were wet and glistening.

I felt a moment of judgment, of my life, my soul, my choices. The sweet son of mine in my veins was screaming questions in a pitch I could barely detect, and I had no answers. I was at the mercy of this mysterious god.

My wife grew impatient and made a demand.

"Take him, you can have him, my son is in Heaven, but his ashes are in my husband. Take the ashes, take my husband."

A pause, as if the Well was deliberating, and the whole land outside waiting on it to respond.

"You believe your son is in Heaven," the Well finally spoke

with a powerful voice. "Your son—*our* son—the one who you conceived in our waters, our fertile waters. Should he not return to us?"

My wife said with conviction, "He is a child of God and returned to his Father."

"Ah, but your God is dead. You killed him by degrees when you killed each other, a species of Cains, a slaughter of Abels. But we were here before, and will be here after. Tell me, do you still hear His voice?"

"No, I do not. I will again, when I join Him."

"And how is it you think you'll join Him?"

"I'll join Him in Heaven."

"But those words you heard were not from Heaven, but from your child's soul in the ash. Your son is not in Heaven, for his soul remains in the ashes."

The tentacle sprang into action, contracting like a muscle spasm, and swung from my face to Lilith's. It wrapped around her neck in an instant, latching itself onto her, writhing around her jugular, her mouth unable to scream in horror, her air blocked.

"YOU THINK THIS WILL SUFFICE?" the Well's voice thundered with a might I'd never heard before, certainly not from God. The tentacle clenched tighter. "You take from me my riches, then try to fool me with your deceits."

Like a whip retreating to its wielder, the tentacle snapped back, dragging Lilith into the Well. So fast, so quick, it felt like a trick of the eye, a magician's deception.

She was gone. I had no words, nor did the Well. I began to cry, teardrops full of anger. I howled into the night like a starving wolf. The stars stopped their twinkle and the flames of the lake stopped burning.

I fell to the ground, leaning up against the Well, and continued to weep. The insects quiet, the earth stopped breathing. I banged against the rocks and stones with my fists and elbows. They mocked me with their sturdiness.

A youthfulness fought back the weight of the morphine inside me. Such freshness in my blood, my veins, my heart, as if I was rapidly aging backwards. I began to rise, a corpse crawling from its own grave in the dark of night, ready to live again.

I wasn't like I was before. My muscles were all flexing, a snake was moving through me, tensing, contracting, hissing. The morning sunrise made the lake sparkle, birds chirping announcing the new day. Species in the forest that were afraid to show themselves now moved about freely, and before I could demand an explanation, she spoke to me.

"Your wife is ours now. She will be trapped in the waters of this land, for we are but a vessel of the lake. She cannot leave the water, for if she tries, she will burn like your son. And she will do our bidding. She will live in the lake, she will fetch and retrieve when we ask, she will never know her son again.

"And should you touch the waters where she lives, your flesh will burn as if the water is flame. A true lake of flames.

"And as she is trapped in the lake, your son is trapped inside you. He will crave the souls of humans insides the ashes of the dead, and you will do his bidding.

"You will know what it is to ache with the need for more lives, more ash, more souls. You will smell them everywhere and need them inside you, for the child in your heart will suffer if he is not replenished.

"You are the Well now.

Go now. Seek out the dead, seek out their souls, and learn the curse of eternal life and eternal ache."

CHAPTER EIGHT:
OF SHARON MURPHY AND HER WALK AWAY FROM CAMP

SHARON WALKED WITH long strides, rapid fire steps just short of a run, away from Camp WaakWing, down Torch Lake Road. She felt banished by Paxton, who admonished her reaction to the missing child, telling her if she couldn't stay calm she shouldn't be there.

Stay calm? Calmness doesn't work. Calm is for those detached from the situation. Hesitating is for cowards. Paxton was accepting the death, delaying. *Don't tell me to stay calm.*

She'd seen the dangers of waiting, of slowness and hesitancy, when trying to save her grandmother but acted too late. She wouldn't be a part of the waiting. *You may be good at life, Paxton, but I'm good in a lifeboat.*

But this was his ship. He was captain, and she was sent away, so away she went.

She turned away from the lake into the meat of the land, moving through the rolling hills and farmland. Heat rose from the street. Each footstep across the hot grill of a road, sweat beading on her head, droplets getting thicker until they streamed down her face. Every bit was getting squeezed out of her.

How did I let that happen? How?

Dylan was in their protection, in *her* protection. What had her grandmother said to her after the consult with the doctor?

'See, the body knows, those fibroids will go away when you're ready to be a good mother. Until then, the body knows, the fibroids will stop things. You got some damaged parts from your mom and dad. God's in charge and doesn't want them removed, for we can't trust you with a child.'

She felt a calling here at this camp to put that notion to the test, that she could *mother*, could help children grow. Instead, she let one drown. She let one die.

She kept seeing the look on Dylan's mom's face when she'd dropped her child off, directly to Sharon's care.

And then she imagined the look of horror when his mother returned back to camp, and Paxton explained the crisis.

Yes, he is lost. Last seen in the lake. It's been hours. No, we haven't found him. We apologize for ripping your heart out. We let your child die. Oops.

The pain inflicted on Dylan's Mom will be unbearable. It has no name—language can't find a word to describe such hurt. The rest of her life will be feigning she's okay. She'll wish she died too when she learns her son drowned in this lake.

The reality will be too hurtful for her to believe at first. *This must be a mistake.* Dylan's mom would go into the lake herself looking for him. She would not leave the waters until she'd searched every part of it, driven by an oxygen more rich than the inevitable scuba divers who would carry the lifeless body from its depths. Tear the dead body from the belly of the beast.

Sharon pictured the boy at the bottom of the lake, alone, wondering, *Why was I left? There is a monster in the lake, and no mermaid in the weeds to save me.*

Sharon didn't even realize she was running just then, her body forced to run to keep pace with her desperate mind. The road was so hot and the sun so strong, a shower of sweat rained down her face. Legs and arms bobbing, like pistons, as she ran up the hills and little valleys.

Top of each hill, she saw miles of farmland in the distance, a token tree in the middle, like a rural lighthouse, *here's the middle, here's shade, here's safety.* Insects buzzed in the brush around her, crickets awakened for this terribly frightened human who didn't want to accept death. The sun looking over her, her speed getting faster, an atom grinder in her gut spinning harder and harder.

She wanted to blow up the world, change reality, because it was the only way to survive.

How can you tell another person their child died? After they trusted you with them?

The pain in her own gut was nothing compared to what Dylan's mom was about to feel, the tragedy beyond words.

Please God.

I'd rather it be my own child — even if I can't have one, but if I could — I'd rather it be my own than be responsible for the death of another. I'd rather take the pain into me.

I'd rather hear the news of my own child's death, then share the news to another.

Please God, I'd trade my own.

An answer to the prayer then came to her, coming from the woods.

"Wish it into the Well."

The voice of a woman, wise, ancient, snaking through the heat, or coming from inside her own woozy head, she wasn't sure, but it repeated, again and again.

"Wish it into the Well."

The words were hot and thick, like heat vapors rising off the blacktop in the distance, every cell of the planet was speaking.

"Wish it into the Well."

She looked towards the voice. An untended parcel of farmland to her left. Beside it, a broken house. The floor itself sagging, the roof caving in.

The family who lived here had big plans. They built this wooden frame that had crumbled after some tragedy struck, she could feel it, so they left it behind. Trying to build a life in God's country but instead found decay and disaster and the rot of time destroyed them.

Just as it destroyed Dylan.

I cannot deliver that pain to another. I'd rather have the pain brought onto me.

She wanted to hide in the woods, rip her clothes off, howl at the sky, go back to the world a century before when death happened often. Like this family who'd lived here before, who likely had many children because they died so often, and so you make more because you need hands to work the fields.

"Wish it into the Well."

The voice, again, summoning her to its source. She ran off the road onto a slight trail that veered into the fields. Grass and weeds and foliage knee high to either side of the overgrown trail. She was sure she saw movement in the forest at the edge of the property, shadows to and fro as if she was being watched by creatures afraid to show themselves.

She was closer to the house, to the wooden frames and stone walls that were either never finished or had crumbled—but the well seemed untouched, unweathered, eternal.

"Wish it into the Well."

The words hung like a mist above the stone well, like steam rising from the ground below. Like lungs breathing.

She was summoned to the voice, the beckoning rocks glistening like gems. Something ancient inside the dark circle suggesting an endless pit into depths of the earth never explored, depths of her own soul she feared, so kept hidden.

And it was from inside these bowels she heard the voice speak so strong and pure.

"Wish it into the Well. You must speak it to me, you must speak it and wish it into the Well. You killed her child. A debt must be paid."

Her head leaned over the Well, the secret voice telling her she couldn't have a child anyway—but she was afraid to think that, or the Well would pull the offer. She said with full faith:

"I'd rather my own child die than be responsible for the death of another."

"Wish it again."

She repeated herself. "I'd rather my own child die than be responsible for the death of another."

Immediately, a bubbling filth began rising out of the Well, brown and chunky. A foreign scent she couldn't pinpoint—that of rich soil, a rusty earthworm, an unearthed tomb. The fluid was rising to the surface, bubbling to the top. It threatened to overflow and she felt the urge to step back—but then she saw a boy, floating in fetal position.

It was Dylan.

Dylan.

He was in the fluid like an embryo, coated in slime, covered in filth, a birthing fluid of sorts. His back was curled at first, but it was slowly straightening. Each vertebrate, inch by inch, elongating, a time lapsed view of a plant reaching to the sun. He raised his mouth and let out a cry, a shriek, as foam came streaming out his mouth.

She reached in, grabbed him under his arms from behind, and pulled him out from the Well onto land. His legs were shaky and uncertain, but he soon stood on his own. With the boy safely on land, the voice of the Well spoke:

"Your child. She will die at the exact same age as the child I've returned to you. Remember if you wish. Forget if it is easier. But when your child is his exact age, she will die."

Dylan trembled like he was freezing, yet he was warm and moist, caked in wet, oily mud.

She held up much of his weight as they walked, arm in arm, down the road, back towards camp. She had so many questions, yet couldn't speak, the atoms of her brain adjusting to a new reality. And her feet didn't feel like they were walking on a road, but on a living creature. This whole area was just a monster that consumed humans, the lake just the mouth, and the Well part of its digestive tract, and like some biblical moment she pulled Dylan from the belly of the beast.

They staggered towards camp, and Kai was there, watching them from afar; two figures moving down the road, ragged, sweaty, the soil all over their skin. He ran towards them, breathing hard, asking in disbelief; "Dylan? Is that really Dylan?"

"Yes, he is found," Sharon answered as he arrived. Her voice seemed that of the Well itself, and her very vertebrae were now made up of stones from the Well. She was carrying its water now.

They were patient with Dylan at first, but then the questions came. *What happened, how did you get there?* Dylan couldn't say if he swam to land and then wandered off and found the Well, or if he fell into the water, or if his legs were pulled as he sat on that raft.

He couldn't say.

Trauma makes you forget, Dylan. It's okay, you're safe now.

And Sharon told herself that trauma could also cause psychotic delusions. That she hadn't heard voices offering a deal, a Faustian bargain, and she had *not* talked back to that voice. And of course Dylan didn't get spit back out from the lake through this Well. The only explanation was that he did leave the group and swam to shore and then wandered off from camp, adventured down this road, as boys will do, and playing in the abandoned place, he fell into the Well.

That's what the report said at camp, right?

Sharon knew better, in her heart where the truths lie and cannot be hidden. The deal she struck with the Well brought him back to life. *Here. He is found.* She had rescued Dylan.

Bad at life, but good in a lifeboat.

She saved the child, but a debt must be paid.

Chapter Nine:
Of Lucas Lamia after Lilith got Taken down the Well

THE WELL FELT so sturdy against my back, as I sat, leaning against it. I didn't want to leave. I didn't want to move. Whatever future lay before me, I could not face, so I sat and waited, the words the Well had spoken my only company. They haunted me in bits and pieces:

"Your wife is ours now.... She cannot leave the water, for if she tries, she will burn like your son. And she will do our bidding...

"And should you touch the waters where she lives, your flesh will burn as if the water is flame. A true lake of flames....

"And your son is trapped inside you. He will crave the souls of humans inside the ashes of the dead.

"You will know what it is to ache with the need for more ash, more souls... the child in your heart will suffer if he is not replenished.

"You are the Well now....

"Go seek out the dead, seek out their souls, and learn the curse of eternal eternal ache."

Through all the curses and afflictions, have I not remained a faithful servant? I have sacrificed everything, but still I've been forsaken by my Love and by my God. After such pain, tragedy, and sacrifice, surely a God of benevolence would intervene in all his grace and restore my life.

But nothing, nobody came, there was no savior or miracle to be had. And the youthful energy that had filled me after Lilith's strange injections began to fade as I sat by the Well and faced a new sunrise. The freshness slipped out of my body, and in the empty space rose a boiling anger.

I gathered what I felt was needed for my journey, and stood in my home for one last time. The silence of it all was tragic. The hours of labor to build this home, with stone and wood and love, only brought evil and treachery.

With one bag slung over my shoulder, I walked into town, hiding my face in shame. Those that recognized me, the local doctor who believed in God and medicine, I explained I was traveling south to further my training, and would soon return. Most who saw me couldn't recognize me any longer. I'd become the stranger.

I took the rails going south, and with each mile, my cravings grew. A burning desire for *more*. Similar to what happens to those who rely on the comfort of morphine with any frequency, they begin to know a new pain, and only more morphine can provide relief. In fact, it was my dear friend, the Doctor Silas Weir Michell, who worked in a Philadelphia hospital treating victims of the war who wrote:

"If any man wants to learn sympathetic charity, let him keep pain subdued for six months by morphine, and then make the experiment of giving up the drug. The nerves, muffled so to speak, by narcotics, will have grown to be not less sensitive, but acutely, abnormally capable of feeling pain, and of feeling as pain a multitude of things not usually competent to cause it."

And so it was in my body. Nerves felt every pain with peak intensity, and my inner ear could hear nothing but my son, Benjamin, screaming with agony. As if stuck inside that moment when he was burned alive by the sun, a witch on the stake begging to be freed. My innocent boy, tortured by pain and hunger, and begging for me to care for him.

'Will the patient live? Will he be okay?'

I can heal nothing, but I can treat anything, and all it required was a human soul within the ashes. This was the only way to appease the aching. Every cell in my body was begging me to find them a soul within the ashes, and directed my thoughts and energy for the search.

Such shame filled my heart, such a curse to move among normal humans as I looked for the dead. The way a wolf hunts prey over miles, I was driven south toward the scent of the brick crematorium, built by the legendary cremationist Dr. Hugo Erichsen. One of the first in the nation.

I traveled with one goal in mind, and when I finally arrived, I had to stand outside and bask in the glorious fumes. The smoke teased me, just a whiff in the air made my desire burn. I stood outside the heartless facility as if waiting for a friend, checking my watch, *they must be late*, but really I was waiting to consume the dead. It was not without embarrassment that I followed families home and snuck into their house at night, detecting the scent of the urns they carried.

Many times I left the ashes in their place, for they were truly dead, no trace of a soul inside the remains, for the spirit had slipped out of the body into a Heavenless existence.

But other times, I found the fresh bounty of a pure soul in the cremains. With my blackened soul it was not hard to hide in the shadows and steal urns from houses in the dark of night. I smuggled urns back to my single room rental, at times so excited I felt my bowels loosen. After I dissolved the grey flakes in water, I filled syringe after syringe, poking my veins for hours. With each prick of my flesh and injection into my blood, my senses heightened. My perceptions became super human, hearing voices from the deceased, feeling what they felt.

The feeding of ash into my veins restored my vigor and quieted the suffering son living within me. Each time it lasted but a few days until my skin grew pale, my muscles shaky and weak. Small aches and pains took root in my flesh and soon grew to agony. Every thought was plotting how to get more, and every cell only obeyed commands that focused on finding a cure for what ailed me. All else was ignored. The ritual of feeding these cravings became holy, the ashes, the boiling, the syringe, and that orgasmic bee sting into my blue veins. As soon as the prick of the needle found its mark, an explosion of youth and love overtook me, such that I began to notice others around me grew in age, while I did not.

What is a person who has a soul forever in their body, but a god? A soul that knows there is no Heaven after death, but only a bodiless existence.

It became evident to me that the human soul fights for the body to remain alive, and to endure any pain in order to live, because once the body dies, the soul has nothing to possess, nor any sanctuary to call home. There is no Heaven for the soul to rise to, so spirits do not go gently. They fight for the body, because it is the very body itself that is Heaven, the afterlife just a purgatory remembering what once was, lost in the nothingness. This is the very reason a soul often clings to a body, even after the corpse starts to rot or is burned to ashes.

I still believed in our Savior and His Resurrection, but certainly Christ had forsaken us, and though God sacrificed his only son, the gates of Heaven were now closed to those made in his likeness. Christianity was lost to me—but not my faith.

I began to study other faiths. Truths of Hinduism, Jainism, Kabbalah, and the Serer people of Senegal. It now fascinated me. The Aghori of the Hindu faith, who smeared themselves with ashes and other unspeakable transgressions, and the demons known as Pishachas, who lurk around cremation grounds.

Have I become a demon, like Pishacha?

Time crept forward, deceptive and stealth. Electricity came, buildings sprouted, metal giants, and the horseless cars moved among them. Mixed in with it all, more crematoriums, more ashes, more options.

I spent generations away from my old home by the Well, but after time away, a hundred years or more, my life became dull and hard to bear.

At one point, in order to end this affliction, I handcuffed myself to a bedpost, just before the cravings hit their peak. Soon after, I found myself possessed by such rage, I decimated my metacarpophalangeal joint trying to break free, but still could not escape. I cursed my previous self for his vain foolishness and this ridiculous endeavor. But with the aid of a screaming Benjamin, I tore the cuffs right off the bed rail and made my way to the crematorium.

I needed out, I wanted out, this laborious war I was fighting. So I once again traveled to northern Michigan seeking a reprieve from the war. To leave the horrors behind.

What I found surprised me.

The cities had exploded into vacation destinations, the lakeshore developed with massive lake houses. Gone were the heathens and torches at night, but the surrounding fields remained farmland and forest.

And my old land remained.

I approached it with caution, the Well before me as the north star must have guided the three kings, shining bright—but my home from more than a century before, now falling and decayed. Barely a roof was left, and the floorboards were busted in where Benjamin once lay.

But the Well...

The Well remained, sparkling in the sun, the stones like diamonds. I sat next to it, at first in silence, and then begging, pleading, on hands and knees, to end this curse, to end my suffering. I waited patiently for an answer, but none came. Instead, she remained smugly silent and judged my dark deeds, perhaps proud of her work. I rested my back against its hardness, watching the occasional car drive by this lonely road, once just dirt for horse and carriage, but now paved for the machinery.

This dilapidated house would not stand much longer, but the Well went on.

And I would go on. But for how long? Who would destroy me? With what purpose to go on into history? There seemed none, no purpose besides avoiding pain and appeasing the screams of my child. I needed out, or I needed a purpose.

The lake glistened an answer, so I left the silent Well and walked roadside to the water's edge, finding public access to get to shore.

Alone on this slice of beach, I could sense her then — my beloved, Lilith — moving under the water towards me. We were two magnets pulling at their source, one severed entity trying to reunite.

Her head emerged from the crystal blue water. Her long hair like strands of seaweed, draped over her body, naked in the water. Her flesh had morphed into part fish, part reptile; barely human. I felt her sadness, her anger, her beauty — yes, her beauty still remained. The heart inside her cared deeply, hated deeply, and the two are not much different.

She emerged like a child from the womb as I watched with both sadness and joy. Finally, I rushed forth to the edge of the lake as she kept a foot planted in the water and reached out to me.

Oh the burn of that water when we embraced, hotter than any fire, branding me like cattle. That glorious water of the Torch Lake had earned its name, for the flame seared me where her skin touched mine. The rancid stench of burnt flesh filled the air.

I held her as long as I could. I felt the agony of her soul, the torture of being away from her son for so long.

"You're still alive too," was all I could say.

"This is not living," she said.

"What do you do?"

"I do her bidding. *Its* bidding. Snatching humans on the surface, watching over the children who live in these waters. Mostly I ache inside for my Benjamin. The one you let die. The one inside you now."

"He aches for you, too. Oh, does he ache."

She reached for me, howling in anger, a quick grab, and I knew she intended to bring me under. I stepped back, and she grabbed just air and fell into the water. I dashed away from the lake.

She could not follow me, could not leave the lake of the torches she was cursed to stay within. So I left her there in the water as I sought out the ash.

I *had* to take her child away from her, I had no choice. But I also took a heavy guilt with me, weighing down my heart. Her sadness, her perpetual loss. Even though she betrayed me, her pain of missing Benjamin scarred me deeply.

If only I could give Lilith her son back, help her feel like a mother again.

But if I could not cure my wife's suffering, might I spare the agony of other parents who were grieving a child? Mothers needed to know that a deceased child was not always lost, it only appeared that way. It was all a deception. Imagine the joy I could bring if I found a way to *return* their children.

During my travels I found one man named Jervis Samsa who, much like the soldiers treated with morphine in the war, became entirely dependent on a substance made from the opium poppy. He had grown quite insane while withdrawing from the drug called heroin and heard the call of his father's ashes, telling him some heroin remained inside his cremains. In his desperation, the young man injected himself with his father's ash, and found himself transformed, with his dad's voice inside him.

Visiting him in Northville Psychiatric Hospital and hearing him talk was the first seed that maybe I could share this love, this spiritual experience of ashes in your veins, with others. It was not just me.

I began to visit more hospitals and offered my services as a volunteer, for what hospital would not want a doctor versed in medical terms who also could provide spiritual guidance? I surrounded myself with the families of the terminally ill, and offered myself as a bereavement counselor. It took some work to forge my degrees and fabricate proof, but the documents and the words from my split tongue gave me passage into the hospital—as well as its medicines—if I snuck around just right.

I had my target audience, and I had my supplies.

The first grieving parent I injected by force, after weeks of trying to convince her of the benefits. I had been listening to her cry and lament over her lost child, watching her neglect her own well-being, not eating, not bathing. I spent weeks getting close to her, whispering words that her own brain was trying to say and that her mind's eye clearly saw, but she ignored these truths. *The child is there, her soul in the ashes.* She seemed comforted by the sound of my voice rather than the content of my words, and so I had to do what was right. Sometimes we have to force the goodness into others if they refuse what is necessary. Same as we held down patients on the battlefield when taking off a limb, I had to hold her down (and she was no small thing).

And thank goodness I did, for the look of joy on her face that followed after I injected her child's ashes into her veins…oh how words fail to explain. Her grief washed away, and her amazement could not be contained. So much so that she began to rip at her eyes, tearing at her eyeballs until they were at first deflated, and then dripped out her sockets altogether.

I learned from my mistakes. I learned to be selective, to choose, to carefully filter through who would receive such a blessing. Soon, I became God's vessel again.

I learned the power of having those who were grieving let me in. If I could convince them to invite me in, just as a vampire needs to be invited inside before entering one's home, and if they agreed to the procedure versus being forced, the results were much improved, though still complicated. I earned their trust, I whispered truths in their ears, and soon they heard their child's cries in the ashes, and agreed to let them into their veins.

Lilith, even though you betrayed me, if I could return your son to you, I would. For now, I seek out other lost mothers, doing God's work.

I moved about Northern Michigan with my new mission, while my wife was stuck inside the Lake of the Torches doing the biddings of the Witch of the Well. I now knew my true purpose. It was not just to fill my own veins, but to find mothers who had faced the devastating heartache of losing a child.

If I could share with them the act of injecting the ashes, it was as if I'd brought their child back from the dead. A gift God Himself could not offer.

CHAPTER TEN:
OF KAI WATCHING SHARON RETURN WITH DYLAN

KAI HAD BEEN looking out for Dylan's mom driving down Torch Lake Drive towards camp when he saw the two tiny figures walking down the road. He squinted, certain it was a mirage, but then the miracle came into full view. Sharon found Dylan. He sprinted out to greet them, throwing his arms around them both.

Dylan was covered in a gooey mud. A bizarre stench of soil and rust surrounded him in a cloud, a dazed look spread over his face.

Dylan returned okay; Sharon returned a hero.

Medics arrived and checked his vitals. The terror spreading through the camp gave way to joy and relief. A feeling of confidence from the campers that everything will always be okay and the adult world has things under control.

Dylan's mom did arrive. She listened without interruption to the explanation. *Your son wandered away from camp. He was missing for probably an hour. It was our fault, not his.*

Dylan's mom took him aside to talk in private. She knew how he ticked and that he needed just her for a bit, but after some time, the decision was made for him to remain at camp. After sharing a meal at the cafeteria with the other campers, she drove home.

Sharon never gave a full answer about how she saved Dylan.

Because she is the mermaid who saves children. The hero who fixes everything, but how? Kai wondered.

Her explanation of what happened was just a cover. Her face betrayed her when she spoke about her journey away from camp. But whatever she did to save that child, Dylan returned a different person. He no longer clung to Sharon during activities, but moved about like her colleague, not a camper. He walked with a swagger. With an 'I know what life is about now' expression on his face, like he'd lost some brand of virginity.

The lake speaks most honestly to those willing to drown. An expression Kai had heard from Paxton himself. Dylan had certainly seen and heard truths from the lake he didn't think anybody else would understand, and kept them secret.

Sharon and Kai had a trauma bond. They'd faced the death of

a child and brought him back to life, it seemed, and a symbiosis was born. He felt her hunger, and knew her tastes. When she jumped into the brisk water, his skin felt the shiver. When he woke for the day, her dreams ended and the day began.

The rest of that week was filled with laughter and campfires, sunshine and hikes, games and songs. They all seemed intent on praising the heavens, for someone is always watching out for us, especially in our darkest moments.

End of the season came and Kai was relieved to learn that Sharon agreed to return the next spring to ready for another season. He allowed himself to imagine her as his life partner, and they'd face every challenge the same, solving it, confronting it.

That's what he believed.

Kai was promoted to Director of Programming at Camp WaakWing, and spent his winter revamping the schedule when he wasn't plowing roads for the county. He worked fourteen-hour continuous shifts, blasting through the snow. Sharon went south for the winter, a snow bird, a skylark, spending one more season working art fairs from Jacksonville to Alabama, to Texas and south Colorado.

But Camp WaakWing and Torch Lake never left her mind, she expressed more than once during FaceTime calls.

She eagerly returned the next few summers, and learned how blessed it was to be part of this sacred place. She saw why others returned. She saw why Kai lived on the lake all year long, so she joined him inside his lakeside home for weeks at a time, then months at a time, until eventually she didn't leave. The most separate they were was when they were in camp, sleeping in different cabins.

Others whispered about their relationship. They could see the glow they had around each other, how they worked in tandem, how they continued to face each camp crisis.

There was the high ankle sprain on a hike an hour away when the agile and crafty Laura Grossman climbed that tall, crooked tree. Every camper was cheering her on as she climbed higher towards the sun, Sharon and Kai just as amazed. But the branch she chose to jump from on the way down was much too high, and she landed with a *snap*. They splinted her leg and carried her to the road. *This may need a cast, not just some ice.* When Mrs. Grossman appeared on video chat, she shared tales of her daughter's litany of broken bones. Mom stayed home, Laura stayed at camp in a cast, and a hero to her peers.

Camp WaakWing Lore.

Paxton encouraged Kai to step up and be the campfire storyteller at times, and so Kai worked on his own tales to delight the campers. He wanted his own brand, different than Pax, and one of his originals was *The Tale of the Cribs*, the backstory of the wooden structures that rest on the bottom of Torch Lake. These were logs, bound together and piled in a square, like a crib, with rocks placed where the mattress might be. Kai heard they were built to shelter fish, but in the glow of the campfire flames at night, it was wonderful fodder for dark Torch Lake lore. Kai told a story of a rare breed of fish that look more like water-children and sleep in these underwater cribs as babies. When they are mature enough, they leave the cribs to go nip at the heels of kids who are foolish enough to swim after dark.

Another story was about the *medicine man* who lived in the nearby forest, who, while working on his potions, spilled acid on his face. He now runs around in a rage at night, his flesh still burning, his ferocity and anger triggered by those who make loud noises at night. So please, do not cause mischief after bedtime.

And when the kids were quietly in bed, asleep for hours, more than once Sharon and Kai broke their own rules and snuck down to the water at night. Paxton not aware, or pretending not to be. They left their clothes on the dock and slipped out of the night air into the cool water, every bit of flesh at attention from the chill. The last embers of the campfire had died out long before, the stars so luscious in the sky, their embrace so smooth and slick. Their lips tasted so fresh.

That moment he entered her they both felt like gods, taking in the seven seas and all the mysteries of the earth. Tiny splashes in the water with each thrust, muffled noises out both their lips, his life swimming into her, every being in that lake leaning towards them in love. After, they pulled on clothes, struggling to slip them over their wet skin, then tip-toed back to their cabin.

The next morning in private moments they joked about camp counselors in horror movies sneaking away for sex. It was amazing a child wasn't murdered by a Jason due to their negligence.

But no child was harmed. In fact, a child was made.

It was a complete surprise when she became pregnant, since

she'd been told the type of fibroids she had would likely interfere with conception. *'It's the gods' way of saying you're not ready, your parts are damaged,'* said her grandmother. They had offered her surgery to take care of them. *Not yet, someday,* Sharon had decided.

But that choice was no longer hers to make. Something in the water had helped them conceive.

Sharon's love for Kai had grown, her purpose in life renewed, and she no longer remembered the day with the Well and the deal she made. It only came back to her moments after her miracle was born.

For just after the birth, after her whole body cramped and spasmed and a new liquid of life oozed out of her. After the exhalation and tears of joy and relief and excitement, when she first held her baby girl, the moisture that covered her was filled with that bizarre scent.

She noticed it immediately. Unmistakable. That mucky soil aroma. That scent of earthworms bathing in rust.

It was the same scent and the same substance that covered Dylan after she pulled him out of the Well.

The baby was cleaned, the scent and substance washed away, and for a while, after many sleepless nights taking care of this new wondrous being, she forgot about the insanity and fears.

Of course there was no curse.

When Julia was just six months old, Sharon pushed her in a jogging stroller down Torch Lake Road, then up the hill towards the Well, trying to mock the stones from afar. She walked past it, again and again, daring it to speak a word.

The Well remained silent. Just a circle of stones. As the nearby house decayed into the earth, so did Sharon's fear. Each time, she was able to dismiss the threat to her daughter, a bit more, a bit more, a bit more. Because *of course* it was insane to think something in the ground could come get her baby.

But when she first took Julia out of the stroller to touch the Well, Jules about five years old then, everything changed.

Jules was happy to be free of the stroller straps, and raced around the circle, a stick in one hand, the other hand touching the Well, tracing its edge, moving faster around the circumference. She started singing as she ran;

"Wing around the wosie, powcket full of pozies, ash-is, ash-is, we all fall—"

"DOWN! WE ALL FALL DOWN," the words boomed from the earth before she could finish.

The voice was a shock. A slap across Sharon's cheek from a spiteful hand. It had deeper bass than she remembered. It had girth and a streak of meanness that wasn't there years before.

"Oh what a special child you are. Our lake has many rooms, and we have prepared one just for you. Both of you. If this were not true, why would we tell you it is so?"

Jules pulled her hand off the Well as if she'd touched a hot stove, and went directly to the jogging stroller and sat inside as if to say 'I'm done here, let's go.'

Sharon could not pretend the voice was a delusion any longer, because Jules heard it, and was clearly terrified.

Sharon stayed away from the Well after that, and living on the lake, she was happier, more content, and more fulfilled than she ever thought she'd be in this life. The three of them were the envy of guests who visited, of those they took on pontoon rides, who they had over for Uno games or campfires or ice skating.

It wasn't until many years later she started to hint to Kai, subtle at first and then more direct, that they needed to move. *This home is amazing, but there's a bigger world out there and Julia is missing it.* Over time, she would get more direct, more forceful, trying to pry her husband away from this lake. Of course she had tracked down Dylan's birthday, and did the math to the incident at the Well. Dylan was exactly ten years, five months, and seventeen days old when she bargained for his life. She had a few years until her daughter reached that age.

But there was no way in hell Sharon was staying put until then, even if she had to leave Kai and go back on the road.

Because she now had a purpose in saving this child.

PART TWO

Chapter Eleven:
Of Sharon and Kai's Daughter

Call me Jewel. I was born Julia, sometimes they called me Jules, but now I like Jewel.

In all sorts of ways, I'm not like I was before. It all starts with the lake.

Torch Lake.

The lake is alive. The water has thoughts and feelings and memories. It plays and sleeps and dances, but most of all, it loves.

Every time I jump in, I feel a special embrace. The bubbles tickle my skin as I sink under the surface. The chill shocks my spine and shoots blood to parts of my body that only wake when I'm inside these waters.

By the time I bob up to the surface, I feel completely new again.

"It's so cold because it's so deep," my dad says.

"How deep?"

"Nobody knows, too deep to know."

"How cold?" I ask.

"Cold as hell, Jewel, cold as hell." And I feel privileged to hear a swear word such as *hell*.

My parents know a lot about Torch Lake, especially my dad who's been on this lake since he was born. He met my mom as a camp counselor.

But there are some things they don't know. I've seen things. I don't talk about them.

Sometimes when we're cruising slowly on the pontoon and I lean over the side, trying to graze the water with my fingertips, I see shadows swimming deep below. Something big, almost like a whale, moving slowly, as if floating in space.

But when it feels my eyes on it, the big monster fish dives down deeper. I catch the flicking fin before it fades into the depths

What did I just see? I wasn't supposed to see that.

It's not just the big monster fish. There are other secret things living in the water. I first saw the Woman of the Lake when I was learning to water ski.

We were on the west side of the lake where it's more calm, less choppy. I'd fallen five times in a row. Every time the engine fired up and blasted forward, I fell on my face, but this time, when the pontoon boat yanked me forward, I leaned back just enough and stayed upright on the water.

My legs were quivering like a baby giraffe. Mom and Dad were way ahead of me in the boat, Dad cheering with his fist in the air, Mom's smile shining in the sun. I was proud of myself but felt so alone. We were going too fast and my skinny legs on those skinny planks and the water so uncertain below me. It was just me, and below me the water seemed a million miles deep. I could sink and they'd never find my body on the bottom.

I looked down and saw her. Saw the Woman of the Lake.

She was swimming upside down, like a human submarine just barely below the surface. She was looking up at me and her eyes seemed so wise, like they knew everything, a godmother who'd been there since birth. She even smiled at me, a fractured smile with shades of aqua blue. Each strand of her long, flowing hair was like a living sea serpent, hissing at me and helping her swim.

I needed to scream for help and get back on the boat to stop her from hurting me, but before I could, she put a finger over her lips to say, *shhhhhh, be quiet...* I knew if I cried for help, she would do even worse things to me than whatever forbidden, dark things she had planned.

Don't fall, don't fall, don't fall, I told myself. *She's under there.*

I kept up on my skis, my first time ever staying up this long, with water bouncing me up and down, my knees acting like shocks, the boat pulling me ahead. Mom and Dad had no idea what was below me.

Stay up, stay steady, stay balanced. Don't fall, don't fall, stay up, stay up.

The monster woman had silver fish eyes and old skin full of scars and slices. I hated her face, her eyes, the way she was so focused, like she'd always been there. I didn't want to look, but I couldn't help but glance down at her face instead of straight ahead at the waves.

I did my best to not be scared, gripping on to the tow rope handles, bending my knees over the waves like they were speed bumps in the water. I wouldn't fall, I wouldn't be scared, I wouldn't look in her eyes, because these waters were mine and she can't change that.

But then she reached for me, one single hand reaching out of the water, fingers not fully human but maybe they once were, and she grabbed my ankle. I did scream then, just before I went flying forward face-first into the water. My ears flooded with rushing water, I didn't know which way was up, rolling and rolling in the lake. The water had soaked into my brain.

Which way is up? The life preserver helped find the way, but then I was alone in the water. Both skis fell off and were scattered far away. Mom and Dad slowed the boat and were circling in the water, so I bobbed up and down, waiting, just waiting for that creature's hand to come up and grab my ankle and pull me under. I kept imagining I felt her fingers on my skin, slimy like fish, grasping me by the foot and pulling me down to her lair where nobody would find me

Hurry up, Mom and Dad.

The boat was so slow coming to scoop me up. I waved my hands, like they told me to do, so another boat won't hit me. I kicked my feet in the water, bicycle style, each time imagining if her hand got close to grabbing me I'd kick her in the face.

Dad circled the pontoon so the tow rope would float over to me, but was still far away. I paddled to it with all my might, swimming as if a Great White was behind me, and gaining.

Finally, I made it, wanting to cry with relief when I climbed up the ladder and the last of me was out of the water.

"You want to go again?" Dad asked.

I didn't say a thing about the lake woman. She had shushed me. Her life was a secret.

"Not yet. Not now," I said, but I didn't say why.

Because there's a woman in the lake.

\#

First time I heard the Woman of the Lake speak, I was in the water by our cottage. I was only up to my waist, Mom and Dad checking on me through the back window sometimes. The sun was near the horizon, not long until it would go down, and the blue water was changing colors into a mysterious purple. I felt something swimming towards me, sensing it in the water the way a blind bat sees in the sky.

Her face emerged right in front of me without even a splash. Blue blood vessels wound through her flesh, her skin all doughy and full of scars, like a fish that died and washed to shore after a thousand fish hooks had snagged her face.

My heart thumped. I was terrified, but pretended I wasn't.

I'm a lake creature too, you can't scare me.

She rose from the water and was standing before me, a dead body brought to life. She was naked with long hair flowing over her like a plant, each branch alive and slithering around her skin. Tiny clam shells were attached to her skin and weird breathing sounds came from her neck.

I needed to leave, but I felt like stone. Her gaze froze me in place.

"Who are you?" I asked.

"I am Lilith of the Lake. The Mother of Benjamin. The mother of a thousand more. They bathe in the love of this lake. They'll be bathing here forever. You shall join us."

"What are you doing here?"

"Watching you. Your mom made a deal. I'm bound to collect." Her voice was a whispered gargle.

I started to make a dash to the shore, pushing my legs through the water, but she put her hand on my shoulder and stopped me still. Her hand gave me a shock, like a lightning bolt hit me in the water.

"Stay," she said. "Stay here with me. Please stay. I cannot follow. The air will dissolve me. Please. I have to speak to you. I have more to say."

She looked at me with eyes as silver as a fish, but when she heard my mom scream my name from the back door, she slid back under the water and swam off. I could see her for just a minute, a shadow going deeper into the blue, me in the light blue aqua of the shallows.

I know she's real because my mom ran down from the cottage, firing questions at me:

"Who was that? Who were you talking to?"

"I don't know," I said.

But that night at dinner, it felt like Lilith of the Lake was there with us as an invisible guest sitting in the empty chair. I felt her presence. It seemed so real I was sure that she would drip water next to me on the floor, and I'd get blamed for not drying my feet before coming inside. Mom sensed her too, I think, because we were all nervous and I wish we could have talked about why. Mom kept saying things like, "There's a whole other world away from this lake to go see," or "Families weren't meant to live forever in a lake house," and "Until we move, I'll be here watching you around the lake."

And she did, all summer, protecting me, watching over me more than before. Sometimes, when Dad was gone, she took me out on the pontoon boat for a sunset cruise. We traveled up and down the lake, eating cheese and crackers, but wherever we were, I knew the woman was following us. She was swimming behind us, underwater, following the boat, following us home. When we docked, she stayed in the water nearby, just off the beach, but too deep to be seen.

She wouldn't show herself with my mom nearby, but I knew she was there.

I sensed her when I was eating fried pickles at Dockside, a restaurant right by the water, where the canal goes from Torch Lake to Lake Bellaire. A parade of boats going slowly by, back and forth, all the while Lilith circled underwater. When I crunched the fried pickle, I know she heard it.

And I could sense her swimming not far from the shore as I ate mint chocolate chip ice cream in Alden, sitting on the bench by the water, licking the drips off my fingers. She wasn't far away, I know it.

When winter came and the water froze over, I loved to play in the snowbanks just off our beach. Dad walked with me on the ice in the shallows, taking slow, careful steps over the areas I used to swim. We looked at ice-fishing shanties farther into the depths, wondering how people could stand the cold just sitting on the ice, me wondering how the Lilith of the Lake could still live underneath.

Was the woman frozen?

There was usually some water visible in the middle, but not this extra cold year, a coat of white covered the lake up and down and across.

"What happens to the fish and other things in the winter when it all freezes over?" I asked my dad. It was a conversation I know we've had before, but my mom always told me if you want to know the truth, you ask more than once, and then see if the answers remain the same.

"They stay in the water. They live under the ice. It's okay, their blood is already cold."

"I never see them," I said.

"They stay too deep to be seen."

"Are there any things in the lake you haven't seen?"

I squinted at my dad through the blinding reflection of sunlight off the snow, waiting for him to answer. His cheeks were red from cold.

"I've seen a lot of things. There's more than just fish in this lake."

"And that's why Mom wants to move away?"

He squinted back, his eyes piercing into mine, wondering why I asked. A gust of wind made me shiver — no thick jacket could hold that cold out.

I shouldn't have asked. He doesn't want to tell me.

"We can never really leave here," he said, "even if we move. We've put so much of ourselves inside the lake, we can never get it all out. It stays in the lake no matter what happens."

"Frozen over," I declared, and smashed my feet against the ice. It cracked, just a bit. I brushed the snow aside to the clear the ice. I was scared I'd see her face in the water below, pressed against the ice and looking up at me, but not so scared I didn't look.

I didn't see her, just sensed her.

Waiting for the ice to thaw so she could get me.

#

Later that day, my mom made apple cinnamon tea, and we sat by the crackling flames of our fireplace watching the day grow dark. The snow was piling up on the icy lake and the sky was changing colors, from brilliant white to grey and then pitch-black darkness. Outside felt like one big deep lake of mystery, with even more snow falling down. Dad was gone on a long, fourteen-hour shift to plow and salt.

"What happens to the fish and other things in the winter?" I asked my mom, because if you want to know the truth, you ask more than one person, and then compare answers.

"They get cold, real cold, but they don't die. I think they like the cold, actually."

"Do you ever get to see them in the winter?" I asked. "Are

there any things in the lake you haven't seen?"

"Oh yes. This lake is full of so many things. Too many things for some of us."

"And that's why you think we should leave here?"

Mom didn't want to answer that one, I could tell, so she sipped her tea. I could hear her thinking about what to say next.

"There's just more of the world to see, Julia. I don't know that we should live on a lake forever. It takes too much of us. Don't worry, we won't leave anytime soon. We have a couple of safe years around here, and then just imagine the places we can go. I've seen so much of the country, and you need to see it too."

"Dad says we can never really leave here, we've put too much of ourselves in the lake already."

"He's right, and it will always be there. But we can't let the lake take all of us.

Chapter Twelve:
Of Jewel Jordan and her Last Meeting with Lilith

THE ICE MELTED when the spring came and each day the sun grew a bit hotter in the sky. The grass greened and the trees got their leaves. Even the water of the lake grew a lighter shade of blue. All living things seemed to wake from their sleep.

"Every soul smiles towards the burning flames of the summer sun," my Dad said his mentor, Pax, used to tell him. Dad was never more happy than the day he put our boat in the water for the season.

Mom even thought we had a couple more safe years, but that summer, I saw Lilith of the Lake for the last time.

I was building sandcastles on our little beach, just at the end of the surf, while the sun scorched my skin. I was going to get sunburn, but I didn't mind. Sometimes I like it that way.

My hands were the bulldozer, carving out the trench, making a moat to protect the castle from invaders. Water slowly came rumbling in, bubbled and foamed, and then retreated back to the lake. For those few moments when the castle was standing, I imagined a fantastic universe inside, much better than my own.

Behind me, I heard something emerge from the depths. The splash of footsteps, going from deep water to more shallow.

I sensed her moving closer but pretended not to notice. When the shadow was cast over me and the sky went dark, it felt like an eclipse. The heat from the sun on my back vanished, and a chill came in its place. I looked up and saw her seaweed hair dangling over her face like limbs of a weeping willow, her fisheyes beating down on me.

I wanted her gone.

"Stay in the water, you have to stay in the water you said," I told her, and looked back down at the sand. I could only see her feet, one of them in an inch of water, the other on the beach.

She didn't respond so I kept working on my castle and ignored her. That's what you do with bully creatures like her. In the distance, I heard a boat accelerate from the shallows towards the middle of the lake. The hull crashed against waves; *boom-boom, boom-boom*. The noise faded, leaving me alone, my mom and dad were somewhere inside, the neighbors were nowhere in sight. Hot dogs on the grill soon for lunch. But not yet. This creature standing above me needed to have her time.

"You've been growing. I've been following you. It's time for me to tell you why."

The tiny clams stuck into her skin were alive and chomping onto her leg like leeches.

"Tell me why what?"

"Why your death is coming."

I looked at her feet. Her toenails were thick, like the talons of an eagle. Flesh connected each webbed toe. It was like a fish and a human got stuck in a boat propeller and blended together.

There was nothing to feel but scared, but I wouldn't let her do that to me again this summer by looking strange and saying scary things. I ignored her and waited for this eclipse to pass, but instead the shadow remained, so I had to say something and cast her out.

"This is our beach, so please leave," I said without looking up. My hands shook as I dug my fingers as far as I could into the sand. I felt the rough, crunchy parts with my fingertips deep below where the little rocks and shell parts sunk to.

"And when you die," she said with her gargled voice that sounded like someone slit her throat and she was choking on blood, "you will meet him. You will meet Lucas Lamia and he will try to ingest your soul." She inhaled deeply just then, and I could feel my scent get lifted right from my body.

I waited to hear my mom or dad running out to scare her away, but nothing. I pretended it was nothing, too.

"Go away, please," I demanded.

"Your mom made a deal, and I'm bound to collect," she said.

"The deal *is*," I said, "this is *our* beach. So go away, please," I repeated, and acted like I expected her to obey my command, but my heart was beating so loud, she could certainly hear. I kept building my castle, but I was angry building, slopping big clumps of sand, trying to patch things but doing it too hard, making walls cave in. "Our beach," I repeated, heavy on the *our*.

"This beach cannot be owned," the woman said. "There are things in these waters stranger than the likes you've ever known."

"I've been in this lake more than you," I said, but I realized she was maybe the only person that this really wasn't true for. I patted the side of the castle. I drew a little window with my finger to let the people who lived inside see out.

"The lake wants you back after you die, Jewel, you need to know this. You need to come back. But before that can happen, your body will die and burn first. It's not fair to you, you did nothing to deserve what's about to happen, but Jewel, I'm here to share the news of your death."

She knows my name. How does she know my name?

My death?

I thought of ways I could kill her first. She had one foot barely touching the water, the other in the sand. I could grab her and pull her all the way out of the lake and she would disintegrate. That's what she said would happen.

"So I die, so what?" I said with defiance. "You die, we all die. Fish die and wash up on the beach. The birds eat them, the crayfish eat them."

"Indeed, Jewel. A scavenger seeks out the dead, and so it is with the Lamia who consumes dead things. His curse is to ingest the ashes. He will learn about you, he will be there when you die, and he will try to devour your soul. Don't let him. Come live in the lake with us. Know him by his pale white face, by his green eyes and jet black hair. You'll see him when you die, sometime soon."

The more words she said the less gargled she sounded, and some little part of me wanted to hear everything she had to say, because she knew secrets. But I refused to look back up at her, so she just kept talking to the back of my head. I didn't want her to think I was scared, but I was. So scared I wanted to cry or scream. Did dying *sometime soon* mean in the next few minutes?

My vision was hazy.

I knew this was wrong. I was supposed to scream for help, to run, to cause a commotion, but I didn't want her to have that.

I clutched onto a handful of sand, filling up my fist. I would throw it up into her eyes. Nothing hurt as bad as that, to have a bunch of sand in your eye, where it soaks up your eye fluid and burns into your eyeballs. After I blinded her I would grab her arm and pull her to shore and she'd dissolve and die.

I finally did look up, but I wasn't ready for what I saw.

She was leaning over, her smile raining down, her yellow teeth chattering behind her lips, which were opening, slowly. Her skin a coating of fish scales. Her eyes didn't blink and were open so wide. Tiny pupils dashing back and forth, reading my thoughts like it was a movie screen on fast forward.

I cocked my arm back, ready to throw the sand into her face and pull her from the water and she'd burn like a vampire in the sun and then I'd run for home and have hot dogs on the grill and then swim in the lake that would be all my own again.

But before I could, she reached out her hand, fast as a blink, and grasped the top of my head. Clutching my skull, she tried forcing me back to the ground.

So strong.

I grabbed her arm, it was immovable, unstoppable. She kept pushing me down. I opened my mouth to scream, *Mom! Dad!* but nothing would come out. Her long fingers wrapped around the top of my head, like some helmet with tentacles was over my skull. Her nails dug in and clenched tighter and tighter, her hands like crab claws, and my brain ready to pop.

I felt it then, a lightning strike from the creature's body zapping into me, like I was wearing one of those electric chair helmets. My body started shimmering and shaking, my teeth clenching together, my hands flailing at her arms to make her stop. The scent of burnt hair surrounded me.

I was going to die. My brain was a metal bowl in a microwave, zapping and zipping and ready to...

But she stopped. And I didn't die. I fell flat on my back when her fingers released. The water came up and encircled me like some chalk outline of a murder victim, only I was alive—or at least thought I was. I could sense things, the water on the side of my face, the sound of the monster woman wading back into the water, submerging, barely a ripple when she swam off.

I thought the surf might take me back out with her, but it left me there. Alone.

My body started shaking then. Bile in my gut burned and boiled and came bubbling up out of me. I lurched over and threw up, my throat scraped raw by the rancid grey puke that came shooting out my mouth, splashing down beside me.

I didn't see Mom and Dad running out of the cottage, but I did feel them finally standing over me. Mom's hand on my back.

"Jewel, what happened?"

"Jewel, slow down, breathe—can you breathe?"

I had no answers, only more bile and vomit. When they realized I was powerless to speak, they just held me while more poured out of my body and splashed into the lake. Each time I heaved I thought I was empty, but there was some deep, endless well inside me, and it got pumped and pumped into the lake, boiling hot and sizzling my esophagus. Burning everything, burning me alive.

#

We went to the hospital that night because I kept throwing up more and my thoughts kept spinning dizzy and delirious.

And then more hospitals, and doctors—so many doctors, and tests after tests followed. For days, weeks, months, years.

I had brain cancer. The fast and aggressive kind. Lots of IVs were stuck in me. Mom and Dad cried during treatment, talking to me sitting bedside or standing at my doorway, arguing with each other when my door was closed sometimes. Opening the door to hug me, to cry on me. Buying me more things than they needed to, promising me I'd be okay. Promising me they wouldn't lie. Doctors and nurses who smiled more the worse I got over the next couple of years.

I almost died around ten, my parents arguing with muffled voices, trying to stay quiet, Mom leaving out to go on her walks, coming back quiet and pensive. Then they went to their separate corners, but always came together to cry and hug on each other, and then hug on me.

Then the medicine suddenly started working again, and I didn't die! I was going to live.

"You're beautiful like that, you know," my mom said when fuzz grew on the back of my head and I was a shade less bald. But saying it made her cry, and she sniffed while her hand ruffled my hair. "You've got a light in you that can never be put out. See, the doctors were wrong."

They *were* wrong, and something kept me alive longer than doctors thought. I spent another year at the lake, a summer watching over the water, not going in because my immune system was low, and because *who knows why*, so I threw rocks at it from the shore. Each time I imagined the rocks were hitting Lilith of the Lake. Nobody knew about her but me, so I had to hit her right in the temple, the place they told me at recess it can kill you with just one shot.

I imagined telling people about her so they could go on a hunt, all of them with boats and guns and nets, hunting her down like Jaws, but I didn't tell anybody. I didn't hit her with the rock, and the cancer made me have more seizures. It got bad again, so bad, and so fast.

I was stuck and trapped inside the hospital. Lilith of the Lake would be free for whatever she did, because I was going to die. They declared I was in hospice, the lights kept dim, the air like medicine, sad smock-wearing people everywhere. The last bed I'd lie in. Slipping in and out of different places in my head, the blankets were warm, the pillow soft, but the death that wanted me was warmer, softer, and I opened my eyes to look at life for the last time before I went there.

There was a coldness by my bedside, like the eclipse that day at the beach. I squinted my eyes, and I saw him.

Who are you? I asked to myself, unable to form the words in my mouth.

His hair was pitch-dark and hanging over his pale skin, his eyes green like a cat. He was holding Mom's hand, rubbing her fingers with his long fingers, and as he smirked at me with his piercing eyes, his mouth was quivering.

Where's my dad?

I wanted to see my dad. I knew he was near, but it wasn't his face I saw — it was this man I knew was the Lamia I was warned about. He looked at me knowingly, a secret only he and I knew, that nobody in the room would believe and nobody could protect me from. He waited eagerly for my last breath, a dog waiting for his dinner bowl. He feigned sorrow and offered false condolences to my mom.

My mom found comfort in his fingers, but I knew he was wrapping his hands on hers like an octopus, suction cups stuck to her skin, ready to squeeze her to death. She was his prey, I was his prey, and I wanted him gone.

Dad, where are you? Get this man away. Mom, Mom get away from him, stay away.

But I couldn't talk. The room spun just before I died, in and out of focus. The last things I saw were his quivering lips, moist, salivating; a monster waiting for me to die. His black hair hung over him, a veil covering his evil eyes, his mouth with a whisper; "You're dying, Jewel, and very soon, I'll inject your soul."

CHAPTER THIRTEEN:
OF SHARON GRIEVING HER DAUGHTER

WEEKS AFTER JEWEL had been cremated, Sharon still felt haunted by the image of her daughter's body set on fire.

The cancer and chemo had already burned her from the inside out. Her blonde hair was no longer there to cremate, her smiles had diminished by degrees. Most of her weight had wilted, not ready for the fire. She was an ant who'd been slowly sizzled in the heat of a malicious magnifying glass called chemotherapy, until hospice came and then...

"You felt the flames inside you when she burned, didn't you?" Pastor Lucas Lamia asked. "You are as one with her—but they want to separate you. Don't let that happen. *You need those ashes back.*"

The words were thick from the mouth of this pastor, of what faith, she wasn't sure, but he had been by her side, summoning unspoken feelings, pulling them from her mind, moving them about in the air like a magician with his cards.

She had at first refused the invitation to his support group, but now here she was, standing in the doorway of his place just a few miles from the lake, and waiting for his words to take root.

"You need to hear this clearly and respond as if everything you love is at stake. Releasing those ashes would be a terrible mistake—for the soul of your child, for the health of your heart. You are her mother; your rib is her rib. It would be a mistake you cannot reverse. And I certainly hope you don't believe those rumors regarding the lake."

He was talking to her with one hand on her shoulder. Surely, he could feel her heart beating, full of confusion, drumming to a song with no sheet music, traveling down a road with no map.

Sharon scratched an imaginary itch. She looked to the ground, looked to the ceiling, her hands struggling for something to fill them, as if noticing the absence of the urn, so she crossed her arms and squeezed tightly across her chest.

The pastor's frame towered high, and her head was slightly bowed as if waiting to be pulled into his chest in an embrace. She was just under the doorway, one foot in the room, the other on the front porch. Three members of the Eternal Life Support Group sat in the circle at the middle of the room, all parents themselves. Some were cradling their dead child's ashes in their laps, urns like little trophies.

Unlike Sharon, with her hands empty, her heart was lost. She was a compass spinning erratically in each direction, never settling on one.

His way to her core had started in small truths, a thousand first slices. He was there at the hospital after the diagnosis, speaking to her in a way that none of the doctors could. She shared almost everything with him—except for the secrets she wouldn't even share with her husband—and the pastor shared of his own loss many times:

"My son died young, just like your child. I also saw over his cremation, and miss him with an intensely deep hurt. But I take salvation in that he remains in my heart. I hear his voice, I feel his presence, I sense his pain. The sun would never rise the same again as it did on his last day walking the earth."

During Jewel's chemotherapy, Lucas was the spiritual seer who whispered words into her ear that screamed larger truths into her heart. *'The medical treatment will damage her body, but her soul cannot be hurt. Can never die, can never die, can never die, can never die... Her body will get eaten, and her heart will stop, and her brain will starve for oxygen. But her spirit never dies, never dies, never dies... Practice knowing this, living this.'*

It was Lucas who helped her through the anticipatory grief, expecting the death, talking openly about it, planning for it, even having her rehearse the day as if Jewel was already dead, for practice. He invited her to the support group even before Jewel died.

"He's pulling you away from me," Kai had said. But Kai wasn't by her side when Jewel died. It was Lucas Lamia who held her hand at the moment of death; Kai couldn't get himself to come inside the room.

Luca Lamia was the mesmerizing Charybdis, sucking her down, but was she ignoring the inevitable crash against the rocks? She wasn't sure, but no place felt safe, and this crash felt as good as any. Because she lived with her secret, and couldn't even tell Kai what she'd done, the deal she'd made—and that his death was next.

"Kai and I are going to return her to the lake," Sharon explained to Lamia as if he hadn't already been told. "It's where we met, where we first fell in love. It's a place so special to us, a place just as special to Jewel. She was never happier than when she was inside that lake, and now we want to scatter her remains and make her part of it forever. What's wrong with that?"

"Your answer is in the question and the sound of your words. As you ask me, I hear your doubt. You are about to watch her die a second death, about to watch her drown in that lake."

The three members of the Eternal Life Support Group watched Sharon from their place in the circle, sullen but stubborn faces, more well put together than her.

Was this her future?

She looked at them, arranged in their seats, a perfect circle, their best faces forward, stuck in such sadness but confident to address it, like they slipped on a new skin and it fit. One woman just nineteen years old, still just a child herself; another sixty-seven, lost her grandchildren though she was the only mother they knew. Not a single one of them shared the same guilt Sharon did, not a single one killed their own child. None of them held her secrets.

They just vomit out their stench of grief for all to see.

Sharon wondered if this was the pastor's game, to seduce those stuck in grief—but that wasn't it, she knew it. There was nothing sexual about this, but this emotional affair was intense, and ever since he was by her side she was just a moon in his orbit, stuck in his gravity. At times, he beamed with life and vigor, his weathered skin full of zest and energy, that fresh scent of nature after a rain. Other times, he seemed the color of dying leaves, flesh aging and shaky. He couldn't hide the two extremes. He was certainly not handsome, but his face was intriguing and complex. In a sense, like Mick Jagger, she thought. She could certainly imagine him introducing himself as a man of wealth and taste who'd been around for many, many years...

"Trying to take care of all these people is killing you," she said to him, deflecting. "You look more tired than I am. Anyone tell you that?" That sounded more judgmental than caring, the way she wanted it to, but his skin seemed so weathered in this light, the tired bark of an aging tree.

"I'm good," he dismissed her. "When people like you do well, I feel better. And I don't think you'll get the right guidance elsewhere. Stop me if I'm wrong. Your husband can't comprehend this. It's not his fault he's unable to, and I think you know this. The threads that connect you with your daughter should always stay tied. *The ashes should be saved.* And please do not believe those voodoo stories about the lake."

She looked into the circle one last time, deciding if she belonged with this group or not. Kacy's face stood out most, the young woman who wore witchy dresses and Birkenstocks, smelled of patchouli, tattoos up and down her body. On her arm, a sleeve of flowers, on her leg, a sleeve of barbed wire. She held the golden urn of ashes on her lap, so shiny she could stare at it and it stared back with her own reflection.

And when it's quiet enough, she says she can hear her child from inside.

'She still cries for me, still cries and cries, cries for me... And when I hold the urn in my hand, and I look at it with love, and I hum to it, sing softly, rock it or walk it about the house, the cries fade away, and I can feel her fade to sleep...to sleep...'

"You're wondering about the whispers, aren't you?" Lucas spoke into Sharon's ear as she stared at Kacy. "You're wondering about the whispers, because you have heard them, too."

Sharon would never admit it, but she wasn't about to deny it, because she didn't want him to stop talking.

"Let me explain. Our souls remain in the ashes after the body is burned, at times, with souls such as hers. It certainly does not happen often, but when the human who died is so unique, and at times the result of an untimely death, like Jewel, and when the soul is not ready to let go onto its presumed trajectory, that's when it happens. I've heard it burn during cremation, crackling at a dog whistle pitch. I've even seen the brilliant explosions like a magnificent star detonating in the vast expanse of the cosmos. The dust of these spirit-bits settle and are returned to you in a golden urn of ashes. The remains contain her essence, the soul remains, and I suggest these things are not to be scattered, but rather held dear.

"You do not need to believe Kacy, you do not need to believe me, but believe your own mind. Return here with the ashes, and I can take you a step further. I can promise, with the Gods of every faith as my witness, you'll hear her voice again. Go fetch them, go fetch your daughter's ashes before they are dashed into the lake."

Chapter Fourteen:
Of Lucas Lamia and the Eternal Life Support Group

THOUGH SHARON MURPHY had left my small home, the scent of her wounds bleeding with grief were left behind and loomed large. As much as a shark smells blood, my gut was thrashing in excitement over her hurt and sadness. Little bits of it floated in the air, dust particles glistening, and I breathed them in, deep into my nostrils, like a shot of cocaine they went straight to my brain, coursing through my bloodstream.

And then gone.

So I needed more.

God I was tired of always needing more. More death, more remains, more souls. What other choice did I have, but to consume and serve others?

The mothers remained in their circle, like grains of salt protecting something sacred. They saw themselves in Sharon, this woman new to their group, still living in the outskirts. They knew, as I knew, she'd be back. And when she brought back the urn with her child's ashes, the first time might be with embarrassment, but eventually, it will be as natural as bringing her purse.

And soon after, I would empty her urn and share an injection with the poor mother, both our veins eager for the bee sting.

I returned to the circle, walking with a touch of dizziness, my hands shaky, that voice of my hungry boy inside screaming to be fed.

I sat in the group, and as I often did, posed a theoretical question: "What would your morning be like if your child were still alive? Not sick, not pale and weak from chemotherapy or in palliative care, but alive and thriving." I was poking exposed nerves, some fresh ones, and could feel the pain dripping.

Each mother answered and it summoned forth the soul of their child, their grief rising together like steam from a boiling pot. I was a conductor with his symphony, asking one side of the group, then the next, to speak on their child. They spoke with voices cracking from tears, a mixed of sadness and joy.

But all the while, I was bringing their children back to life in a world that sucks us into death, sometimes with black hole speed, sometimes in the slow, dark specter of aging, many times before a child's skull has even hardened. The arc of life bends to death in its own time, but I'd learned to hammer it flat. For as they talked, their dead children seemed to run around the circle, like some ghostly game of duck, duck, goose, laughing at each other, skinning a knee, crying for their mother.

I couldn't help but tremble. My flesh on fire yet cold as a corpse. Shaky, sweaty, impatient, eager. *Yes, hear them, see them, feel them...they are with you, and they go with you when they leave.*

The climax came naturally, when it all hit a crescendo, when their emotions popped like a champagne cork, then settled back into their bodies, confetti falling to the ground. Then they shuffled off towards the door, too lost in themselves to notice my flesh trembling.

"Wait, wait Kacy, Kacy Baker. Don't leave yet. Kacy, come here."

My hand on her shoulder, I guided her back inside. Her flowered dress flowed, her movements fluid as a breeze.

I studied Kacy's face. That she lost her six-year-old child was evident upon a glance. She'd been beaten, shell-shocked, moving about the world because she had to, not that she wanted to anymore. Every reaction, every breath, was done out of an unwanted duty, an obligation.

During the grieving group, Kacy's lips had been moving and murmuring, responding to a voice others could not hear. She was responding to the stimuli from her lost child, the psychosis just a whisper to start, then gaining some volume, and the group, many who had seen this before, envied this and wished they were the chosen one.

I took her by the hand. She was melting inside, her flesh hot and mushy, while my body was in a cold sweat. The contrast made her hand seem on fire. I guided her to a table as if a seduction, and there was indeed something sensual at that moment, an intimacy that separates the spirits of humans from beasts in the wild.

We sat in chairs near the table, facing each other, knee to knee. She set the urn on the table. It glowed, majestic, the very ark of the covenant. I took both her hands in mine and turned them over, veins facing upwards.

"Kacy, you hear him, don't you? The voice of your child. That's how this works. Mothers can hear their child's pitch when others cannot."

"Yes, yes! I can, I can!" Relief changed her expression into something hopeful, less pained — but only for a moment. "I'm scared. This isn't right. I'm not right."

"No, you are as right as a human can be. Never apologize for a miracle. Be as still as you can, close your eyes. It will get louder. As I suspected, your child's soul... Your child's soul remains in the ashes.

"Breathe that in, he's *in* there, Kacy, I'm telling you he's in there, and he can *grow*. Imagine his voice, imagine him saying 'Mama.' What would it be like to feel him with you again? Instead of being trapped inside this tiny metal coffin, separated from his mother."

I rubbed her trembling hands, pushing my message deeper into her heart.

"Bring him out, it will only get louder, clearer."

The urn beat then, all three of us syncing, members of a band tuning their instruments.

She held the urn in her hand, tried to twist. It was sealed. It needed some hard taps to loosen it. I let her decide, and she presented the urn to me, pleading for help to open it.

I opened the top with shaking hands, brain telling every nerve to have patience, to resist the impulse and be patient.

I handed it back to her, and she poured the ashes onto a pile on the table. Chunky grey soot, but there was a majesty there, they were golden to me, not grey.

A near seizure hit Kacy's face, her lips mouthing words but not in English, speaking in tongues. The roses on her sleeve of tattoos seemed to be growing, flourishing, the reds reaching out to bloom, the barb wire on her leg tightening.

"Kacy, you can hear him now, so loud. I know it."

Emotions seemed to bead on her skin, like sweat in a sauna, steam filling the room. She did try to speak, but words were impossible, she could only nod her head — *Yes. Yes.*

"Good…good…he is crying for you to be closer, the same way he used to, at your breast, in his crib. He suffers without you. We need to put him back inside you. He will be alive again. He will have your five senses, and you will have his. More than just in your womb, this will place him in your bloodstream, in your brain, your soul.

"You need me as your guide. It's what I do."

Her head was nearly bowing, her eyes looking up at me with deference. Her jaw hung slack. She tried to mouth words again, and was clearly frustrated that she couldn't say a thing.

"Shhhh…" I whispered, "this is what happens. What happens next, that is up to you. If you want to see and feel your child grow…it may be more than you're ready for you. Unless…unless you feel you are ready?"

She nodded again.

My spine shuddered. The beast in my chest yearned to destroy this woman and take all her child's ashes for myself. Living for over a hundred years and always needing to feed, constantly craving, the best moments of my life were but a momentary relief of this suffering. Sometimes I wished my next one was the last, that the Witch of the Well would give me a reprieve and say, *We will remove your curse, just one more, and then it's over.*

I was tired from saving so many during the war. Tired from saving generations of grieving parents.

It was only moments like this one that helped me push forward, sitting before the pot of gold, the treasured prize, the tiny specs of dust from a young child so fresh.

"I'm going to show you, to guide you, I need to..." Words started to fail, but I'd said enough. She was feeling the same as I was and would allow what was about to happen. I placed the supplies on the table, each synapse salivating over the spirit I was about to ingest.

I sprinkled the sooty ashes in the water of a deep spoon, flame to the bottom of metal, that sweet scent when the water boils and the ashes soak into the potion, the essence of the soul aroma, this fresh young soul. Then finding the blue vein to prick, *ah, the bee sting*, once safely inside, draw some blood, and push the plunger.

It was like breathing out poison and pain and breathing in nirvana. Every atom of my being reveled in the young soul coursing through—the boy's organs, his flesh, his spirit, his memories, reborn inside my soul. *I don't look so tired anymore, now do I Sharon? In fact, I am fresh, renewing and reborn once again.*

I wanted more, I wanted it all—but if I took all the ashes for myself, the guilt became too much. My benevolent heart would not allow it. I was a doctor and a pastor and that would not be denied. I would be of service to God—whatever gods are left to serve.

She held out her arm. I smacked her vein. The prick of the

needle found its mark, pulled some blood, pulled her essence into the tiny chamber, then pushed the remains of her lost child through.

Kacy's eyes spun and swirled and then stuck in place, frozen, all her attention looking inward at the explosion of stimulus within her blood. Her limbs moved with a billion lightning strike twitches. Her lost child had been returned to a deeper womb within her spirit, and the love they shared glowed like a thousand hot suns. She was breathing for two once again.

But soon she'd go mad.

Experience made it clear that this explosion of stimulus would soon become too much. In the days that follow, Kacy would slip into madness, becoming increasingly psychotic, making bizarre statements that family may see as a one-off—until it becomes two, then three. She'd hear coded messages on the radio. She'd disrobe and walk in the street. She'd think she was pregnant with Jesus. Hospitals would try to treat her with medications, and after multiple failed trials, she'd spend the rest of her days in psychiatric confinement.

But what a gift I was giving to her.

Wouldn't Kacy make this same trade to experience her child again, even if she knew what came after?

Yes, she would. She would want it even if she knew what it was.

Kacy was still unable to speak, but eventually was able to stand and staggered out the front door. She'd be lucky to make it home.

I had to move on, too, for I knew the only way to survive was to tap into this newfound energy, to line up my next fix. I needed that next urn with traces of a soul inside, because those barren days are a torturous hell.

That next fix was to be Sharon's daughter. I'd worked Sharon so delicately and patiently for this moment. I had commanded her to return with the ashes before they were dashed into the lake. I expected her to comply and bring me the urn.

But if not, I would happily pay her a visit and indulge myself.

I'd offered her a gift that only a god could deliver for her final days.

Sharon, and her special child, who died a death touched by his own wife, was next.

CHAPTER FIFTEEN:
OF JEWEL JORDAN'S SOUL IN THE ASHES

CALL ME JEWEL.

I was born Julia, then they called me Jules, but now I like Jewel.

In all sorts of ways, I'm not like I was before. It all started with the fire.

"You're dying, Jewel," said the black-haired man as I lay in the hospital bed.

Dying, Jewel…

The words faded, like the person was falling down a deep well. As the words fell into black so did I, dying after three raspy inhales of air.

A weighted curtain was drawn over my eyes, and a dark, cold, dreamless sleep enveloped me. I was completely unaware of the deep slumber until it was over. It may have lasted two hours or may have lasted two centuries, impossible to tell, but when my casket caught flame my senses came alive. As the casket burned, I could sense the history of the wood and the forest where it grew.

The wood came from brilliant walnut trees, growing for decades in Illinois. I could even feel the earth the trees grew from and the bugs and worms burrowing within. I felt the storms that raged against its limbs, the frigid snow, the thawing of spring, and the birds that lived on its branches. All of it, every fiber of its being, even as it succumbed to the flames.

And as the wood casket burned, my own flesh blackened and bubbled.

Of course, I felt the pain, but no, the pain did not hurt.

You will learn what I mean someday.

For two hours the flames made a bonfire out of my body, boiling my organs, the liquid bubbling inside even before my flesh was gone. My bones resisted as long as they could, until the marrow itself began to melt and the tendons and cartilage all turned to ash. I was still in the shape of a body when the flames died, and soon after, once the ashes cooled, my cremains were ground into finer bits, then siphoned into an urn.

Despite the darkness inside this urn, I was aware of such a

spectrum of colors outside. Some colors have no name, they're shades I haven't seen, but colors and feelings and thoughts and memories are expanding.

Because for those two hours my body was being destroyed and burned, it was also being cleansed. Like there was a part of me that was kept secret and hidden, it had to be, because if it was ever revealed while I was among the living, I wouldn't do anything but gaze with slack jaw and mind reeling. With this cleansing by fire, I could sense it all. I'd been reborn into such wonder. It was like my spinal cord was growing roots, and each root was stretching and stretching into other spinal cords, soaking up the nutrients of every other living being, and bringing them all to my brain. It's all a part of me, and I'm part of it.

I could even read what was etched onto the brushed golden sides of the urn:

Julia Jordan
5/8/2012 – 8/4/2024
Forever in our Hearts

Why didn't they spell it 'Jewel' on the urn like I wanted?

If you were to open up the urn sitting on the table of my dad's cottage and look at the ashes with the eyes of the gods, you'd see tiny sparks in my ashes. You'd see transmission between heart and mind and soul, like a downed electrical wire sparking with the stimulus of all that surrounds me.

I'm either twelve years old, or as old as the mother who gave birth to this universe, because I can see and feel and use languages long ago forgotten.

But I'm stuck in this liminal space, no Heaven to take my soul, no body to move or live or swim with. Inside the urn on the kitchen table, in the darkness of our lakeside home, while Dad's in the bedroom wrestling with a sleep that won't have him, as if he's unworthy. He gives up trying, ends the torment and rises from bed.

He walks out of his bedroom, through 4 a.m. darkness, within arm's reach of my cremains. He opens the back sliding door of our house. The life outside instantly greets him, air sweeping over the top of the water, gathering the lake's essence, and then delivering it to caress his cheeks and fill his lungs.

98

He inhales it deeply as he gazes across the surface. It's too dark to see details, but he can sense the lake under the dark sky. He hears its edges, small waves lapping gently at the shoreline, the heartbeat that's proof of life. He's heard the lake rage and scream in darker times, but now, the waters are calm as a coma.

Lights from the two miles across the lake are barely visible, just back porches lit up amongst the dark. The lake, so much longer than it is wide, nineteen miles north and south, two miles east and west, but holds a universe in its grand depths.

Dad loves the lake's presence. The lake never lies, never hides, always shows her true mood, without judgment or intent. Nothing is right or wrong, no justice, no injustice, it's simply one of many colors in a spectrum, the full spectrum of colors, thick blackness, or playful aqua blues, red sunset reflections on purple fractured moonlight. It's well aware of its immortality, as mortals play inside its depths.

Like Paxton told him, *Water* is the supreme example of acceptance. It never struggles, it simply flows. It does not resist. *Water* nourishes all things without trying to. It is content with the low places that people disdain—*Be like water*.

I can hear these words from Paxton, his most trusted friend.

Dad stands in the doorway, one foot still in the living room, the other on the back porch, waiting for one side to pull him. He wants to stay with the lake, for it to take him forever. I can understand that feeling, but the world wants him back inside. He slides the back door wall shut, the *click* when it shuts like the locking of a jail cell.

He feels alone in this room, one big couch, one old kitchen with appliances near antique, but familiar. He needs to sleep, or maybe start the coffee intake now. The coffee maker isn't plugged in. He spots the cord dangling there like an exposed nerve, a loose connection.

With a hazy brain and staggering gait he walks over, plugs it in, and imagines for a second that everything returned to normal in his life. *Ahhh, there it is. Found the problem.*

He imagines I'll come back to life and he can live and love on with our family together, like he used to, like he had planned to.

Mornings like this one, Dad used to chop up a cantaloupe for breakfast, leaving it outside the fridge long enough to reach room temperature, not cold where it hurt my mom's teeth. On summer days we played under the sun in the magical water. At night, we were dazzled by sunsets, or watched storms come in from the lake, thunderous explosions in the clouds, lightning zapping the water, making everything inside come alive, a million Frankenstein monsters.

Mom and Dad fell in love here as camp counselors, nearly children themselves. Then they had me, their only child—but the brain cancer ate me from the inside out. The chemical therapy couldn't kill the cancer. Only the flames from the crematorium could.

On the table where we used to dine sits my golden urn full of my ashes. If my dad would just try hard enough he could sense me surveying the room from inside. This room that used to be full of love and smiles, and a carpet tracked with sand from the beach carried inside between my toes. (*"Wash your feet Jewel"* – but I usually didn't.)

I wonder from inside the urn: *What has become of you two?*

Dad wishes it was different.

I failed my family, he thinks, but to fail means he had a choice, that he could have faced me during my last breath. But he found it impossible. (I knew you were near, Dad. I knew it.) But he could not fight that pain enough to even be in the room.

I'm in the same kind of urn you are, he thinks. *Just as metallic and cold, nothing inside can get out.* So he let Pastor Lucas comfort my mom, and he is right when he suspects the man is not as he seems.

Dad hopes somehow my mom will forgive him, that she'll stay with him for a while longer before leaving—he can sense that she is leaving—but he'll take any bit of her before she does. He's losing her, and she's been staying away from home. Today she is coming to be with him. Will she even spend the night? Who knows. First, they plan to scatter my ashes in the lake.

Scatter? Terrible word. *Scatter.* Dad hates that word. So many wrong words. Why not a different word? He doesn't know which one, but it's not 'scatter'. This was to be a ceremony, grand and majestic, sad and tragic. A union of the two souls—the lake, and that of his child's remains.

He remembers how I splashed in these waters and played on its beaches and tubed and fished and made sandcastles in the sun. For years I was baptized by this lake with water so fresh and mysterious and clear and inviting.

He remembers when I cried at this hour of the night as a young babe, and he went to console me in the nursery, holding me until I fell back to sleep.

But on this dark night instead of holding me he picks up the urn and holds my cremains. The urn feels heavy in his hand, firm edges, solid and permanent. I want to feel the warmth of his flesh but instead I feel his rage growing, like he's afraid to hold it—to hold me—like he's undeserving, and wants to propel it, fire it like a cannon shot.

If he'd just listen he would hear the lake asking to receive my ashes, to take me back where I belong, speaking in soft whispers: *We hold all her memories, all your memories, and we will hold her too.*

Take me there, I whisper back to ears that deny they can hear.

There will be no more sleep, he decides, he'll be awake until the sun rises. He turns the coffeemaker on, and while it brews, he carries me in the urn to the back door. This time he steps outside all the way, and closes it behind him.

Back outside, that feels better. Even in the darkness of the urn, I can feel the spectacle of constellations sparkle with brilliance. It's beyond the hour when crickets chirp, the waves lapping have seduced them back to sleep.

He carries me closer to the lake, and I feel the lake pulling at me, like magnets getting closer, until soon enough—*snap*—we connect and unite as one.

I wonder about Lilith of the Lake. She's out there somewhere.

My dad sees a porch light across the water…but then realizes it's moving, coming closer, gliding steadily towards shore. The faint sounds of an oar splashing, the light flickering, and he realizes it's a flame. An orange, flickering flame. Nothing electric here, this is fire. A torch burning from the rowboat of our neighbor, Garcon, who lives across the street.

"Can't sleep," my dad says when he's close to shore.

"Don't sleep," Garcon answers.

A fishing pole towers over him like a scythe, and the torch is burning, mounted at the bow. The reddish orange flames are reflected by the surface of the dark water below, the colors dancing about.

Garcon's house is actually an RV that sits across the two-lane street and has been there for nearly thirty years. It was originally set up with a little garden, a well-manicured lawn surrounding it, but now is full of knee-high grass. Only the street-side grave marker where his child was hit is tended to. Dad made sure Garcon knew he could keep his dinghy tied to our dock.

"You bringing it in?" Dad asks, ready to reach out a hand and help him ashore.

"No, I'm here to take you out."

Dad stands hesitant after this presumptive invite. He's promised to go out with Garcon so many times, but it was one of those things to say to be polite, never expected to happen. He's only been inside Garcon's RV one time, and never been in his dingy. Never wanted to be that close.

But they had something uniquely in common now; both with a child lost before their time. Garcon's son died shortly after I was born, and there was an unspoken connection of the sadness they shared. My dad was fine to keep it unspoken where it was safe, sharing concern in conventional pleasantries. *If I get too close to Garcon, I'll become him*, Dad thought, *living like a recluse, letting life go to waste.*

"I don't know. It's late, and I should sleep."

There would be no sleep. Dad had already surrendered to waking. The torch shows no signs of fading, burning bright against the darkness.

"What you got there?" Garcon asks.

Dad realizes he's still holding my urn. This boatman had come out of the night to take him and his daughter away.

"It's Jewel. Jewel's ashes."

"Why you holding them?"

"Sharon and I are going to scatter them this weekend."

Dammit...*scatter. What's a better word?* He hates that word.

"You know, I did the same with Dion. Come on, my friend, I'll take you both."

Garcon's child, Dion, was even younger than me when he died. Cars come up around that bend in the road so fast, no time to stop if something is in the road, and if you're trying to cross, you have just seconds to get out of the way. His little boy was in the road, but never got out of the way. My dad never talked to him about this much, but since I died, he just imagines the look in Garcon's eyes saying, *Now we both know.*

"Best to scatter the ashes up the lake a-ways. Northeast side," Garcon says. "Get the best results there. And best row with the oar and turn off the engine, don't want to scare away what's below."

Dad carries me onto the boat, the torch at the helm of the dingy lighting the way. They're venturing out at night as was done in the ways of old, holding a torch to summon the fish to the surface, because the water is so deep. So blue, so cold, and so deep.

"Things okay for you?" My dad breaks the silence when we got farther from shore, but immediately regretted asking that, opening the door for a long boat ride when he should be in bed. But the lake is like that—it brings things out that you can normally keep hidden, freedom from the gravity of land, floating above the universe below.

In the daylight, the water's so clear you can see the lake's bottom even a hundred yards from shore, but at night, it's all infinite and dark. Whatever comes out at night seems just below the surface, waiting for bait.

And Lilith of the Lake is just below the surface, too, because I hear her, whispering: 'Jewels. You're back. Come swim with us.'

She knows I'm back.

"Yes sir!" Garcon finally answered my dad's question. "I'm okay. It's all A-okay. I like the nights, now."

Now, and Dad assumes the *now* means *now that he's lost a child,* and my dad feels that there is a *then* and there is a *now.* An implausible now that should not be, but can't be undone.

Within every one of his thoughts, I can hear my dad tormenting himself about my last day alive in the hospital.

I was in the hallway when she died. I couldn't take it. I couldn't stay by her bed when she died. What is wrong with me?

Garcon's rowing starts to slow, the torch flickering in the breeze. Soon enough, he slips the oars out of the water, but we still glide from momentum like an astronaut floating. He takes the torch out of its holder, and places it just above the water, leaning towards the surface, having his moment.

Dad wants to turn back time, be like it was before this decade when life got ripped from him. He suddenly feels more alone than ever, holding me in his arms, holding his guilt even tighter.

And I long to be back in the lake. To answer the whispers. To join them, join the whispers that sound like children, so I whisper back: *I'll be there soon.*

You need to come now. It's not safe back on land. The Lamia will get you.

I'll be back soon. They are going to scatter me.

Dad senses me, even though he doesn't realize it, because as the lake beckons me inside, the ashes of my essence start to vibrate. Each flake and chunk is ready to jump into the water, to be accepted into its arms, a longed-for mother.

My yearnings peak, the ashes in microscopic motion. My dad feels the urn slipping from his hands and imagines he's a wide receiver with a tipped ball, fumbling the urn in the air, desperately trying to grasp it but finally dropping the urn entirely. The golden urn would sink to the bottom, trapping me in the dark depths inside this urn forever at a bottom too deep to rescue. Dad's final mistake in a series of mistakes, and my mom shaking her head, *our daughter at the bottom of the lake* — dark, cold, alone, rather than scattered.

He prefers the word *scattered* suddenly.

I fear for what my dad's life has become. His sadness is a thick, dark fog and he wanders in it alone, eyes closed, afraid of what he'll see. Stuck, unmoving, not understanding the eternity of existence.

Because he wants to join me. Wants to die and be at the bottom of the lake with me.

How can I make him see and understand?

I cry out to him but it's at an octave his ears cannot detect. He didn't want this nighttime fishing trip, he wishes he was on shore.

"You're not going to put your line in the water?" my dad asks, trying to fast forward through this awkward moment.

"I just like looking," Garcon says, his head leaning over the dingy. The flame he holds has cast its magical hue of orange and red onto the dark water.

"You want to look. I think you need to look."

Dad, don't you realize why he does this?

But my dad doesn't want to look, he wants to go back to shore. He imagines jumping in and swimming to land, buoyed in the water by the urn. He needs me to stay afloat, and I will do what I can to keep him from sinking, even if he wants to sink.

Join us Jewel — but just you, not him yet.

I want to.

"Come on, my friend. Look, just look in the water," Garcon urges my dad again.

"I'm good," Dad declines. That was the final riff, the split, the rumbling earthquake that tore us apart.

"Someday," Garcon says, "someday you'll need to look."

Without saying a word, Garcon puts the oar back in the water, the torch safely in a socket. He rows for a bit, then fires up the engine, just barely above an idle, the torch flickering in the slight wind.

I hear the voices again from the lake.

Don't let them take you back to shore, Jewel. It's not safe for you there. It's not safe for your dad. He'll fill his pockets with heavy stones and jump in the lake. He will be dead on the bottom. And the Lamia will get you on land. Stay at seaaaaa...stay with meeeee...

The woman's voice is like a snaky sea serpent, fading as the boat gets closer to shore.

When the boat's grounded, Dad steps off to solid ground, me and the golden urn in his hand, but Garcon isn't done. "Gonna go back and stay until morning. Who knows how many nights on the lake I have left?"

My dad watches as he pushes back off from the shoreline, the soft sounds of oars in the water and then the lake fades into the night.

I was in Dad's hands, but I wanted to comfort *him*. I needed to comfort him, because I could feel his darkest thoughts and see a terrible future. Once Dad had put my ashes into the water he wanted to stay with me, inside the lake forever—and I saw him there, with an anchor tied around his ankle, stuck on the bottom, a lake that is so deep, and so cold.

Chapter Sixteen:
<u>Of Sharon Returning from Lamia's</u>

SHARON WAS DRIVING back home, fearful the lake house was not where she belonged anymore. It felt less like a home, and more like a tomb. A mausoleum. Dead daughter inside and a cloud of haunting memories, the distance in between Kai and her growing colder each day, so cold it would soon freeze over, like the lake.

How long until it cracks and she drowns inside?

She was clenching the wheel tightly, letting go only to grab the Dr. Pepper from the cup holder to take a swig, wishing it was a pint of Jack Daniels instead. To her right, the lake kept peeking from behind the houses, diamonds glistening off the blue water, sparkling and shimmering.

Such a gorgeous drive, but she had this urge to keep going. To drive south down 75, head west down 80 or 90 to Chicago, Sturgis, Cheyenne. Get away from here, fully break. Start anew.

The rest of the country, the wide expanse of the world, was calling, like it always did if she stayed too long in one spot. It had been a dozen years now — though Kai wasn't lying when he said the way the landscape changes through the four seasons on the lake, you may as well be traveling: from the hot sunny summer days to the explosion of color and splendor of fall. Then, in the winter, the lake out their back window became a frozen tundra, waiting for the rebirth of spring, when the greening is enough to prove to even the biggest cynic of the resurrection of all dead things.

Living on this lake, you see as much change as you do living on the road, all by just staying in one spot, and letting the planet spin under you.

Truth was, she was scared, and needed to get out of there before the Woman of the Well took another loved one.

Sharon had wanted to get Julia away from the lake, and thought she had more time (she was nearly two years younger than Dylan was when she made that bargain) But it seems the Well sensed this, so got to her daughter early.

And now this place would never be the same.

Would leaving be running *towards* something, or *from* something?

Of course leaving Kai now was running. She knew she couldn't take Kai with her, because he'd never leave. She literally imagined him dying in the seat next to her if she drove him away from a fifty-mile radius of the lake. Flopping in the seat like a fish, drowning outside of his blessed body of water.

Instead, the lake was going to kill him, and when she did the math, she knew it would be soon. He had no idea he was living his last days. So many secrets. And it would be her fault.

Before she turned into the long driveway to the lake house, she was greeted by a crooked cross that jutted out roadside, a tattered red ribbon draped around it, and plastic flowers that would stay colorful for eternity. The sad father had put up a noble fight to stay a memory for the boy who died roadside in front of his dilapidated old RV. That RV would likely never leave this parcel of land, but foliage might cover it up. The man just a version of Kai's future.

"Can you imagine her dying like that?" Kai once asked, as if the pain of Jewel's cancer treatment was any less than what Garcon's child felt upon impact. Sharon hadn't answered. She held back the dam of anger at everything he said and found her way to forgive him. 'Forgive yourself for anything,' as Lucas Lamia put it.

But it's the accumulation, Kai, it's the accumulation that kills you, that's too much to plow through.

If they put the ashes in the lake, he'd probably be afraid to enter again, same as he feared the hospital room during Jewel's last breath.

She parked in the front, turning off the engine, wondering if Kai was watching from the window.

With a deep breath, she went to the door, opened it with a faint, "Hello?" She ducked her head as if a memory would take a jab at her face and she'd miss it like a boxer bobbing and weaving. No sound greeted her. It was empty, silent, a shell, everyone gone. Kai wasn't there, and she didn't want to yell for him.

Out the back window, she saw the diamonds sparkling off the blue lake. They seemed to twinkle even more brightly and rapidly, greeting her.

Welcome home.

She set her bag down on a chair. Next to it, on the table, sat the urn. Front and center, like a centerpiece. And today they planned on emptying it. It was what Kai expected. He'd be shocked if she said otherwise.

She hated the idea of debating where to put the ashes. Leaving her daughter in this lake was a way of saying she would never move on from this house, right? How could she? With her daughter permanently tied there?

Kai, you need to understand what's coming. We need to go, you don't understand, I killed her, I should have gotten her out. She wanted to confess to Kai, and then share that she had cursed him too, but he'd never believe her, and even then, would not leave this place.

'*You're about to watch her die a second death and drown in that lake,*' was what Lucas Lamia said.

Lamia really expected her to return to the support group, and even bring the ashes, but she was so torn. Jewel was conceived in the lake water, raised in the lake water—why not return her to her source?

But Sharon agreed with the pastor. She didn't want the lake to have her ashes. She wanted to keep them.

Because Lamia was right; she *could* hear the ashes. Not words, not sentences, but the murmurs of Jewel's voice. The sound of her sighs. The way she breathed and smelled. Sharon still felt all of this and more in the air. Even if she couldn't make out any words, she felt the tone, the volume, and could feel her child's memories inside the faint sounds.

Coming from the ashes? Of course not. But removing the ashes and the urn was taking too much out of this house.

"Every time we look out over the lake, we'll know it's Jewel shining," Kai told her, but what does that mean? For the rest of their lives they'd be the guardian of Jewel's tomb—pretty soon, their tomb. Staying by this lakeside for eternity.

Why not just fill our pockets up with stones and join her in the lake forever? Sharon thought this more than once but dared not share with Kai—because he thought it even stronger, and certainly much louder.

It was so much easier with her Gramma, who died slowly, then all at once, as they say.

She was in South Dakota with Gramma, eating lunch roadside (ham sandwiches on white bread with mustard—not mayo, mustard, because it keeps better on the road) when her grandmother had the stroke. It was like watching a Netflix show with poor Wi-Fi, Gramma suddenly glitching. Her words stopped, mouth drooped, eyes spinning and spinning and spinning in place, waiting for a connection.

The connection didn't come. Their roadside picnic was over. No cell service.

Sharon was good on that lifeboat. She made quick decisions, as much as the urge was to sit there and cry and hug on Gramma and hope for rescue, she acted.

Even at thirteen years old.

She'd driven an ATV on an Oklahoma ranch, driven Mario Kart on a handful of Wiis, and drove the Jeep Cherokee in a few empty parking lots, but that was it. She had to do her best with guesswork while fighting tears to get the car to *just go forward*. Nobody was coming down this road. She had to decide:

Go back down the road they came, or go forward?

Going forward saved her grandmother's life, they told her, but did not save her brain. Had she gone back, she wouldn't have made it in time. As it was, Sharon found her way to a service station and called an ambulance. It still took twenty minutes until the EMTs were there.

Years later, after some real shitty care in a nursing home, after words to Sharon that she would never forget, then being non-vocal the second half, her gramma passed.

Cremation was the cheaper option. The service was attended by a party of twelve, eight were friends from the nearby Cheyenne art show. Soon after, they released the ashes into the wind, and now her dust was in every breath Sharon took.

If her gramma was in the wind, her daughter should be in the lake.

It was that simple. Sorry, Lamia.

Sharon picked the urn up, felt its weight, figured it would tell her what it wanted if she just listened. Sharon was sure she heard Jewel's sweet, infectious giggles coming from inside. Though the laughter was of course coming from a memory, not the urn, emptying the ashes into the water seemed a sure way for the laughter to fade.

How can I let go of the precious thing inside this?

You're exactly right, Lamia. Don't scatter the ashes. The tennis match of decisions continued.

She twisted the top of the urn but it wouldn't budge, packed tighter than a pickle jar. It took some light banging of the lid, and some twists, but soon she opened it up.

Inside the urn, the red velvet sack reminded her of a Crown Royal bag filled with overpriced liquor, drawstring included. Sharon pulled it open, and revealed a plastic bag, sealed, and the ashes inside.

She unsealed the plastic and poured the ashes out on the platter that once displayed fruit, but now sat empty and lonely.

The white platter never looked so glorious with those ashes on top.

Sharon was alone with her girl, staring at the finely ground remains — grey-white bits of death, not the rainbow that her daughter really was. So many dreams Jewel had, forever deferred, so many bedtime stories unfinished, a world unexplored. The depths of this lake was her world, and they were about to put her back.

You do need out of this urn, Jewel. We'll release you, we'll set you free. Maybe the wind should take you beyond the lake.

She left the ashes on the platter. Let Jewel feel that freedom for now.

Sharon slid the back door wall open and stepped through outside. Diamonds sparkling off the blue lake began to twinkle so bright and rapid she was blinded for a moment. The lake's sparkle seemed so excited to see her, like a child greeting Santa Claus.

She saw him then, wading in the water, the moment just before he broke from a walk into a swim, taking the last few strokes before climbing aboard the swim raft. The water made her more nervous now — she expected to see Kai start to spasm, start to vomit the way Jewel did. Poisoned inside from swimming in poisoned water. She wanted to scream a warning to him, the same way she wished she'd screamed at Jewel and taken her away. But when you have secrets nobody will believe, you're stuck keeping them.

I'm soon going to lose you too, she wanted to say, *and can't bear to watch. That's why I have to leave before I watch the lake take you. God knows you'll never leave on your own.*

He noticed her from the raft, and she figured he expected her to come to him, but she would not, and maybe a bigger fear was he would come rushing to her, asking her with a glorious love in his eyes to finally share her hidden truths and fears — *don't you remember who I am? It's me. Your mate. Why are you hiding? I know you're hiding.*

She stepped closer to the lake, and watched the ripples on the shore. The lake never stops, always active, never dies. Full of life. Swimming underneath, flying above, floating on top. One death inside the lake wouldn't matter, the lake lives on.

Sharon gave Kai a wave, both of them pensive, staring across the water at each other, too far apart to really read each other's expressions or to gauge each other's temperature. Both of them waiting for the other, neither one acting, stuck in their safe spots, stuck in fear.

He would stay out there, and her on the shore. Good on a lifeboat, but not good at life.

Chapter Seventeen:
<u>Of Kai in the Lake</u>

As a plant needs water, Kai needed the waters of Torch Lake for nourishment just the same. He felt healthy in these moments, planted in the water, but leaning towards the flame of the sun above. As if a spiritual photosynthesis, he soaked in the rays like a solar panel, gathering energy, fueling his spirit, his desire to go on.

But now he was a solitary plant. No forest. No friends. No daughter (save the ashes left in the kitchen table). He'd be sprinkling part of himself later inside the lake, and it couldn't come soon enough that the lake would take all of him.

The darkness of last night's late night, torch-lit cruise with Garcon was just a dream. Up by the house, he heard the door slide open, felt eyes on him and caught some movement. Sharon was back earlier than he thought. They looked at each other from afar.

She waved, and he gave her a wave back. His hand flailing, unconvincing, with low enthusiasm since he was certain she was looking at him with disdain.

How he wanted her to walk out to him, wading through the waters, a priestess ready to give a baptism.

But she wouldn't. Instead, after the obligatory visual announcement she had arrived, she returned inside.

He stepped off the raft, lying flat on the water, afloat, setting himself still, becoming part of the water the way Paxton told him how. Flowing, flexible, accepting. Letting the sounds of the lake take him over, his head just above water, sanitizing his poison heart, his poison body, that would create such a beautiful child only to become sick, such imperfect creatures they were. With ears just below the water, he imagined he could hear everything inside this gigantic lake trying to speak to him.

With some dread, it felt time to leave, to go back ashore where the danger of sinking seemed even higher. He emerged from the water, toweling off as he made the hopeful march back to the house.

Beach towel draped around his neck like a prize fighter, he pulled the door open and stepped through. Sliding it shut, felt trapped, a jailer slamming himself in the cell, sentence undetermined

Every time he stepped inside from the lake, he still felt Jewel there next to him, like the itch of a dismembered limb, and he was taken back to summer days of running up from the lake, water dripping off them both, ready to grab some sour cream and cheddar chips and root beer before dinner.

Jewel was gone from his side.

Sharon was standing inside, arms crossed over her heart.

"Hey. I saw you. I saw you from the raft," he said.

Obviously — we waved to each other.

"I was going to take a walk," Sharon said. "You could have stayed. Didn't mean to interrupt your swim."

"Hot as hell out, you'll want a swim after. I was thinking we can order out. I'll pick it up and be back when you're home from your walk."

"I'm not up for a lot. Sorry."

They were talking on either side of the table, across Jewel's urn. It felt like a game of kick the can, both of them equal distance to the urn, waiting for the other one to make a move, draw their weapon, and then a race to see who could snag the child and take her for their own.

"I've been thinking a lot about this," Sharon said, interrupting the silence. "Releasing her ashes. Letting them go. Feels so…final. Doesn't it?"

"It does. We can wait, if you'd rather, wait until tomorrow. Morning calmness might be nice, or even wait until dark," Kai said.

She walked over to the urn, his eyes followed, and he finally noticed she had taken Jewel's ashes out. They were now neatly gathered in a pile on a white ceramic platter, sad, grey, and dry.

Sharon was in a different spot today. He could feel psychic energy fluttering like a punch drunk butterfly.

"Do you think it helps to see them like that? Because I…Well, I'm not sure it does," Kai said with a wince.

"'People should be forgiven for anything.' You remember when they told us that? We thought it sounded so good, and we both wanted forgiveness for it all, but never gave it to each other, did we? Should we?" Sharon asked.

Kai was tired of this line of thinking, even if the questions were rhetorical.

"You're doing that thing where you pretend to be owning up to something but it feels like you're taking me down," Kai said.

"Just not sure what's right," she said, and proceeded to put the tip of a single finger onto the ceramic platter, and slide the ashes in a swirl.

Horrified and fascinated, Kai found himself wondering about tiny bits stuck on Sharon's flesh, not sure if he was angry about this or jealous.

"I'll miss her," she said, eyes fixated on the ashes. "Even this, I'll miss it."

"You're not ready, I understand. Let's wait, then."

Short sentences, afraid of truths, and every breath that filled her lungs, he blamed the pastor for poisoning it all, with his words poisoning the air she breathed.

"Do you ever think we did something that killed her?" Sharon asked, this time the question was not rhetorical. It had been asked before in a hundred different ways, but usually less direct.

"We did everything we could to keep her alive," Kai answered

"But what if *I* did something that *I* shouldn't have?"

"You can't keep doing this to yourself, Sharon. Remember how hard we worked? Took out loans for the consultation. Drove to Ann Arbor, Chicago. Never gave up. We never did. There was no health care that could have saved her."

"You maybe excuse me for everything," said Sharon, "because you excuse yourself for everything."

"Yeah Shar, you're right. I forgive myself for times I wasn't perfect. I need to, God knows you'll never forgive me."

"You don't want to be with her now, do you?" she asked. "You're ready to just put her away. Well, I love her too much for that." She kept her finger in the ashes, her statement inferring she loved their daughter more, her finger revealing she is mine to keep, born of my body, not of yours. "I feel like we're killing her again, putting her out to drown. Don't you see it that way? Don't you want to feel her as close to us as we can?"

"I'd do anything to feel her nearby, anything to see her again, to look into her eyes. I'd gladly do that. We both would do anything. We both did do everything."

"And we'll all be in the lake together, won't we?"

They paced back and forth, boxers on either side of the ring, the urn in the middle, their temperature rising. These little micro aggressions between them, fires that burn, were easily put out in the past by diversion. One of them would start a line with 'remember when she would…' or 'remember when she said...' and revel in the love and memories surrounded by melancholic joy. But the sadness of releasing her ashes into eternity engulfed them. This was too much.

"I need to go," Sharon said. "I'll be back and ready to have one last night as a full family."

CHAPTER EIGHTEEN
<u>OF SHARON WALKING BACK TO THE WELL</u>

SHARON SHOT OUT the same front door she'd just an hour ago walked so pensively inside. Now she wanted *out*.

They were at that stage where they both had such simmering anger and blamed each other for more than their share. If she stayed in the house for one moment longer, she'd find herself yelling such hurtful things, finding all his faults. Better to give guilt than receive, sometimes.

But was he holding as many secrets? Certainly not.

She moved briskly down Torch Lake Road, going north towards Camp WaakWing.

She read the names of cottages written on mailboxes as she moved: Sandy Bottom Bliss, Lake Daze, Summer Breeze. Nearly all had been in her house for lunch, or shared a glass of wine at sunset, an ice cream cone after a chance encounter in Alden. But all of them went somewhere else to live. They didn't stay here. *People don't stay here.*

She finally hit the road that led away from the lake into the meat of the land, rolling hills through farmland.

Heat rose from the street, the pavement a hot grill. Sweat started beading on her head, droplets getting thicker until they streamed down her face. She had to pick up the pace, and turned her walk into a run, as she always did when she needed grounding, running away from the water, away from the source of tragedy. She needed the firm surface, the fertile ground, the rolling hills, the solitude.

She saw the crumbling home in the distance. It was being destroyed by the elements, always sinking and slacking and falling, one atom at a time, turning to dust.

But the nearby well remained firm and stout. Long grass surrounded it. She took the nearly disappearing trail that veered from the road to the Well. As she got closer, the colors that seemed a bit muted from the road, sparkled just the same as her first visit a dozen years ago. The sun couldn't bleach it, the snow couldn't bury it.

If only she could destroy it.

She walked around the circle, looking down into the darkness, her finger caressing the stones, and with each step she imagined what was down there. This mystical hole in the earth, on this hilltop, the lake in the distance, always pulled her back. This spot was as much her home as any. The church confessional that knew her secrets.

When Jewel was just a few months old Sharon ran by this spot, pushing Jewel in a jogging stroller, trying to mock the Well from the road. As Jewel grew, she still walked by the Well, gazing at it from a safe distance. As the nearby house decayed into the earth, her fear faded. Each time, she was able to dismiss the threat to her daughter, a bit more, a bit more, a bit more.

Because *of course* it was insane to think something in the ground could come get her.

But some truths you can't fight, no matter how hard you try to deny. She felt it in the water. In the air. Within her spine. She knew the reality she moved and lived and breathed within was smaller than the larger expanses where the Well existed. Her world of physics and matter and language had been slipped on top of something deeply cosmic. A smaller part trapped in this larger Russian doll.

Sometimes, when she saw a certain gleam in Jewel's eyes, both their spirits in communion, looking so far into the depths of each other where the truths sink and stay anchored forever, Sharon had to look away at that last second. She could not let her six-year-old daughter feel the full honesty that her time was coming.

Sharon made up for that guilt by parenting hard. Playing on the beach for hours beyond what her patience would have called for, never saying *no* to a story at night, so many hours of Uno on the deck at night with the neighbors. S'mores to feed a village.

Why not tell Kai? she of course asked herself. Her answer was that no human would believe this secret who hadn't witnessed what she had. And how unfair to unload this burden on to him. *Isn't it mine to bear?*

But another answer was she didn't want to take the blame from Kai, if he never knew, she could slip into moments where she pretended it never happened. *Don't go back, go forward to save a life.*

So she made plans, forward-thinking. She'd get the hell out. As Jewel grew, Sharon started to hint to Kai, subtle at first and then more direct, that they needed to move. *This home is amazing, but there's a bigger world out there and Julia is missing it.*

The hints grew stronger, but just slightly, as she aged. She had time. Dylan was ten years, five months, seventeen days old when she had pulled him from the Well. If she had to, she'd leave with Julia a few weeks before she reached that age. To take Julia and drive away from her father was cruel to both of them—but that idea was the parachute strapped across her back if she had to jump and save them both. She and Kai had never married. "We're connected by something deeper," one of them had said, she forgot who, and Kai never pushed the idea of marriage further.

But as if the Well knew her plans, it infected her daughter with a terminal disease before she could make her run.

Sharon was rinsing out grapes in the sink when she was hit with the instinct to look out the window and check on Jewel. By the time she had, the strange woman had already risen right out of the lake and had her hands on Jewel.

Sharon dashed out the door in time to see the woman submerging back in the water, leaving Jewel in a puddle of her own grey vomit. And that vomit floating in the water had that unmistakable stench of the fluid that covered Dylan when she had found him. A rusty water, earthworm soil scent.

So many tests followed: scans, MRI, blood draws. Radiation, chemo. Doctors argued over what type of cancer it was, spitting out words like diffuse intrinsic pontine glioma or medulloblastomas. "Yet your daughter's symptoms differ, quite unique, the neurocognitive impairment is not as pronounced and..."

Each of these words gave Kai more to Google each night, writing emails and friending other families on social media. He paced at all hours of the night with a whole new breed of insomnia. No sleep, lots of anger, frequent hugs. Sharon's mouth wouldn't make saliva to digest food. She lost weight, lost hope, lost direction.

Sharon visited the Well a few months after Jewel was first diagnosed. An expected meeting between the rivals, a decade in the making. The very ground she walked on was the Well grinning like a mischievous demon.

"You're taking her as promised!" she'd yelled.

There was no response, but she was sure the words reached their intended audience.

"You went for her *brain!*" Sharon yelled again, and this time, the response from the Well was immediate.

"And yet, she is still alive."

The voice spoke in a tone familiar to Sharon, though she had not heard it in a decade.

"We will kill the brain slowly. She will take her last breath at the exact age of the life you exchanged for. Is that not fair?"

"But you're making her suffer first. Why not just take her quickly? Why make her suffer?"

"Do you not let that boy suffer?"

"He doesn't remember a thing."

"And your daughter will not remember her pain."

"Who *are* you?"

"We wish to remain nameless. Mother. Creator. Destroyer. The door to the lake of fire."

"And you are evil and cruel giving her this disease."

"You were to take her away. We had to reach out and touch her before you did so. We will not accept such deceits."

Sharon fell to the ground then, crying, silently, not just for her daughter but for the farce the treatment had been. All the oncologists with their tests and their efforts and empathy—none of that mattered. She already knew the day that Jewel would die. She imagined taking them to this very spot, by the Well, and telling them the story of her first encounter to make them believe why she was the killer, why the blood was on her hands. She'd beg the Well to validate her story of how it all started with a boy she thought she let drown.

If I hadn't walked here that day, this would not have happened. If I never came here I would be able to live with Jewel the rest of my days.

"That is not true."

The Well answered as if it had read her thoughts.

"What is not true?"

"You would never have conceived had you not walked here. It was only because you promised to sacrifice your own that we blessed you with a child. Our child."

"You?"

"Your womb was not ready. It was these nutrient rich waters. We had to give you a child so we could take it back."

"You gave me a child just so you could take it?"

"Is that not how all gods work?"

"You are no God. You are a devil."

"I am who I am and I am who I am not."

"What if I give you my own life, will you let her live?"

"You would kill yourself to have her back? "

"Without hesitation."

"So what kind of sacrifice is that? It's not one at all."

"Tell me what sacrifice I can do, then, tell me."

"The boy. Bring us back the boy, that same boy. Dump him in the Well, and your daughter's brain will return to full health. The debt will be paid."

"You want me to kill him?"

"Oh no, do not kill him. A dead body would be poison. We want him alive, we can make plans for him. We make plans for everyone who joins us."

Sharon hadn't given an answer; her silence signaled her agreement.

She went home and let the dark idea stew, lying in bed, scrolling through her cell. Sending Dylan into the Well, and still alive, meant she would have to get him to the spot somehow, then push him inside to fall into the darkness.

Is that not just a murder?

But he'd already lived longer than he would have if not for her.

Wasn't that fair?

She could lure him back up to camp—*We're having an alumni week.* She could convince him to walk to the Well again—*I think it would be good for you to revisit, good for your trauma.* He would walk circles around the Well, mesmerized, like us all—*No, have a look, you have to really look in there.* Then the final shove over the edge.

She was just one push away, of one young man, from having her daughter for the rest of her life. Just get Dylan back up here.

She found his social media, stalked his Instagram pictures. He was still so awkward looking. He wore cereal box t-shirts, clearly ironically. His hair was long and shaggy up front, his face pocked with acne that refused to stop even in his twenties. A gamer, she saw, and he had a YouTube channel with 632 followers to watch him play first-person shooter games.

She followed the breadcrumbs to his mom's page.

Dylan's mom mythologized him with her Facebook pictures, most of them were him of a young boy. No sign of a dad for him, or partner for her.

Sharon kept searching and scrolling back in time until she saw ten-year-old Dylan at camp. One was a selfie of Dylan and mom in front of the Camp WaakWing sign, before the incident. Another was a picture of Dylan, Kai, and herself, after camp was over. They were loading up the car with luggage just before they drove back home. Caption read "reunited with my boy."

She'd really saved the mom's life when she made the original deal. The Well knew she couldn't push the young man back into the depths after she had rescued him.

She knew it too.

She felt so alone, avoiding eye contact for too long with anyone, afraid that all of them saw her lie, her fakeness, hiding these secret thoughts, these secret deals. Kai knew she was hiding and tried to joke his way in, tried to *force* his way in, but when it didn't work, he retreated back into himself.

It was only the pastor who seemed to understand her.

Lucas Lamia had lost his child, just like she did, and he read her so well. They thought in the same font and same cadence. He said words that she was tired of hearing from the nurses and social workers, rearranged to sound new and with meaning, not just slogans. Lived experiences are all that matter, and Lamia had them. She wanted to be held with him at times, imagined him as her partner for life, but thought how trite to fall for a grievance counselor.

When Jewel was clearly near death, sickly, pale, and the test results came back showing the treatment wasn't working, and clearly modern medicine no match for the curse she bestowed upon her daughter, Sharon went to the Well to beg once more.

"I need more time," she said.

The day was cold, wet, overcast. A glimpse into winter.

"You made your deal."

"More time. I'd trade my life. Why not take me?"

"That is no fair trade, we shall have you soon enough, we need others. Who else do you love?"

"You know who."

You'd give him up, your partner, your child's father, for your daughter?"

"Yes," she said, surprising herself with how fast.

"One year for one month. Your daughter stays alive for one more year, but one month after her death, I take her father. Surface the Morbid, let the miracles shine."

The moisture in the air, so cold and alive, crept deeper into her skin, into her bones, chilling her to the core.

She'd willingly offer her own life for another year of her daughter's; would not Kai do the same if given the chance? She thought of how many times he'd inferred he couldn't live without her, how he wanted to go with her, how he needed to know right away if there's an afterlife because he can't bear to never see her again.

So of course she said *yes*. Hadn't every deal she made just extended the inevitable — death for them all? But she was pulling the strings, as if she was the god, or so she imagined, not this deity in the Well.

She was doing him a favor when she said yes.

"I need a drip of your blood to seal this agreement. Cut your finger, squeeze some drops."

She still remembers the sound of that *drip, drip, drip*.

Jewel's health improved overnight, and though far from perfect, she spent another year alive, as the Well promised. The doctors grew suddenly proud about how their efforts were working, Kai talking about how life might be worth living.

Jewel died a year after, one month ago to this very day.

So here Sharon was, ready to beg and plead for more, to keep Kai in her life, because she couldn't take another loss.

"What can I do?"

The Well was silent. She could have asked again, but the absence of a response was the answer. In fact, she swore the voice felt sad for her, for humans, for all mortals, but this is the truth of being alive: your body is a short-term rental.

She walked back home slowly, imagining she might find Kai's body, cold, having died alone, when she opened the door.

Instead he stood by the kitchen island, chopping up strawberries, washing raspberries, certainly preparing fruit with whipped cream on top for their dessert that night. Their favorite.

She placed her hand atop his knife hand, to his surprise, followed by an embrace, the knife released and clanking on the counter. She imagined she could protect him, but it was the very earth, the very water that he was attached to, the deeper truths of this lake, that was going to kill him very soon, probably that night.

How can I fight that?

Or might the Well even trick her, get *her* to take his life somehow, as if it wanted to make her the Woman of the Lake. Wouldn't that be justice?

If she had more courage, she would reveal all to Kai so he knew. She would end their long embrace, take him by the hand, and lead him on a walk down Torch Lake Road. *'Come with me. I need you to hear something,'* and hope the Well itself would confess her secrets.

Instead, she prepared for one last night by the lake, because that's what he would have preferred on his last night alive. Spending it together, unburdened by these truths, eating fruit salad and whipped cream, watching one last sunset by the lake of fire.

CHAPTER NINETEEN
OF LAMIA ALONE IN HIS HOUSE

I SAT AT THE mahogany desk in my small home. Solitary, but not alone.

Before me sat the glorious ashes of Kacy Baker's child, scraped together into a perfect pile. I coveted the bits of grey flakes as a drowning man craves air. Every move I made was deliberate and slow, for just an exhale of breath too close would blow these delicate flakes off the table, lost forever.

I couldn't let that happen. I treated them as a loving God would treat his creations, for without them nothing could hold back the inevitable and eternal onslaught of pain.

I'd done what God does not—I'd given Kacy her child back. She felt it with an intensity grieving mothers could not imagine. She should be grateful. I would never get a trace back of all that I lost. My wife, my family, my home.

I missed living in the home miles away and closer to the lake, where the Well of my past that burrowed so deep still stood, where the house I built with such dreams had withstood a century of seasons but now was losing its battle to the elements. I remembered the way the long grass played like a string instrument when the wind blew. The music from the cicadas at night, an orchestra of the earth. I have witnessed generations of mortals suck their last breath since I first came here to settle, fleeing the war, hoping I could raise my son in peace.

Benjamin, my son. Always feeding my son who's hunger never waned, and I was cursed to this life of hunting and gathering for over a century, sniffing out scents of when the souls remain in the ashes.

Despite this fresh wave coursing in my veins, and the euphoric sense of youthful zeal, my bones and joints and ligaments elastic, I was tired. So very tired of this life, and alone.

For it always fades, and I would have to find more.

The ashes of Kacy's spawn would last a month, but by the end of summer my skin would pale, my muscles weaken, my cravings— my son's cravings, really, would beg and drive me for more.

But with ashes freshly in my veins, my senses so acute, so

heightened, I could *feel* it when the car pulled up to my home. I could sense the driver's anger. I knew how such moments played out, and I was about to be confronted with unpleasantries.

A car door slammed, first one, then another, and two sets of footsteps approached.

With careful, deliberate purpose, I carried the tray of ashes to the metal cabinet, placed them with precision, not risking a tilt or for a single grey flake to fall off. I locked the metal cabinet, and then got ready to face the three knocks on the door.

CHAPTER TWENTY:
OF MIKE BAKER AT LUCAS LAMIA'S FRONT DOOR

MIKE BAKER GAVE THREE firm knocks on the front door of the secluded home of Lucas Lamia, and immediately regretted he hadn't knocked harder, knocked longer. Something to message his urgency and anger.

His sister, Kacy, was at his side, and after the night they had together, he feared she may bolt into the woods or start talking to the trees. God *damn* his edible-munching, mushroom-eating, hippy-loving, Grateful Dead-listening, Commie sister. Hadn't she embarrassed him enough? Now she found an even worse pastor, and she'd finally gone completely crazy.

Why should I have to take care of her? I have my own family.

Next stop was the emergency room so she could go to Munson Hospital's psychiatric floor, but she begged to be brought here first, and since Mike wanted to unleash his anger at this man himself, he agreed. He rehearsed what he was going to say, but when the tall man with the black mane of hair answered the door, the ground beneath Mike became unsteady, his balance uncertain, and his words of fire got watered down.

"I was going to call, but I needed to see you. Sorry to be a bother, but this is important," Mike said.

The pastor looked at them both, clearly noticing that Kacy was troubled. She was muttering words softly to herself as if speaking in tongues. One of her hands was swatting at flies, the other picking at herself like she'd walked into a spider web.

"I'm at your service, what can I do for you?"

"You may not remember me. I'm Mike Baker, Kacy's brother. You know Kacy, here." He pointed towards her nervously. She was oblivious, suddenly spying a spot on her shoe, one foot trying to scrap it off. Her hair unkempt, muscles twitching. "She's been coming to you for grief counseling."

"Of course I remember you. I saw you at the funeral service for Kacy's child."

Mike remembered the way the pastor worked the room at Stephen's funeral as if at a grad party, reveling in condolences, fawning over Kacy.

"Kacy came home yesterday and she just ain't right. She's talking crazy, acting crazy. She's always been a little off, I'm sure you can see that, but now it's all nonsense. Keeps talking about the *empty spaces* and *five senses* aren't enough. Talking to people who aren't in the room. Seems like she's speaking backwards. Hasn't slept at all. Hasn't eaten a thing. And she's got a mark on her arm that—"

"I get it," Lamia interrupted. "She's distraught. I'm glad you're with her." Lamia stepped back, opening a walkway for them to enter. "Let's see how I can help. Come on in."

Mike fought the temptation to step inside. He refused the offer. Lamia was working him.

"I don't think you understand," Mike said with more force. "I'm not going in there with you until I know who you are and *what* you are. Are you a pastor? Are you a doctor? Which is it? I know some things, if you really want to know the truth."

"Mr. Baker," Pastor Lamia interrupted, "talking falsely is a crime, please speak freely."

Mike couldn't find the words and his thoughts were distracted by Kacy's whispering, her mouth and lips moving so fast, words too rapid to decipher, like some priest praying in Latin, her head moving to the left, to the right, her hands flapping.

"When I ask her what she's doing, she keeps saying, 'You need to forgive me for anything right now.' Apparently, she got that from you."

"I do, I do say that. I believe in letting her speak these things without judgment when a child passes."

"But she's been acting bizarre for so long, and she gets that *from you*. She's been carrying the urn with her. Puts it in her bed at night. Whispers to it. Says *nothing ever dies*. I get it—life after death and Heaven and all that, but..."

Kacy started scratching her arms frantically just then, each hand on the opposing arm, nails dug in, a sandpaper coarseness, and it seemed she'd scratch her tattooed arm sleeve right off.

"But something happened last night. She came home without the urn and we think she used drugs. That's the thing. Not just drugs, we know she smokes weed, but *heroin*, with needles we think. And this is more than you can address, because the thing is...I started looking around about you. I read about investigations and complaints with the licensing board. It seems you used to be licensed but aren't any longer. What the hell?"

Mike realized his summary was in first draft form, not polished, but finally delivered the last statement with the confidence he'd been seeking.

"So, pastor, or doctor or whatever you are who has no license to do this—look what you've done! We're not coming here anymore, we're through."

Mike didn't want a response, he wanted to leave right then and there, just a quick verbal slap across the jaw of this tall man. Then he'd take his freak sister to the hospital and get back to his own kids.

"Mr. Baker, we have a lot to discuss. She needs help, I can accompany you to the hospital. I'll go there with you. I volunteer at the psychiatric unit, they know me, I visit patients. I can talk to them with you. And I'll suggest a new grief counselor for her. That's not unusual. I am sorry I failed you."

"Well, we're leaving. Follow us there if you will."

Mike put a hand his sister's shoulder and guided her to return to the car when the pastor's voice suddenly spoke like some command from a wizard, shouting, "Kacy, you hear him! Go to him, go to him now!"

Kacy started twisting and turning her body, breaking free from Mike's arms, and before he could get her under control and stop her, she was gone, dashing by the pastor and running deep into the house.

Mike was suddenly lost and alone on the front porch, his sister inside rambling and rummaging, the Pastor grinning and showing his teeth.

"Kacy. Kacy get back here!" Mike yelled to his sister, alone on this man's front lawn. The grass had been manicured to beat back the nearby evergreens which were closing in. A large barbeque pit took over part of the lawn, one picnic table nearby, and his sister now being eaten up by the home.

He had to get her and then leave.

"Mr. Baker," the pastor asked. "How much would your sister have given to have her baby Stephen back?

Lamia's tone had changed. This was wrong, it was nauseating.

"She'd give anything. Anything, of course. What's she doing

in there? Kacy? Kacy. Come on, let's go. I'm serious."

"'She'd give anything, anything,' wouldn't she, Mr. Baker. And imagine if I reunited her with her son again, closer than they even were when the child was in her womb."

"You're talking that same bullshit way she talks." Mike was shaking his head, ready to dash past this man, and drag his sister out.

"Well, I apologize to have let you down, but I gave your sister the best grief counseling one can give. The opportunity to *feel* her child."

"Can we go now? Kacy! Kacy come on..." Mike screamed over Lamia's shoulder, unable to see much, only hearing echoes of her babbling screeches and smashing around inside. *I gotta stop fucking around, letting my little sister control my life.* "Kacy, now!" Mike yelled, his highest pitch yet.

"She doesn't need saving, Mr. Baker, *I* saved her from a lifetime of sadness and depression, traded it to have her son coursing through her veins, all well worth it, even if it led to this insanity."

"What the fuck are you saying?"

Mike tried to dart by the pastor into the house but Lamia reached out a hand and stopped him, hand clenching so tight on his shoulder, it felt electric, like being tased.

"I saved her from a lifetime of sadness. You need to hear that. I want you to be aware of that before we take care of things here."

Mike was just inches from the pastor's face, staring up at him, unable to move, feeling the intense eyes burn, the iron claw on his shoulder. The moment was on pause, but the sounds from inside got louder, more violent, more destructive.

She was hurting herself, banging her head against a cabinet.

"Kacy, stop that!"

The doctor released him with a roll of his eyes, and Mike rushed inside.

The small house, mostly one big room, center coffee table, chairs surrounding, an adjoining office with a large desk and cabinet.

And it was this cabinet Kacy was attacking, smashing her fists against the metal, banging her head against a drawer.

Mike ran over, grabbed her from behind, and tried to pull her back by the arms. She cocked her elbow like a shotgun and smashed it back into her brother's jaw. *Smack!* Followed by another into his nose, *smack!* Then her elbow jammed into his eye, *smoosh.*

Blood covered her fists and the cabinet doors, but she'd given up on using her hands and started with her head, banging the flat of her forehead against the cabinet, smacking against the metal, making the whole room vibrate with every *BOOM.*

She's gone mad. She'll never be normal again. She'll be in a hospital for life. Mike felt a small relief in this. Nobody could deny she was crazy, but first he had to get her the fuck out of there, to a hospital, and then she was someone else's problem. *BOOM,* her head kept smacking the cabinet, bone on metal.

Lamia stepped inside, walking slowly, but speaking surely. "I have something for this, sir," he assured Mike. "I have something, but do I have permission?"

"What?"

"Can I use an injection?"

"What does it do?"

"Calms patients to a near sleep. Hospitals use it. It makes the next steps so much easier."

The struggle was a flurry, and the longer it went, the more energy Kacy had, throwing elbows, hollering words as if possessed. "Your evil must stop! He's alive. He LIVES! But not you. Not YOU! You'll die in the fire! You'll die in the lake! He LIVES!"

"Do it. Please, do it," Mike pleaded.

Lamia opened up a drawer from his desk, pulled out a small briefcase and snapped open the lid. It revealed five syringes, preloaded, tucked inside foam cushioning like loaded firearms.

Every time his sister's skull hit the cabinet, Mike cringed, that horrifying sound of bone on metal, blood splashing from her forehead. He'd never forgive himself if her brain was being damaged, but it must be bruised by now.

This had to stop, the needle had to work.

Lamia wielded the syringe like a sword—then like a scientist—holding it up to one eye, squinting with the other, and then, when he seemed satisfied with the potion inside, sunk it into the flesh at base of the neck, just above the shoulder.

Into the flesh of Mike Baker.

Mike's face melted, his mouth in the shape of a silent gasp. His muscles went slack, his body faltering, muscles of rubber, he fell to the floor. The tall man with the black mane stood over him.

"A sweet Haldol Ativan cocktail for you, kind sir, compliments of these magical wands," he said, still holding the syringe with love.

Briefcase back in the desk, drawer slammed, and Mike slid to the ground. His sister continued her attack on the cabinet, completely unaware, oblivious.

KACY help! Mike wanted to scream but couldn't, as the tall man reached down and picked him up, the way a husband might carry a bride, and Mike was carried out the front door. His mouth wouldn't make words, his arms wouldn't obey his commands, his eyes grew hazy, focus fading. Out the front door, the sun felt hot on his skin, blinding him. The insects in the trees witnessed whatever horror that awaited him at the mercy of this man.

What is happening?

Kacy, Kacy, he tried to mouth, but the words just soft murmurs.

"Don't worry, Mr Baker, you will feel this. I promise you will feel this."

Lamia laid Mike on the ground, spun the man so he could grab his arms, and then bound Mike's hands behind him with twine. He picked Mike up, carrying him like a package, and placed him inside the large barbeque pit. The scent of charcoal and ashes filled his nostrils, the horror of what might be happening was too unreal.

This will stop. Someone will come by and rescue me, Or I'll wake up. Or this pastor will stop at the last second and give some explanation of how this is a teaching moment and part of his unusual practices.

Instead, Lamia grabbed the white plastic bottle off the picnic table and squirted lighter fluid on Mike's chest.

The fumes burnt his eyes and nose, the cold liquid a shock to the warm sleep that was dragging him down.

"These drugs in you that I was kind enough to share. Haldol, Ativan. The same used for a psychotic patient in the hospital. They don't miss what I take, but I added a bit extra, just for you."

When Mike saw the square box of Diamond Strike matches on the picnic table, he tried to scream from deep in his gut, but with his muscles so lax, all he could do was drool bubbles on his lips.

"Mike, I understand. I know what your screams would sound like if you only could. I've heard such screams. I've seen such sights, operating in a field of war, not a lovely field like this is on a beautiful summer day. Amputated limbs piled in puddles of blood, muskets and flies and diseases in the air. But through it all, such bravery, oh such bravery to live on, the iron will of the human spirit."

"But why fight death when it would seem a relief to die and the soul ascends to Heaven? Why, oh why? If there's an afterlife, shouldn't the soul rejoice in the passing of the body? Why not just let the body die and go to Heaven?

The Pastor looked to the left, to the right, then up to the sky, as if waiting for a response. None came. They were alone.

"Because the soul is wise, and knows more than the body, that's why. It knows after death there is *nothing*. No Heaven, no Hell," the pastor said, holding out one match in the air like a professor lecturing at the blackboard. "All that awaits is to drift about in the spiritual world, lost in that ethereal place, the coldness of being without a body, but remembering what it was like to walk on this earth on a sunny day such as this.

"No, souls do not want to leave. Your nephew's soul, it did not leave, so when Kacy decided to cremate him, I did what a good man would do with the cremains. I took what I needed—I hope you don't mind? Consider it a tax—and I injected the rest into your sister."

Lamia scanned the horizon while Mike's mind was lost in a hazy terror, already feeling the horror of the burn on his flesh, praying to God for a hero to rise up, commanding his arms and legs to move but they were jelly and refused his orders.

Lamia went on: "So, let's see how your soul responds, my friend. After you start burning, we need a hole, an escape route, or the soul stays trapped. The Hindus know this. I'll hammer a hole in your skull as your body burns. We shall see if your soul is strong enough to stay or if it slips away. You're not as fresh as a child, but I hate to waste your life."

On the table, Mike saw the hammer and stake. This pastor wasn't just practicing a deception to teach a lesson.

"Should your soul remain in the ashes, I shall burn you to dust and invite you to live in eternity, a delicious Well inside me where my son awaits."

Mike summoned the power to make himself move, but the response wasn't there. Instead, a cold grip clutched at his core. The icy hands of the drugs pulled him under.

This can't be happening. I have kids at home, a family, he wanted to say, begging for mercy. Instead, just bubbles of drool formed on his rubber lips.

The pastor came closer, pressed his ear towards Mike's mouth. "What's that? You'll have to speak up. My ears are old."

He was mocking, laughing, then held forth the box of matches.

After a lit match was pressed against his chest, the fire went *poof.* The small funeral pyre caught flame.

At first, just the fluid burned, but the second his clothes caught fire, his skin began to blister, then turn black. Soon, his very nerves caught on fire.

He fought against the flames. He sucked for air among the smoke, but inhaled only fumes of his own flesh on fire. The blistering, the melting. The hell of being roasted alive, begging for a rescue but there would be none, trying to twist and turn with such fury, but his body not responding to his wishes.

The doctor leaned forward, eyeing him in the pit the way one might a steak on the grill. Then he placed the metal tip of the iron spike at the center of Mike's skull and pulled back the hammer. The last sound Mike heard was the bang of metal upon metal, the spike driven into his forehead, puncturing both bone and brain, driven to the core of his thoughts. Releasing them.

And his soul slipped from his body into a cold, dark eternity.

Chapter Twenty-One
Of Lucas Lamia and the Burned Body

I STOOD AT THE FIREPIT outside my small home, solitary, but not alone.

Before me the burning body of Kacy's brother lay in state, the skin turned charcoal, the terror and pain gone. The soul, also gone, escaped from the body through the hole in his head. His was not one of the spirits that remained in the ashes.

If the soul was still present, I'd be able to detect that sweet scent from the charred body, and hear the subtle cries on a dog whistle wavelength. I would hear the slight hum, feel the vibration. But there was none. Instead, just the cawing of a far-off bird, the sun burning down, the fire pit burning out. The soul had left the body, the ashes lifeless.

Even the ruckus coming from inside his house, caused by psychotic Kacy, had faded. Who knows why. I would find out in a bit, but first, I watched the sun slip a notch towards the western sky. Another death to clean up. And soon, two deaths.

How exhausting. So exhausting, this eternal life I'd been cursed to live.

This was a slaughter that I had no desire to clean, but I must. I'd killed here before, but it took work to clean. And this man had a family. I saw the children running around him at Kacy's son's funeral.

Police would be here. They'd ask questions about both missing people.

Because I also needed to take care of Kacy inside, unless she had already killed herself.

I turned and took a step inside the house, expecting to see Kacy's bloody head, her skull damaged from the pounding, perhaps unconscious on the ground. I prepared for the sad deed of a mercy killing, euthanasia is often the best route.

But what I saw terrified me.

Kacy lay on the ground, her head all purple and blue and dripping with crimson. And in her strength, Kacy had busted through the cabinet. The tray of ashes, which I had set deep and firmly in the cabinet to keep them safe, and with enough air for them to breathe, were now splattered about Kacy's face. It was like a drunken Catholic priest had missed her forehead on Ash Wednesday.

Kacy had tried to snort them. Or she did snort them, that was clear.

You fool.

You wasted them.

The ashes were useless! Gone! All of them. All my work, and now I had no supply.

My skin burned with fury. I grabbed the poker from the fireplace, stormed over to where she was shaking on the ground, her eyes distant, her consciousness gone. *I'll torment her like a demon from hell.* My grip tight on the poker, my fury imagining a thousand different tortures for her ingratitude. I'd flay her. I'd peel off her skin, one tattoo at a time, making her suffer for what she'd done. I missed the days of operating on a human body, why not quench that desire?

"After what I did for you!" I screamed.

I looked into her eyes, watching her shake, tremble, eyes unable to focus.

"I brought him to you and you do this? Do you realize what you've done?"

She couldn't understand me in her state on the ground with every limb shaking in a seizure. She didn't even feel it when I stabbed the poker right into her chest; through flesh, through rib cage, spearing her heart the same way the savages must have speared their fish from Torch Lake, the living thing flopping on the end, frantically, before dying, flatlining.

I felt her life leave her, a soul gone mad, no direction, nothing worth saving, and it lifted to the ceiling, out of the cracks of the walls, into nothingness.

Her dead body lay before me, and for that moment, I wished I could join her, to leave my body, stay adrift in some liminal space. A purgatory, instead of this hell. How I wished this curse would be over.

I could scrape together at least one fix from the flakes of ash on the ground, the smears on her nose—but then I needed to move on to the next.

Where to find it?

I had hoped to wait for Sharon's return.

Go fetch your daughter's ashes before they are dashed into the lake, were my last words to her. I thought for sure she'd be right back. I saw it in her eyes, same as I saw it in a hundred others, but she was not as complicit as I'd hoped.

She had no idea what she was refusing.

Decades ago, I didn't have to work so hard. This age was different. These people wanted everything brought to them, instantly, and when it arrived, they pretended they deserved more.

I didn't know how to get by anymore. My season had passed. How could I go on?

The house felt so still just then, everything stopped, with only me alive, only me, all existence over. *Why go on?* So tired, carrying the burden of my aching son. I'd been feeding this parasite for over a century. This son, begat by a mother with no loyalty, and there was no end in sight, and the people of this age ungrateful.

And instead of Sharon coming back to me immediately to share in the ritual, I had to go to her to fetch what I wanted.

But first back to the Well, and begging to make a new deal.

Chapter Twenty-Two
<u>Of Pastor Lucas Lamia and his Return to the Well</u>

I PARKED ON THE SIDE of the road near my old home, marveling how overgrown the fields had become, how my house was ready to finally collapse. The next strong wind would certainly knock down the remaining boards that clung onto each other.

I moved through the tall grass, and as I walked towards the Well, I heard whispers rising, like all the insects were chattering — *the doctor is back, the pastor is back, does she know?*

Should we tell her?

Yes, please do tell her, I thought. *Tell her I'm done and will do what it takes to end this suffering.*

I'd been here a century before these monstrous lakeside homes were erected by men who could never haul the material or do the work, instead just propped up symbols of their wealth, all just to stake the land, rarely to use it. I imagined going door to door and ridding the area of the invaders. A new civil war. My last good deed.

The stones on the Well continued to change, shift, sometimes pale, then suddenly sparkle. Tiny bits of what seemed ancient gems twinkled from inside the faded stones, beat on by the sun and rain. I felt a circle of gravity around the circumference, pulling things into its darkness, a seduction if you'll make the sacrifice. Sometimes I could sense the bottom and feel whatever was beneath there breathing. Long breaths, deep inhales. The lungs of one who is ancient and lives for eons.

It knew I was there. Of course it knew. I got down on my knees to offer my humility, my pledge.

"Please," I said, hands clasped. "I can't do it anymore, I want out." I felt myself sink into the earth, hoping for a grave that would not keep me. Suddenly I thought of George Alexander Hanna, the Union soldier who shot himself in the leg, perhaps not wanting to die, but not wanting to continue his life in the same trajectory.

"I can't do it anymore," I repeated. And finally, a response.

"Then don't do it anymore."

"You know what will happen."

"Tell me anyway."

"My son will hurt and suffer with the pain; *I* will hurt and suffer with the pain. He will torture me with his screams. The ache will be unbearable, and it will be worse than anyone could endure."

"Can you heal the patient? Will the patient survive?"

I stood up, kicked the stone with my sad leather shoes, felt the crunch of my toe, imagined the laughter of the impenetrable forces inside.

"Just take me. Take me down with you. Kill me, destroy me!"

"You can do that to yourself."

"And what of my soul? My son's soul. What of us, of him?"

"You never paid your debts."

"I will now. Just end this. I'm tired of this life, tired of living alone. I have helped so many mothers, only for them to go mad. What must I do? I will do it now. End my existence or remove my curse, deliver Benjamin to his mother. I have lived 150 years like this and do not want a day more."

"I will say it once more. This time listen on how to end your suffering. You never paid your debt. An amputated limb was promised."

'Will that make a difference?"

"That is hardly enough."

"What you want darkens my soul."

"Virtue chokes the soul as much as vice. Predator and prey in balance and harmony—that is the song I sing. To listen and live and breathe is to sacrifice, to sacrifice is to live and listen and breathe. The dead fall, life rises. Miracles spring from morbid soils."

"What is it you need of me, speak plainly!"

"Come back here with two limbs of her mother, and with that child's ashes in your veins."

"Which child?"

"That child you are chasing. It is her, don't pretend you do not know. Deliver us two limbs from this mother and bring us the ashes. All of them. All the ashes of the child, two limbs of the mother. You have until the midnight hour. Make this effort, and your suffering will end."

I glanced at the sun. It was close to taking its dive into the western sky. Soon it would be dark. I didn't have much time, I had to go directly there, I'd have to amputate two limbs. I'd have to collect the ashes.

The mother never brought me the ashes, I would go get them. I would inject the child's soul into mine and return here with bloody limbs in my bag. I will return with the limbs and ashes and end this 150-year curse. My last Torch Lake sunset.

PART THREE

Chapter Twenty-Three
Of Sharon Walking with Kai

THE SUN HOVERED above the horizon, another brilliant Torch Lake sunset.

Our last Torch Lake sunset?

Something about the sun seemed so omniscient to Sharon. No dirty misdeeds of your past can be hidden from such a life-giving entity that knows everything, knows all. That orange ball of flame is a giant eyeball seeing through you. The Torch Lake's tranquil blue water paid homage to the sun by reflecting the stunning spectacle above. The water was a living canvas, paint shimmering from the work of its master. As the sun descended, falling to the earth, as all living things fall to the earth, the water took on darker blues and deeper purples. The lakeshore bathed in the soft glow, the distant silhouettes of trees stand witness, day after day, and darkness began its nightly reign.

Nothing gold can stay, Ponyboy, Sharon thought, *but it can resurrect, as it will tomorrow.* Another day of pure magic at Torch Lake, and she was fortunate enough to witness it.

Kai would never leave the lake, that was a given, but the lake may take him. Was that really so bad? Was she being selfish, worried about losing him, when really, having the lake take him, since it already took Jewel, perhaps could be what's best? And here she was jealous father and daughter would be together while she'd be left alone.

Stay in the moment. Cherish this night. Stay in this day.
Treat this night like it will be your last with him.

Because it is the last night, based on math. If not tonight, close enough.

The embrace after she'd walked through the front door felt like a weight lifted. He stood confused, nervous. *Who is this woman? Where did her anger go?*

"That walk did you well," he said.

"They always do."

"Never return the same."

"And sometimes not alone."

Nostalgia. Kai loved stories about their time at Camp

WaakWing together, and if she wanted to forget her return with Dylan, he wouldn't let her.

They did order out for dinner; deep fried pickles as an appetizer, one of Jewel's favorites. Her ashes on the white platter remained at the dinner table as they ate.

"What do you think about us doing a season as camp counselors again?" Kai asked.

More nostalgia. *It's his last refuge*, she thought, *but all he had*. They stopped working at camp after the diagnosis.

"Those were such good days. So many kids we got to know. So many fantastic memories."

They were fantastic. That was no lie. The years after the Dylan incident, every year became charged with joy. The drunken euphoria of being loved and loving another. Her spirit filled with energy, her mind with laser focus. They came up with new games, new songs, new campfire stories. They often stood shoulder to shoulder, campers flocking around them. They finished each other's thoughts, read each other's cues, knew each other's feelings. Smiles came often, warm glows of happiness, interpreting each other's tone of voice and body language.

That intuition at times seemed a curse, for no bits of resentment could be hidden from each other. Every muscle twitch on their faces meant to stifle a resentment, unable to be concealed.

"Lots of kids will still remember us," Kai said, a flicker of excitement in his eyes. "What if we went back there next summer? That spot on the lake is somehow different than here."

"Yes, I love it there."

"Well, let's go back. In fact, Garcon suggests we should go there with Jewel's ashes. Best spot on the lake, he says. Not sure why."

Kai crunched a fried pickle.

"Where did this Garcon suggestion come from?" she asked.

"I boated with him last night. He asked me to go and we talked a bit. It was good to talk to someone. You've got your priest."

"He's a pastor. And a doctor. And a parent who lost his son. He's one of us."

"So is Garcon."

Kai was right, Garcon had survived an experience, but Pastor

Lamia had opened up some channel in her heart, freed her to be in tune with the music that emitted from Jewel's ashes. Lamia had beckoned her to return with Jewel, as if there were more to be had—but she wasn't going anywhere. She was staying with Kai.

"Yes, I love Garcon," she said, "though I barely knew the man. But I'm not like him. He was ready to let his child go. I'm not yet ready, I've decided. I don't want to scatter her tonight. Let's just stay here with the ashes nearby."

Kai narrowed his eyes and took aim with his words. "You speak as it's actually her. Like it's really, really her."

"Oh but it *is* her. If it's not her, what else is it? It's her and I don't want to scatter her."

"How much of this is you and how much is that guy? What did he tell you?"

That it would be like watching her die a second death, she thought, but didn't say, and she wasn't sure Lamia was wrong. The water had had enough of her. And more importantly, she feared being near the water with Kai. Not tonight. She hoped they could enjoy this moment and the lake from afar.

Looking at his eyes, she saw his awareness of her lies. But he wouldn't believe the truth if she revealed it, so lies it would have to be.

"You don't understand, you've been angry at the pastor as if I don't have my own thoughts. It's not him. Besides, I go there as much to be with the other parents. I feel them. I feel less alone."

Somewhere hidden in those words was that she felt alone, even with him next to her. Yet still, she needed him. They needed each other. He was the only one who held the dear heart of their child in his flesh. They loved each other as best they could after the product of their love died, taken from them.

They went on with their dinner over fried pickles and a big salad and decided to stop punishing each other. They took a walk after dinner along the shoreline.

She held his hand and they moved in the darkness. Even if they couldn't be seen, she felt like they were being watched. She knew it. God from above, insects on the lakeshore, people out their back windows from the two miles across the lake, the nineteen miles up and down, all of them were holding their breath waiting to see what this couple would do.

"You don't go in the water much anymore, I noticed," Kai said, as if the cover of darkness set him free to share. "Since Jewel's seizure. You've taken some boat rides, but not been in the lake since. You even look at it different. I can see that. I know it's changed for you. As if waiting for the next tragedy."

"Once a child is taken from you, you feel cursed. You blame yourself. You wonder who's next?"

She squeezed his hand as she spoke, hoping he'd read her mind, each squeeze some sort of Morse code of what she could not say.

"I think we should go back to camp, Kai. Your roots are so deep in that part of the lake. If I'm not ready yet, go on without me. I'll always meet up there later when I am ready. Our permanent meeting spot. People need a safe meeting spot in case something happens, where no matter what that's where they'll see each other."

She felt his steps grow uncertain, like her hand was all that was holding him up. His legs seemed quaky, her message confusing. She wanted to meet him there in the afterlife, but what he heard was she wanted him there without her company.

The walked in silence back to the house, but even with no words spoken, they heard each other's silence, as they always had, just as she could hear the breathing of Jewel's ashes on the platter, the hum of the crickets, the echo of the long gone sunset, and burning of the stars.

She decided she wouldn't deny him more time on the lake, so agreed to take a nighttime boat ride. They first pulled off the canvas cover, working together, Sharon portside, Kai starboard, as always. They brought wine, a bowl of fruit with whipped cream, but left Jewel's ashes at home. A very slow cruise, barely idling, not disturbing the peaceful night. The hum of the engine soft, the wine in her glass gulped quickly. Cruising north up the lake, they came within eyesight of the camp. Kai was purposely taking them by WaakWing, half mile from the shoreline.

As they slowly went by, they could see the campfire flickering, the kids' laughter traveling over the water, as it does. The kids saying goodbye to their counselor, Sharon decided.

They continued north, past the camp, just as Paxton was likely pouring water over the flames, kids shuffling back to their cabin for the night, but Kai steered on in silence. She wondered when he would turn, how many miles they'd travel along the edge. His choice, but she didn't take her eyes off him as he steered the boat.

As the night grew darker, he grew more into a shadow. Bugs danced near the pontoon's sidelights. No other boats in sight.

After a slow turn of the pontoon, they took a faster ride back. She poured half a glass, he poured a full, both emptied shortly after. They returned home, docked, and wrapped up in silence.

She understood why Kai was somber. He'd been preparing for this night to drop Jewel's ashes into eternity. Sharon would do that in the coming days if needed, but not tonight. Tonight, they all stayed together.

They cleaned up just a bit before going to bed for the night. A warm heartfelt embrace in the middle of their king-sized bed, and she felt an urge to never let him go. She wanted to know he'd be okay, whatever came next, fearful that they'd been split, forever split perhaps, disconnected from each other. None of it was fair.

Old boards in the house creaked, resetting into this shifting land. This area of Northern Michigan, where the huge canyon of Torch Lake had been dug in the earth, deeper than any in-land lake in the state by far, was built by the slow movement of glaciers. This land isn't dead. It lives on, constantly moving underneath them.

But once the world stopped shifting and darkness settled, she felt comfort in Jewel being on the nightstand next to her.

Kai had shook his head in disbelief when she brought the platter of ashes and set them next to her bedside. He didn't know that she could hear and feel Jewel's warm breath, as if her soul was sleeping a forever sleep in the ashes. Perhaps they were not sounds, but just emotions in the air, picked up in wavelengths, undetectable by those who didn't feel the same love.

Am I just torturing myself? Maybe. But wasn't this a sign that loved ones are in your life forever? Even if their bodies are burned to dust, so young, our children never die. Whatever God made us and watched over us wouldn't be so cruel.

As she felt the ashes breathe, she could also feel Kai's anxiety and restlessness. He was unable to relax, and his troubled thoughts penetrated her own. If she was dreaming of him waking up, getting out of bed, and leaving his insomnia behind, she wasn't sure, but she sensed him moving about the room, rustling near her headboard, then a warm, soft kiss against her cheek. More rustling, and soon after, she heard the back door sliding open. She pictured him walking out into the dark night, the pallbearer of his own weight, out the back towards the lake, closing the door behind him.

Stop him, stop him! part of her screamed. *Warn him*, but how could she explain that he was not safe?

So she stayed in bed, living as she dreamed, alone. Defective mother, defective womb, damaged parts, unsound egg, cancer child.

And now did I kill my husband?

Not long after Kai left, the back door slid open again. Someone from outside had slipped inside from the dark night. And the cooler air slipped into Sharon's room as she slept with deep dreams.

CHAPTER TWENTY-FOUR
OF LUCAS LAMIA WATCHING THE BACK DOOR OF THE LAKE HOUSE

I GAZED OVER the dark lake, wondering about the living creatures beneath the depths, swimming in the blackness. There were no torch-lit canoes moving about like a century ago; instead just tiny flickering porch lights of expensive abodes on the shoreline.

No moon, no stars. And this was not a lake as much as a claw scratch that had ripped the land open, exposing things that should not be, and the nearby Well where the woman waited.

I sat patiently, watching the back door of Sharon Murphy's home, a stakeout of sorts, the air off the lake caressing my cheek. A mistake to call it a breeze.

I refused to get closer despite the beckoning calls. I kept my distance from the water that would burn me like flames.

But I was not here for the water. I was here for the ash. And her limbs.

I carried a briefcase of works and syringes in hand, some loaded with Haldol and Ativan, some empty and ready to be loaded with cremains and fired into my bloodstream. I eyed the back door of Sharon Murphy's home the way a hungry tiger eyes the most vulnerable of the herd. Waiting to attack.

I felt a stirring in my stomach, like a fetus kicking, and I wondered if Benjamin could feel his mother in the waters close by. *Don't worry, Benjamin. I'll fix up one last time tonight, one last injection into my blood. Then, if I can get the limbs, I will end your suffering, my suffering, the way an honorable loving father would.*

A light then appeared, as if coming from the dark of my memory.

The sound of one dingy, a little boat, and this one did have a flame burning on board, moving about like Charon on a skiff ready for a journey to the Underworld. These gods of the Greeks, the Sikh, the Hindus, all these gods were as real as my Jesus. The Jesus I had loved so dear was likely walking the waters of a new planet now, dying for the sins of a species who would care, who would have more faith, who would not have such evil intent. A race whose Creator will not regret the making of them.

And so I did not refute the idea that the gods of all faiths were

148

here on this night, one with a skiff coming ashore.

Then I saw movement in the house. The back door slid open, the man stepped out, turned, closed the door slowly, trying not to be heard. He walked towards this ship, not noticing me spying from the darkness. I couldn't make out the words, but some exchange took place before the man climbed aboard, and they were off.

What are you up to, Kai Jordan, traveling into the lake at these hours, torch flame to light your way?

Abandoning his wife, that much was certain, and as the torch light faded, the boat moving north up the shore, I moved towards the house. I slipped open the back door, precise as a surgeon, like opening the flap of flesh, and I entered the house. Floral scents from the young girl's soul drifted in the air, greeting me, inviting me to their source, and I followed. I moved to the back bedroom, briefcase in hand, blood flaming in my veins, saliva puddling in my mouth. I moved so softly, just a small shadow and a part of her dreams.

I stood over Sharon as she slept. She was a beautiful specimen; if God had only made more like her, he would not regret his creation.

One silky leg was exposed from the blanket, her body splayed, as if she fell to this mattress from the sky. I imagined for a bit if she had been my love, if someone like her was with me when I traveled north from the war.

She would have betrayed me just the same.

Next to the bed, I could hear the ashes stirring, restless, reaching, calling out. I recognized the scene, the tone, the feeling of the child's spirit nearby. I was there when the daughter died. Her eyes met mine at her moment of death in that hospice bed, my hand caressing her mother's hand as the cowardly father sat in the hallway.

I had thought Sharon was under my command after that moment, but she'd declined my order to bring me the ashes. She would regret her defiance.

My lungs were in unison with her breath. I moved like a shadow in the dark, and then I was the darkness. If Sharon was aware of me in her sleep, she was at peace with this.

The ashes were exposed, and I was certain that Sharon had been listening to them, communing with them. I had convinced her to believe her motherly senses. But she was so damn *ungrateful.*

Oh, but if she knew what was coming.

Why was this one so special?

I knew the answer, it was in the air like incense smoke — my wife had been responsible for this child's death. I knew it. Reached from her place in the water, and touched this girl.

My wife brings death, I bring new life.

We are your family now.

If I had more time, I would convince this grieving mother to do this willingly, but as it was, I would have to fill Sharon's veins up with a Haldol cocktail, weighing her down. Pockets full of stones in a lake full of sorrow.

My briefcase held all my works. I would boil up the ashes, take them into me, and then take from her the limbs the Well demanded.

Sharon's eyes popped open then. It was clear she didn't believe what her eyes saw, they must be deceiving her, but she would soon believe so much.

Just as she realized her space had been invaded, the syringe was stuck into the meat of her thigh. She cried out, her hands reaching for where the thick muscle had been pierced.

She used those few seconds before it took effect to unleash a tirade of curses, of screams, that faded as if she was falling.

"You hear your daughter, I know you do," I said. I placed a palm on her cheek, felt its warmth. It reminded me of standing over my own son's bed, feeling for fever. "I hear her, too. I'm going to take her from you, and then take some limbs. You'll learn it's better to have damaged parts than no parts at all."

Chapter Twenty-Five
Of Kai Sneaking Out Into the Lake

JUST A DARK OUTLINE of a past self, that's all I'll ever be, Kai thought, standing on the shoreline. A shadow of the human he once was, no real definition, just faint, fragile lines holding his sad self together. No longer the loving father who played on the lakeside with his daughter, splashed in the waters and grilled hot dogs and sliced watermelons. That was his real life—this was the shadow one. And he felt more dead than the ashes he held in his hands.

He had scraped half of Jewel's ashes into this Tupperware, lid attached securely, and gave Sharon a soft, warm kiss on the cheek before walking out the backdoor to stand lakeside. He left her with half of Jewel's remains, and carried the other half in this Tupperware, like some herbs you'd collect in a plastic container to keep them fresh.

Only this was his daughter.

The lake was quiet, no wind, no breeze. Stars dotted above were no match for this darkness, but the approaching flame burned brighter than them all. It was as if Garcon knew Kai was there, waiting, because the flame on his boat was gliding straight towards him, nothing except the fire was visible. Soon the shadow appeared on the shore.

"You ready to come out, my friend?" Garcon called out from his boat.

"I am, I am ready."

"What you got there?"

"Jewel. Jewel's ashes. Some of them, at least."

"You planning to just keep taking her out for boat rides?"

"Well, no. I'm going to let her go. Scatter her, as they say. Finally."

"What a grand night it is then. Like I said, best to go to the northeast side. Calm night, I can take us there."

Kai gave his agreement and stepped inside.

"No Sharon?" Garcon asked, pushing off from the shore.

"No Sharon," Kai confirmed, and clutched the container, as if Sharon might come and take the ashes back.

Garcon rowed with long strokes, leaning with his weight, propelling them forward, before starting the engine to help them move along faster. Kai watched his house getting smaller and smaller, and it was as if the shadow of his own death slipped in through the back door.

How can we heal the hurt, and fix what's broken? Kai thought. Seemed too hard, they were in too deep. Easier to just sink to the bottom than try and swim out. Easier to not be reminded. What glued them together was gone. Jewel was a gem mixed with the best of both of them, and to look into each other's eyes was to look into the face of what they'd lost.

How can anyone stay together after that?

Kai suggested the idea of having another child together after some time passed, but they were beyond that. They were going their separate ways.

Sharon's new peace after her walk took a second to translate, but after just a few words, it became obvious.

She was leaving him.

And since she made her decision, it was suddenly easier for her to show love. Like someone planning suicide who feels at ease with their self-prescribed fate, and since the fight was over, an odd reprieve from depression followed.

Well, he also felt a bit at ease after he split the ashes in two.

They both wanted the same thing; to be alone with their daughter. He was going to be with her into eternity. No longer passive, he wanted to do what was needed. Place the child into where she was happiest, and he would join her.

Moving along the water, incredibly still on this calm night, gazing up at the shore, at the houses with slumbering people inside. *Why did cancer strike us, and not them?* He asked this often. He often got bitter at random people who seemed to have escaped tragedy, and who had no idea the burden others carried.

He felt an urge to talk to Garcon more than ever, to inquire what made him tick, what made him still have a sparkle in his eye, living on the edges of the world, across the road, beyond the divide, on the same street that killed his child.

They were approaching the campsite, closer to WaakWing. He felt like an assassin creeping in the night to perform some clandestine military operation. One more bend, and they'd be in view of WaakWing's towering flagpole, the kayaks, the swim raft in the water. The campfire had certainly been put out by now.

If he listened, he imagined he could hear the echoes of Sharon on the raft the day Dylan went missing, the splashes as she dove in, again and again.

He was expecting her to save Dylan that day. He knew it had to be her, not him. When he dove in to look, it was as much because he wanted her to see he was doing something, but he had no faith he'd be the one to rescue the child. He didn't have what she did.

He listened to the oncology staff with less questions, he supported Jewel through the treatments with less words, he did his work quietly, searching for the specific brand of soup that didn't make Jewel nauseous, talked to her specifically about things other than her cancer treatment, since if it was so much inside her, she needed a reprieve.

But he never thought for one moment they were to blame for her death. But Sharon, life-giving Sharon, who could save lost souls just by a walk into the countryside, blamed herself for not saving Jewel. How many times did she ask, infer, and wonder if she'd done something to cause her death. He didn't understand why, but he could feel her engine of guilt so often just idling.

"You tell me when to stop, boss, just know I was around this place," Garcon said, still looking forward.

"This is good."

And it really was. The memories of where he fell in love with Sharon, swimming together after hours, an embrace of wet skin, warm lips, soft flesh. Playing games with the kids all day, the best of both of them for each other on display. Each season a new layer of love.

Garcon gazed sideways across the lake, leaving Kai alone as he held the Tupperware extended over the water. *Goodbye*, he said to himself, *goodbye*. It was all he could think of to say: *Goodbye*.

The ashes seemed to sprinkle like snow flurries, drifting into the lake. In the darkness he imagined sparks of electricity as they hit the water, just quick flashes, too fast for most eyes, but his could see them, as her father, as part of her soul forever.

With each speck that landed, ash into water, his own memories sparked of her. Jewel's eyes, shiny and bright when she was happy, or that pensive look when she was thinking, biting her upper lip and deciding if something that happened was just or unjust, and how to frame the right kind of question. Something that would stump the grownups and was really a condemnation of how they'd created the world. That aura she got when she wanted to be alone, the private world of hers spinning and spinning, a universe in her mind deeper than the one she lived in, all wrapped up in that brain, that brain of hers that became cancer-ridden, her vomit that day just before the diagnosis like the lava of the poison that erupted.

All those memories, and all her possible futures never to be known, were all part of the lake now.

Ahhhh. Big sigh, from an exhale he'd been holding in since the diagnosis, a toxic breath, full of poison left him. That felt so right. So complete.

Next time the water sparkled in the sun, it would be the sparkle of his Jewel.

If only he could see her face sparkle once again.

He dipped the Tupperware into the chilly water, as if cleansing every last fleck of her. Every bit he took from the platter, were now part of this lake.

The two fathers sat in the dark silence, floating atop the lake, Garcon letting him have his moment. Kai's face hovering over the water, staring into the depths as it soaked up his beloved daughter.

#

"Okay. I'm good now. I'm done," Kai said after the volume of silence became too much.

"Oh, no, you're not done, my friend. You're just getting started."

Garcon softly rowed away, digging in deep with the oar, as if he was moving dirt, digging graves. All of it less intrusive than the engine, and Kai was thankful for that.

Is Sharon awake back at home?

He imagined her running out to the lake, stopping the boat, diving in after Jewel. *'No she's not dead yet!'* she'd yell each time she came up for air, then dive back down. *That's what Sharon does, she dives in and saves people.*

There wasn't much left at home for him now, besides Sharon, and she was on her way out. Both of them alone with part of their daughter. They'd sliced her in half, ripped her apart. *Perhaps that's fitting.* And he wanted to stay with his half, even if it meant without Sharon.

What did she say to him? *'Don't wait on me, don't wait until I'm ready. Go on without me, I'll always meet up there later.'*

A small anchor was there near his feet. He reached down, the chain link cold to the touch, then cold against feet, his ankles, his shin, as he wrapped it around his legs. The metal chain was clinking too loudly, so he moved them even slower, tiny bits at a time, hiding his intent from Garcon. Still, they seemed to clank and echo to every corner of this huge lake, waking up those deep in slumber; *Come out and see everyone. Witness the death of Kai Jordan!* And they would all take a step out their back doors. They'd talk about the man chained to the bottom, perpetually being eaten by those fish in the deep, the creatures Camp Counselor Paxton told him about.

But he'd be with Jewel, she'd be all around him. A part of him.

With every link of chain that he wrapped around his legs, the lake called out to him. *'Yes, do it.'*

Now that Jewel was inside, it wanted him.

Garcon was rowing the boat towards the center of the lake rather than down the shoreline, and that was perfect. So cold, so deep. This was it.

He was going to join her.

The chain link snake was choking its prey and wouldn't let up if he jumped in, no matter how much he changed his mind when the survival instinct kicked in. Garcon didn't seem to notice when Kai unhooked the anchor line from the cleat.

Now it was free to bring him to the bottom.

Anchor over side, he would drift down, down, down, nothing to stop him until the bottom, 300 feet below? A diver once told him it was twice that.

Nothing ever felt so right.

He hated to think of Sharon searching for him, wondering. He owed her something.

With one hand on his cell, he sent her a text:

I'm ok. I'm where I want to be. With her. Go see the world. Bring her ashes along. I'll be at the meeting spot if you return.

He hit send before reading it twice, and as if Garcon sensed something was amiss, he stopped rowing. He lifted the oar out of the water, tucked inside the boat, and picked up the torch from the bow. He held the flame towards the water and leaned forward.

"Garcon," Kai said, "I never said the words I wanted to say."

"Words don't always need to be spoken," said Garcon.

"Well, they're all we got. And you know the road, the road your son died on. I used to plow that road nearly every day in the winter it seems. Always used to slow down around that bend. Always. Like I wanted your son to know that we still remember him. We will, always. And it's like they're still there, and we pay heed, because they never go away."

"I know, my friend, I know. I used to watch you from my front window. I see. I know. You slow down your plow. You pay reverence when you do that. And you let me keep my boat on your land, those are enough words, words aren't always spoken."

Garcon was leaning into the water.

"And if I was you—and I am you, I look on families with their children with anger. Can't help it. Can't help but decide it's a Godless world where nothing is fair and the good are treated no better, and in fact worse than the wicked. Not a place I want to stay in."

Kai had said his last words, and leaned over just then, the anchor clanking loudly, wrapped about his legs, gathered in his arms. He clung to it, ready to go over, sink into the arms of the lake, so sweet and so cold.

His chest was leaning over the edge, face close to the water, life about to end, when Garcon looked over his shoulder, and with a twist, he whooshed the flaming torch in Kai's direction.

The world on the lake's surface lit up below him. The fire brought out colors so rich and alive. The water suddenly became translucent under the flame.

What's this?

A face. A smile. Two eyes glowing with youth. He was face to face with a child.

A child, in the water.

A wise grin on their face, swimming underwater but on their back, looking up at Kai from just below the surface. It was hypnotizing, mesmerizing, with Garcon holding the flame steady, casting the glow of the flames, the fire flickering. The boy just below the surface seemed preserved, a specimen in formaldehyde, but his face full of emotion and wisdom. An angel in the waters.

"You see, my friend. This is why the nights are the best, what the torches bring. This is why you bring the ashes."

Garcon's boy was in the water. That was Dion. It was clear, Kai recognized the boy's smile. His spiky hair flowing in the lake, his hands moving like little flippers to keep him in place, a dolphin showing off for tourists.

And he knew what this could mean.

Jewel? Could Jewel be in here?

Kai leaned over with feverous anticipation, scared to let himself believe in this miracle.

An angelic shine came under the boat, moving slowly towards his side. The heartbeat in his chest was so loud, a chorus of joy sang into his ears, notes from instruments not made by the hands of men.

Such brightness in the eyes that appeared below him.

The eyes of his Jewel.

She was there, just below the surface, floating upside down. Her eyes brilliant orbs of happiness, her flesh full of colors. No longer pale from sickness, no more chemotherapy baldness, but brown hair flowing in the water, like a crown for a queen.

My girl, I'm sorry. I'm so sorry I wasn't there at that moment. The *moment,* he said, and he knew she knew what he meant, she'd always known. Why should he think differently? He saw in her smiling eyes the wit and wisdom of the perfect human he remembered, not the sick one with chemo in her veins.

Is this what you see before death? This was it, right? The lake speaks most honestly to those willing to drown. The most precious thing of his life was before him. The chance to look his daughter in the eye, face to face, her body floating in this sacred water, the love flowing in and out of them both, the face of God and the proof of the Afterlife. Of course your loved ones stay with you forever.

He saw the beauty of his child and the truth of the lake because only drowning men can see them.

Life had just become so much bigger. The universe he comprehended had been permanently changed in an instant, his understanding so different, his thoughts so small for such a grand design. This lake and this life was something much different than he thought it was.

He needed to hug her, he was going to reach in and embrace her and pull her out of the water and bring her home. *He* would be the one who saved a life...

"Jewel."

"No. No. You can't take her out of the water. You can't—"

He reached for her anyways, driven by the weight of his regret, pulled down by the gravity of his hurt, the depths of this lake, and the depths of his girl's heart. Kai leaned over the boat, closer and closer to his daughter, nearly nose to nose until...

A new face emerged, coming into focus as it ascended from the depths, details fully revealed in the glow of the torch just under the surface.

It was scarred, worn, a human face after a boat propeller had ripped it up. She had long hair like seaweed. Eyes that were cold and hurt looked up at him for just an instant, freezing his joy, freezing the moment, until she shot out of the water.

"She made the deal, sealed in blood," the woman said, as her wet amphibious hands grasped onto his cheeks, his head in their vice grip, and she pulled him down with the weight of her body.

Kai went over the edge with a splash, and with the anchor still wrapped around his legs—unlinked from the clip on the boat, the weight pulled him down without regard or concern for how much Kai's life had just changed. Down, down, through the cold water.

It's so cold because it's so deep.
How deep?
Too deep to know.
How cold?
Cold as hell.

Chapter Twenty-Six
Of Jewel in Ashes

TO HAVE SPIRITUAL roots that tap into those who love me, to be able to sense what they sense, feel their thoughts, see their dreams, changed everything for me. Free from the urn and inside my parents' bedroom, I branched into my mom's spirit. I moved about her soul, trying to comfort her, crying out for her to comfort me just the same. As she slept, we communed.

I felt my dad kiss her cheek, I sensed his spirit next to mine, gathering part of me up and placing me in the same Tupperware we used for the leftover chicken nuggets. He took me outside for a walk. I sensed the fresh air outside the container, the nighttime alive with insects that I don't think the living can hear, but I do. I sensed their heartbeats, and I felt the much bigger heartbeat of the lake as we got closer.

Soon we were floating on the lake in the rowboat of the poor man across the road. I'd met him before—he was always so nice to me. Not a lot of words, but I could tell he was safe.

Like him, I could hear the lake call to me, kind voices of children on a playground asking me to join them. And somewhere deeper in the freshwater depths, Lilith of the Lake, like the playground monitor, watching over. Her words beckoned the strongest.

'Come swim with us.'

I heard the chatter of the children—not words but a music of laughter and play. We were floating above it all, gliding over the surface. It felt like what they told me purgatory is, that space in between, waiting to go to either Heaven or Hell.

Traveling north, the chatter in the lake grew stronger, my own soul felt the anticipation in my dad's arms, and soon, that which contained me was opened.

Ah, the fresh air, bathing my spirit.

I was in my dad's hands, like the days on the swim raft when he threw me in the water. I felt the swirl of each fingerprint, the warm flesh of his palm, and then the slow sprinkle, my soul just a snowflake, drifting into the water.

And as I sprinkled down I felt such a lightness like no soul cursed to be inside a body could imagine.

The lake brought me to life.

The lake was alive. Full of thoughts and feelings and memories, but most of all, love. The love embraced me soon as each flake hit the surface. The sweet chill, the electric rush, like a bolt of lightning hit the water. The lake of the torches was the magical elixir to spark my soul back to life. Not of flesh but of spirit with aqua blue water as my blood. A richness that I never had when I walked the earth.

I felt a tingling like the stars above had all gathered around to shed their power inside me. I heard the chatter of an ocean of happy children.

I was translucent, glowing, nearly like a jellyfish when a horde of children greeted me, all full of love, leaning out to me. They surrounded me with safety and sweetness. The water below me was full of movement—something bigger was lurking while all us small things were moving about, moving in and out and through each other. We had no confines. The water was *alive*, each tiny bit was alive and meant to nourish us. None of us were unhappy. We were part of the cold, deep blue.

You've come home.

A voice I recognized, coming from far away, but getting closer and louder. It was the woman of the lake who had touched me on the beach. The children moved aside for her. Their faces were sweet and full of joy, but hers looked hurt and full of sadness.

Heaven, is it here? I asked.

There is no Heaven.

Who are you?

I told you. I am Lilith, I do the bidding of the Woman of the Well, she is the mother of the behemoth of the deep, she is the goddess of this land.

Why did you kill me?

Your mother asked me to.

She would not ask that.

She asked it before you were born. I tried to warn you your days were few, but you would not listen, you feared me.

So you killed me?

I moved you forward. I am the mother of these children now, I am the sister of the Woman of the Well. I mean you no harm here, but something's wrong with you.

What is wrong with me?
Where's the rest of you?
By my mom in her bedroom.
That's a problem.
Can I stay? I want to stay.
You may be eaten by Mishi. She will eat the imperfect souls.

Lilith looked sad in this lake of love, full of scars and wounds. Clams stuck to her skin, pinching her, a thousand fish hooks had taken their slice, a boat motor had cut her. But something inside her was hurt even more.

And above me, I felt a beautiful glow, a flicker of flames, more life, more love, and it drew my attention its way, forcing me to seek out its center, its warmth. I ascended toward the surface, and gazed up at the orange flickering flame.

Dad? My dad's eyes looked down on me, the same way he must have the moment I was born, in awe and amazement. My spirit shined with love in response.

When he saw me, the sadness left his eyes. An electric current of love passed from him to me and back again.

I'm here, back in the lake, you're watching over me. Go tell Mom. Go tell Mom, please.

But something was wrong. The woman who claimed to be a mother to all and sister to one, dashed by me. She extended out of the water and grabbed my dad by the sides of his head. My dad's face changed to that of an angel to that of a demon, falling from Heaven — falling, falling, falling right into me. Falling right through me. Metal was wrapped around his legs, an anchor shooting down to whatever was below, sinking, sinking, sinking to the bottom. A place nobody has ever been, where it's cold as hell.

Something was wrong.

My soul was imperfect, incomplete, part of me still back at home, not in the lake, next to my mom.

And I felt a dark shadow hovering over my mom as she slept.

The darkness of the bedroom overtook me. In my parents' bedroom, I felt the man looming over Mom, standing tall, black bangs over his green eyes, scars on his body from an embrace that scolded his skin as if being branded.

My mom's sleep was full of restless dreams, her mind a tumultuous sea, but her muscles and limbs were a frozen arctic, everything stuck in place, unable to move. She looked up at this man, towering over her bed, the same man who held her hand bedside while I died. The light was dim in this room, everything just shadows, everything the color of ashes, the color of me.

I found myself as ash in water again. This time not fresh, cold, lake water, but warm tap water, and getting hotter, like a flame was under me, boiling my essence. Like the most terrible water-skiing crash but I fell into a lake of lava, my ash disintegrating into water, then sucked into a needle, poked into flesh that was over 150 years old.

I sensed what was happening.

I was being put into the blood of this man, again and again, my soul was boiled and burned as if in Hell.

I was inside a red sea of pain, hurt, agony and torture. Sailing through his veins, a river of red, in and out the chambers of his beating heart, such an ancient dark soul. And inside him I was not alone. Hundreds of other children were with me, a boiling pit of dead trapped souls, crying out, and all of them coming for me. I couldn't stop it, so many of them, feeding off my freshness, like greedy piranha fish. One seemed the biggest of them all, a sad, sad boy.

How did you get here?

I died and my mom put me here.

I died too.

I know. I know. I've been waiting and wanting you to come be with us.

How did you die?

I was burned by the sun then turned to ash.

I was burned too. It set me free.

You are not free now. You are here now. And we will feed on your freshness until you are no longer fresh but rotten inside just like us.

Who is this man we're inside?

My dad. The Lamia. You and the children are all trapped here. And you will ache for more the way we ache.

They had me surrounded, the opposite of the loving souls of the Torch Lake water, these malevolent children inside this Lamia, made of ashes that would never burn out, but always aflame in this red river of lava, surrounding me with hungry eyes.

What happens now?

We will feed on you until you're like us and then we'll want some more.

What about him, the Lamia, what is he going to do?
He's going to chop up your mom.

Chapter Twenty-Seven
<u>Of Sharon in Bed with Lucas Lamia</u>

LYING IN BED—stuck there, really. Like gravity was that of another planet, one that turned a million times faster, pulling at her, freezing her in place, defenseless. Sharon saw him as a blur, or perhaps she saw him for the first time—his black mane of hair that he wiped away from his brow from time to time, his green eyes, intently burning.

Her muscles were goopy plastic that would not move. She tried to move them with thoughts that were also weighted. She tried to mouth words, but they would not come.

The room fuzzy, her thoughts on fire, nothing but sludge in her veins.

He was at the side of the bed, mixing magical potions together like some alchemist, or at least that's what her brain perceived in this stormy dream. He tied a plastic piece of tubing around his arm, fast and efficient, like someone who's done this a thousand times before. He clenched a fist, then released, clenched a first, released, and then he stuck the needle in the underside of his arm.

She felt him shudder. The whole room was shaking.

He did it again, taking her daughter's ashes from the table, flicking the lighter underneath the water and ash, taking it into the syringe and proceeding.

She tried to swat at him, telling her arm to swing with a world of violence. Instead it slowly rose from the bed but then fell back to the mattress.

Kai? Where's Kai?

He was gone, who knows where. Maybe he'd come back.

A dozen interactions with the pastor flashed through her head, each one now interpreted differently. Words of comfort were just words to con, the reflection of emotions he gave with his eyes, the muscles of his face, all deception.

"Everything I told you was real. Please don't question my words of empathy, my words of insight," he said, as if reading her thoughts. "If you'd done what I asked, we could share this right now. You'd know your daughter again. But now you'll never know. You can watch me ingest her instead. Watch her drown, a second death, but this one in my bloodstream."

The needle again poked into his arm, and the pastor groaned in satisfaction, nearly orgasmic, gory relief. A devil in her bedroom, and hell in the air.

"Nod your head if you want me to stop. I'll give you all the time in the world."

He laughed. He was mocking.

Whatever he had drugged her with kept her body like lead, her head so woozy, bordering on the edge of consciousness. If there was a God, he would wake her up from this nightmare.

"Your daughter really loved her mother, you know that. I can feel it. She misses you. She remembers so much. She loved making those Christmas cookies — snickerdoodles, her favorite just because she liked to say the name. What great parents, you two.

"But I'm her mother and father now. You should have listened to me."

Fuck you, she said, but nothing came out. In her fury she was able to pry herself slightly up on the bed.

He pushed her backwards, and her head slammed into the headboard, her neck vertebrae felt like they wanted to separate, her muscles useless. A dark sleep was hovering, a cloud ready to descend.

He unwrapped a rubber hose piece from his own arm and tied off one of her arms to the headboard. With another piece of hose, he tried off her other arm just above the elbow, squeezing tight. He was like some birthday party clown, tying balloons, pulling pieces of rubber out of pockets, making each do tricks, all of them animals at his command. He pulled out tools from his bag, as all doctors do when making house calls.

One was a small saw. He held it out to examine at eye level, his pupils gleaming with delight, his mouth wet from drool.

She fought to move, to scream, to get away. The weight of his body holding her down, and the drugs inside like shackles and chains.

With one hand pulling her arms sideways, he aimed the saw with his other hand, lining it up just below the tourniquet. A woodworker ready to cut.

And he did cut. The teeth ripped into her flesh, sawing with short strokes. The pain searing, shooting electric agony through every nerve. She was a puppet with him pulling the strings of her limbs, and one he was trying to saw right off.

What Hell have I fallen into?

This can't be happening. Can't be happening. Can't be happening.

She knew this should hurt so much more. Like getting a cavity drilled, and her cheek half-numbed by a careless dentist, the saw ripped apart her flesh and tendons without full feeling. Blood poured from the cut despite the tourniquet, she felt it warm and puddling underneath her, the sheets being dyed red.

In his eyes, she saw the madness that he'd hidden so well. That intense, narrowed vision. But there was something else in his eyes. A familiar sight within his madness. And then she realized what it was.

She was looking into the eyes of Jewel. A trace of her daughter's sparkling eyes was swimming deep inside this man's eyeballs.

Drool bubbled on her lip in place of the scream she desperately wanted to get out. She cursed herself for letting him play on her grief, all his movements, tiny notions of kindness, and each one made her trust him. *He understands me in ways you don't.* She had told Kai that.

Perhaps she deserved this—for killing her daughter, then her daughter's dad.

What happened to you, Kai? The white sheets are bloody now. *Where are the neighbors? Garcon, where are you?*

She had nobody, just herself, but he'd taken that away, her spirit sedated, her muscles so loose. Her appetite for a violent revenge could not be satiated.

The white sheets turning blood red, the saw hacking at her like a logger at a tree limb. Back and forth, harder, faster, nearly finished with the job. He'd severed flesh, veins, and bone, making quick work, and finally finished.

She saw it floating above her before she felt it.

Lamia held up her severed limb, the bone in the middle surrounded by flesh, dripping red drops from the bloody cut. Fingers dangled on the other end as if confused.

Rage in her blood was fighting against the drug. This wasn't over.

"I know that look," he said. "I've seen it. The Battle of Shiloh, The Battle of Antietam. You weren't there. I was. You're like a soldier now. A soldier in my war."

The severed arm was put aside like the limb of a clothing store mannequin.

He was not finished.

He tied another rubber hose piece just below her knee, so tight she thought he might not need the saw, that it would cut off her from shin to toe on its own.

But he did need the saw. And her calf muscle, robust from running, biking, swimming, walking up these northern Michigan hills, was separated from her body. She tried screaming from deep in her lungs, more spit on her mouth bubbling, screams just the faint whine of a rodent, not a mother being attacked by this pastor of some monster faith.

It was just a few minutes, and her leg, her whole shin bone, was held in front of her eyes. Then both her limbs were gathered and placed in his bag, a satchel over his shoulder, a prize for him to keep.

"What I want to know is, if the soul is attached to the body, and the body is dismembered, is the soul not also fractured into pieces? Different pieces, different places? Please tell me. None of my patients were able to share, but if you can?"

His voice had changed. It had become more youthful, decades younger, his skin aging in reverse, lines in his face tightening.

As she bled, crucified like Jesus, bloody and forsaken, he held up the platter, now completely empty of ash.

"Where is the rest of her?" he asked with the voice of a devil. A young demon craving pounds of flesh. "No, don't tell me. I can feel it. I can feel where the rest of her has gone. I know — she's in the lake. The rumors are true. He took her to the lake to set her free, but I need all of her. I will get her and finish my task.

Lamia let out a sigh, standing over her as an executioner ready to swing the sword.

"Please be honored your daughter was my last. I hope someone comes for you soon. Or you go get help, you've got a few hours of blood left in your body — and I have an eternity of your Jewel in mine."

She lost consciousness as he left the room, fading into dark, returning, fading, returning, until the blackness kept her and didn't let go.

CHAPTER TWENTY-EIGHT
OF KAI SINKING IN TORCH LAKE

FALLING, SINKING, DEEPER into the cold depths. His hands clawed helplessly above him, trying to swim up against the weight that pulled him down.

Be like water, flow like water.

He could not be like water, flow like water. The water was killing him.

Falling, sinking, deeper. The lake is so cold because it's so deep—deep as Hell. He kept his eyes on his daughter above, but her image was fading. The light from the torch still flickered just above the surface, but grew smaller as he sank. His daughter hovered just below the flame, no longer dust, but reborn in the lake.

He was graced with a chance to see her again, just one fleeting moment, but it was stripped away. He desperately wanted it back, fighting against the very death he earlier wanted to embrace.

But he'd trapped himself with this anchor.

He frantically tugged against the chain link to unwrap the anchor and drop the weight, but it seemed to react and fight back, as if the metal links were alive. A sea snake, wrapping around his leg, tightening its embrace the more he tried to unravel it. A Gordian knot.

The anchor was alive.

And so was this woman swimming around him in circles as he sank, watching him die, making sure he died.

She made a deal, sealed blood.

Her words echoed, but meant nothing.

Falling, sinking, deeper into the depths. So cold, so dark. The light of the torch at the surface gone, his head woozy, his lungs burning.

Sinking, sinking.

Are there any more angels in this Hell to save me?

No.

He was alone. Swallowed by the darkness, his insides gasping for life, lungs burning for air, burning in pain, until his core finally burst and his mouth sucked for oxygen that was just not there. Instead, he took a deep breath full of cold lake water. Who knew water could burn? An explosion of pain burst from his chest. The lake water had killed him.

But then it stopped hurting, this death of his body, but his soul remained, still chained to his carcass, afraid to leave, unable to leave, so remained inside.

His life was gone.

For one instant his child's face had flashed before his eyes, his beloved brought to life by these waters. And in that moment when his eyes had locked on hers, he wanted to live on, needed to live on. He'd imagined a thousand future summer nights in this new reality — pontoon rides with Sharon as the sun went down, lighting the torch, flame near the water, and then watching their daughter play and swim like a porpoise in the lake, their eyes looking down with love, their hands locked.

But the chains that bound his feet stopped him from kicking and clawing back to the surface.

Why had the monstrous woman grasped his face and pulled him down?

Why?

As if to answer, the Woman of the Lake started circling his body, her strands of hair glowing like neon snakes. She glided to a stop, her eyes before his, silver in the dark.

Why? Kai asked again.

Your life was sacrificed so your daughter could live one more year. Your wife made the deal, sealed it in blood, and I was bound to take you, same as I was bound to take your daughter.

My daughter?

Yes, your wife traded her. After Mishi snatched that young boy from the raft, snatched him by the foot, dragged him below the water so fast and quiet not a single human noticed. She pulled him to the depths, not far from where you are now. Mishi was to devour him, flesh and soul, but the Well commanded the child's return, for your wife agreed her child would be taken at the very same age. That boy was reborn again and returned to dry land. He was unharmed, but your child was taken in return.

Even in this water, Kai remembered the scent from this woman. That putrid smell of spoiled earthworms when she first grabbed his face is the same scent when Jewel was vomiting on the shoreline.

Sharon's guilt, it made sense now.

This woman of the water seemed lonely, like she needed to

talk to someone, like she'd been waiting to talk to someone, and found a captive person to listen.

Who are you? Kai asked.

I am Lilith, born in Virginia in 1823, daughter of a landowner, husband of a pastor and a surgeon. He was banished from the Union army for amputating limbs that were perfectly fine. He went quite insane, it seems — and he kept amputating limbs even after we traveled to these northern lands to settle, lopping off the arms and legs of loggers who swore they were fine, but put under by chlorophyll.

When I saw him ready to hurt our boy, I tried to destroy him.

Both of us tried to outwit the Woman of the Well, but now we are cursed. Now I do the bidding. I care for the children. I give or take life, like I took your daughter's, and like I took yours.

Kai's rapid descent into this cold hell finally stopped. The anchor came to rest on the bottom, the chain keeping him there. He could feel the anchor nestle into the sandstone, leaving him in the darkness like some deep sea creature who never knew the light.

And soon he was alone, because Lilith swam off, dashing away, a fish acting on fear, because something else massive was moving within the darkness. Circling and circling, the creature so big it had its own gravitational pull that tugged at Kai's soul. He felt the behemoth breathing. The mass getting closer, a submarine made of muscle. Too dark to be seen, too massive not to be feared. Big as a weather pattern, changing every atom in its presence, making them vibrate at different speeds, a tuning fork hum that does not stop.

It was Mishipeshu. The myth was true.

This was the legendary creature Paxton spoke about. The mythical beast, the demi-god. Made from dead parts by a sea witch who gathered them from the bottom, assembled them, and brought them to life. Mishi's presence spoke to his soul, communed with him, spirit to spirit; *YOU'RE LIKE ME, OF THE DEAD PARTS NOW.*

Kai was dead parts. His life was over. His soul would not leave his dead body. It clung to his carcass. His flesh preserved in the cold water, his blood growing cold, his body burning in the hell of the cold, wet darkness. His spirit feared to leave. It knew not how.

Mishi owned the bottom, fed from the bottom, and the wide circles she swam around Kai were getting smaller. So close that a whisker of the biblical beast — or was that a tentacle, meant to capture its prey — dragged itself across Kai's face.

Kai never forgot a word that Paxton said, and the ones he heard at that moment were: '*...and Mishi had developed a taste for these humans'*

The scream from Kai's soul made no sound, and provided no relief.

CHAPTER TWENTY-NINE
OF SHARON COMING TO AT THE LAKEHOUSE

HOW LONG IT took until she came to and her eyes opened back up, she couldn't tell, but the Haldol and Ativan eventually released their grip. Sensations returned to her body, slowly, a gradual wake from a dream. With the shackles unbound came the freedom to move, the freedom to feel pain, but not the ability to comprehend what just happened.

What am I now? What do I do next?

Lying there in a puddle of blood, sticking to the sheets. Waiting for help was one option, but maybe the worst one. She had to move, but how? She felt like a snake. Lost limbs, full of sin, stuck to the ground, stuck to this bed.

She started to rock back and forth; left, right, left, right, until finally, she rolled off the bed.

The *thud* she landed with sounded almost comical.

On the ground, a wiggling worm, she grasped onto the bed with her one arm, leaned against it with her chest, and pushed off the floor with her one leg, trying to stand upright.

She slid right off the bed sheet.

Boom.

The blood kept coming, the tourniquets couldn't stop it all. She was just a bloody doll now, held together by bits of rubber hoses, a mistake she was still alive.

She was going to bleed to death and die alone.

But she would not give up. She tried again, pulling against the bed, grunting loudly, a primal roar coming from somewhere deep in her soul.

Thump, she fell again.

On the ground she glanced where her arm should be, where her leg should be, instead only seeing stumps. She felt nauseous, ready to vomit, hoping to vomit. The pain was getting worse as the drugs faded, the pastor never left, but was still sawing, sawing, sawing at her body. Her brain so confused, this reality so wrong. *What to do?* An arm and a leg. Dismembered. *And taken, but where? Can I chase that man, can I catch him?*

That was ridiculous, of course she couldn't do that.

Shock. I'm in shock.

What just happened? she asked herself. And answered.

Your daughter had a seizure on the beach and was given cancer by a touch. Your gramma had a stroke in the car.

A pastor just sawed off an arm and a leg and left with them.

What was left to lose? What to do?

I need help.

She wormed over to the cell phone on the bedside table. She imagined herself in a war, shots firing overheard. Her life was on the line.

Others' lives were on the line. Dylan, Jewel, Gramma.

There was no cell service here in the Badlands. She'd have to get in the car herself and drive Gramma to the hospital, somewhere to get help. Could she work the transmission, the gas, reach the brake?

Why won't Gramma respond to me?

How do I save her?

Drip. Drip.

The blood everywhere, smearing on the carpet like roadkill dragged on the pavement.

She reached for the cell, knocked it from the bedside table to the carpet. With the cell on the ground, she tapped the numbers to dial Kai. It kept ringing. No answer. Wait, he sent her a text. She read it best she could:

I'm ok. I'm where I want to be. With her. Go see the world. Bring her ashes along. I'll be at the meeting spot if you return.

Where he wants to be. Meeting spot. Return. What does it mean? If only she could focus, could think. *Please, come back. I need you.* She texted him "911" with her bloody finger, waiting for a response, but nothing.

Because he isn't alive and I killed him.

She dialed 911 itself and the answer came after one ring.

"911, what is your emergency?"

What to say? Last time she tried to dial 911, when Gramma had a stroke on the plains of Dakotas, she couldn't get a signal, so she took action. She drove, at thirteen years old, with the artwork in the back, carefully stored. Gramma next to her with her muscles twitching, drool on her lips, her head slack. The Badlands ragged and rocky to both sides of her.

Her silent tears, her raging fear.

"911, what is your emergency?"

What to say?

She wanted to start from the beginning. *I was born with damaged parts, Gramma made art, I was her art, we went where the art took us, on tours, then Gramma died a slow death, then I killed my daughter, a slow murder. Then her dad and I killed each other, a double homicide.*

Arm taken from her. A fucking arm. A fucking leg.

It will take a day to explain to 911, it will take another hour for emergency to arrive.

The bizarre and absurd.

I'm good on a lifeboat, not good at life.

"I need help," she said, but could say no more.

Can you find my arm and leg? Of course not. Her body, her soul, her family, everything was splintered. The world wasn't the same now. Her brain itself felt chopped in two. Arm gone. Leg gone. Phantom limbs. But the pain—the pain was real. It felt like the Pastor had a voodoo doll and was poking at her wounds from afar, red hot needles stabbed into her exposed marrow. And wherever he was, he had her limbs.

How to share this when the paramedics arrived?

This is only half of me, the other half was taken by a pastor I let trick me.

She looked down at the stump of her leg, certain this was a trick of her eye and the other half of her leg would appear, but nothing.

She kept trying to use the arm that wasn't there, flexing it.

All that happened was more blood, all over her, all over the carpet. *I'm sorry for the mess, Kai.*

Forget help. She hung up on the emergency call. There was no going back. There was only going forward.

She remembered the crutches buried deep in the front hall closet, left over from her plantar fasciitis surgery. She crawled out her bedroom door to the front hall closet, extended her one arm, then pushed with her one leg. She had to roll over more than once to adjust her course.

Gramma's going to die.

Do I go back the way I came or do I go forward for help?

If you'd gone back she would have died.

Maybe that would have been better.

Cheek to the carpet, she reached into the floor of the closet, felt around for the bottom of one crutch, pulled it to and fro until it tumbled onto the ground, close enough she could grasp.

Sliding her arm and leg against the wall, she was able to stand, a punch-drunk bloody boxer. *Fight's not over.*

The crutch under her one arm, clutching it tightly, she made it to the back sliding glass door with short hops, using the crutch as a leg.

She slid the door open, just a crack.

The night air off the lake greeted her but didn't recognize her. *Who are you now? What happened to you?*

Maybe she was always this way, never fully equipped.

Or maybe I'm perfect now. My damaged parts have been removed. Look Gramma, I'm perfect.

She imagined the air from the lake healing her, cauterizing her wounds. *No evil bacteria can handle our goodness.* The lake would grow her limbs back, a new species, made for the lake, by the lake, and no more deaths. Her old self over, no need for a life. No need for a lifeboat.

The pain and blood washed these thoughts away.

She saw movement on the lake—one figure, two figures, the hum of an engine. The engine got cut, and shortly after, a small boat leaves the shores, a torch burning at the helm.

Garcon's boat. She was left alone.

Blood was gathering on the stump of her arm, stump of her leg, then dripping, staining the carpet with thick, crimson red paint.

Wipe your feet Jewel, don't bring the whole beach inside.

How many times had she said that to Jewel, coming in from outside, how utterly meaningless such concerns were, but how precious that beach was.

Where have you gone, Kai?

If he was with her, they would figure this out. All their resentments would vanish at this moment, no words would be spoken, just a soft look into each other's eyes.

That's not how it works. You don't always get a face-to-face at the hour of death. She killed her daughter, she killed her own partner. Now she was about to die herself, and all alone.

If I cannot express my love for my daughter, I'll express rage at the powers that took her.

She would avenge their murders. She would seek out and destroy the Well.

How to get there?

Car keys on the counter. She could reach them, with some work.

Can I drive? Of course I can.

Every hop with the crutch sent another dash of blood seeping. She was slowly being wrung out, her essence left in puddles.

One step at a time she got out the front door. The crutch was her leg, under one armpit, her arm stressing and bracing. One fall and she would never ever get up again, and someone would find her on the ground in the morning.

Short step, hop. Short step, hop. Short step, hop.

The car was open, never locked in these parts because nothing bad happens here. Leaning against the car, she opened the door with her one hand and swung it open. She swerved into the seat, sliding on the lubricant of her own blood.

One arm to steer, one leg to dive.

The street flickered in and out of focus, her consciousness fading like a curtain begging to close. She lined up the car, fighting to keep it straight down the road, swerving like a drunk but correcting it, moving ahead.

Odd shadows like creatures began dashing back and forth across the street, the whole forest had been called into arms as if protecting the Well from this surprise attack. One arm, one leg, one dizzy brain, she was on course for the Well.

I killed Jewel, I probably killed Kai, and the last thing before I die will be to kill the Well.

The Well had to be destroyed.

A dead body is poison.

She came to a complete stop at the fork in the road. She had to navigate it with one arm, turning the wheel, then pushing her thigh up against it to keep it in place. Twist the wheel a bit more, push her thigh up to keep the wheel in place. A slower process, like turning a barge.

She was just a quarter mile away.

Accelerating up the hill, the stars in the sky glowing brighter on these darker roads and these darker times, her brain skipping and jumping. The eternal sleep beckoned. Dizziness made the whole world tilt, left, then right, a cruise ship on stormy seas.

There. There's the house.

As she approached, the one board left from the decaying home fell to the ground, all to the earth, and just to the side stood the Well. She veered towards it. The stones in the headlights seemed shocked, surprised, and (she imagined) scared to see her coming.

She locked her elbow with one hand and pressed the gas to the floor. She held it there, and veered off the road and onto the land, straight towards the Well. The car bounced back and forth on the terrain, side to side, her one hand trying to adjust, *can't miss it, can't miss it, I'm going to miss it. NO, adjust your arm, there, back to the center of it, here you go.* If this went as she planned the car would explode and the Well would be destroyed.

Keep steady, keep awake and alive for a tiny second and then...

Crash! Metal crunching, glass shattering, piercing the quiet night. The airbag went *poof* and smacked her face.

Queasy and dazed, she counted her limbs, as if another was taken off, or the two were put back on.

Nope, no changes, she was the same monster.

Throwing herself against the door, she fell right out of the car onto the ground, gravity tugging at her, the rag doll, the half human, a creature crawling, crawling, to see the destroyed Well. Then she could die in peace.

But before her was a perfect circle of stones. Immaculate.

The Well was fine.

Unharmed. Undisturbed.

The car was smashed in like a skull bashed in with a bat. The engine destroyed like the brain, but the stones of the Well stood strong and firm. Mocking her.

No.

She cried then, finally, dropping to the ground ready to die, the last bit of fluid in her body came out in tears, there was no more. Both body and soul gone dry, save the last few drops the tourniquets fought to hold inside.

Dying alone. That was it, leaving just a dead body behind.

A dead body poisons the Well.

The Well had a weakness. Her decaying body had a purpose yet.

The way to kill a Well is to poison it with a rotting body.

She wouldn't leave a pretty carcass, but her carcass would rot in the Well.

The rubber hose tourniquets were holding her life together, still tied on, but one pull and she'd bleed out in an instant. She leaned against the Well and tugged the tourniquets free, letting the essence bleed out of her. A grand finale, baptizing the stones with her blood, leaning over the rocks, the one hand finding a grip, pulling herself up, flipping herself over the rock.

She fell down the dark hole, down into the planet, this eyeball of a giant, this lake its blue iris.

And Sharon kept falling, into the bowels of this land, into the arms of the ancient deity who remained nameless, such a cold life, such a cold hell. And it took her in, as it does, dead parts on the bottom.

Chapter Thirty
Of Garcon Rushing Back to Shore

GARCON HAD PUT down the oar and opted for the motor. No need to worry about the engine startling what's below at this point. Let it all surface.

He was rushing to shore with an urgency, as if when he got there someone could help. As if he knew what to do when he arrived.

He didn't.

Garcon had yelled and searched for Mr. Jordan for at least an hour. *He has to be dead, right? Dead and drowned.*

But things aren't the same with this lake.

Maybe he's out there swimming. Or maybe another boat found him. They heard the noise, shined a spotlight, and he's wrapped up in a beach blanket, safely on board.

No, he's sinking, twisted up in the metal chain and then pulled down by some creature.

Why was the anchor wrapped around his legs? What was that *being* that reached from the water to grab him?

He would go to Kai's house, find his wife, tell her what happened (not all of it, no not all of it).

Then what? Call the Coast Guard? Drag the lake for the body?

No way you can drag a lake this deep. Plus, this lake doesn't give up its dead easy — in fact, it stores them.

Garcon was the one who told the sad father best results are scattering to the north. If only Mr. Jordan hadn't tried to pull his girl from the water. Garcon never warned him, *don't reach for your daughter*. Just be content to be in her presence and leave her be.

#

Garcon was given guidance in his own time.

He first heard the story from a utility worker who was doing some line work near his yard. Garcon was laying some red roses on Dion's roadside memorial while the man was working on a pole, thirty feet above.

"You use fresh flowers," the man said from his spot in the sky. "That's good. Some folks use them plastic type. Not a fan."

Garcon looked up, squinting in the sun.

"And why's that?"

The man climbed down the wooden pole, quick and effortless, until they were face to face. The man's skin was weathered, his hide tough, his skin full of deep wrinkles and chasms.

"Real flowers fall to the ground," he explained, "then rise again in the earth. Children fall to the water, rise again in the lake. How it works."

Garcon invited him to sit down. Soon after, they sat on lawn chairs in front of his RV, drinking a twelve-pack of Short's beer.

"You bury your child?" the man asked.

"Had him cremated, wanted him to remain with me."

"That's good, that's good. You want him to rise?"

"Rise?"

"The witch made it possible."

"Witch, huh?" Garcon wanted him to talk, needed this worker from the sky to say more, but feigned indifference. Why Garcon picked that time to be social, when he had been shunning contact with everyone, would soon become clear.

"Yes, Mistah RV. A witch, or a goddess. Same thing. 'Course she delivers. Almost lost her own child. Her daughter, Mishipeshus."

"Mishi…"

The man smiled, a bright white flash that lingered. "Mish-if-e-suss. She swims in this lake. You'll see her if the lake lets you. Long ago, hungry humans tricked Mishipeshus to the surface. Stabbed her. Burned her. Witch made a deal with the tribe. Said leave my child be, and none of yours shall die. End the hunt. Let her live. Burn your own dead. Let your child's ashes rain into the water, then I'll rebuild them from the dead parts. Their soul will greet you when you return with the flame, but they must remain in the water. Leave them be, leave Mishipeshus be, and go in peace.

"'Course the witch delivered. Perfect kids. Perfect kids."

They kept drinking, each emptying a can with nothing but silence, sighs, and swigs, eyeing the bigger houses across the street. Few cars passed. Kai Jordan himself walked out his front door and put up his lawn sign saying: *Keep Torch Lake Blue*, condemning the use of fertilizer.

"You and your signs. Y'all just honoring the goddess witch but you don't know it. Torch Lake is blue 'cause it's nothing but the iris on this big eyeball of a planet. And the blue iris belongs to the witch."

Garcon clutched his Short's beer like a pacifier, a baby hearing a bedtime story.

"You go try, Mista RV. You go try. Sprinkle the ash, like they did. It's true, it is. You've seen the cribs in the lake. Mothers made them out of logs to care for their children. A place to hide, a place to sleep."

Garcon shook his head but he wanted to believe it. "We've all seen the cribs on the bottom. They're fish shelters, made by the DNR."

"No sir. Made by the mothers of grieving children. Now do it, Mista RV. Do as they did and sprinkle the ash and you'll see."

Garcon was skeptical until he saw with his own eyes. He tried to pass on this wisdom to Kai, a kind man who paid Garcon's property taxes once, who gave reverence to his deceased son when he plowed the road, who often paced the lakeshore at night when he should be asleep. Just as the story gave Garcon a reason to live, he wanted Kai Jordan to find his way. *Best results scattering to the north,* he had said, but he should have said more.

Yes, you will see your daughter in the lake at night under the flame. You will want to pull her out of the water and embrace her and take her home. But do not. I tried to pull him out of the water, too, my dear friend. I did pull him out.

Pulled his little human out of the water. But as soon as Dion got onboard he began to burn again, turning from a perfect specimen to a raging demon. His white eyes were popping out, full of anger and insanity. He bit his dad's cheek. He called out names Garcon would not repeat, cursing his father for letting him die on that road, for not watching him, for letting the car shatter his bones and drag him on the road.

The words turned to screams, howling with anger, his skin first bubbling with blisters, then turning black as charcoal. Garcon dropped his child back into the water. The noise it made, like lava to the sea — *hissssss,* as if water had put the fire out.

One more instant, and his soul would have been lost. But back in the water he was restored to a happy child. His glow had a different shade, tainted by the wounds, but once again love beamed from his eyes.

So Garcon returned, every calm night. Never again would he try to reach for him. Grateful to just watch him swim in the love and joy on summer nights, and even setting up ice fishing shanties to catch a glimpse in the winter. He talked to very few people, and they wanted it that way. The world feared him after the tragedy, gave forced pleasantries, but he did not need them. He slept during the day, boated at night, leaving the waters for the shore just hours before sunrise, invisible to the world in the darkness.

#

This was the first time he ever raced back to shore, no longer wanting solitude, but help from his fellow men. The torch light blew out at such speeds. He waited until the last moment to cut the engine, momentum pushing him in, the sound of the boat scraping against the lake's bottom, waves sent lapping against the shore. The night didn't seem calm anywhere on this lake, nothing the same at this hour, and for proof, there was a shadow standing at the shore.

"I lost a man. He went overboard," Garcon said. *How could this man help?* He didn't know, but he was eager to share his misery.

"Yes, he went to the lake with his child. The ashes of his child," said the tall figure with a powerful voice.

"How do you know? Who are you?"

"I'm a doctor, I can help. Please, let me help you."

Such fortune.

Garcon beached the small boat, stepped off quickly into the water, a few inches deep there, slopping and splashing, ready to talk to this doctor who said he could help.

Before Garcon could say a word, before he could share his rehearsed story and hope this doctor could save the patient, lost somewhere at sea, the figure stepped right by him, dismissing his presence. First one, then two legs onto the boat, extending each foot from shore to boat without touching water.

"We need more help. We need more boats. More boaters, call the Coast Guard, we need..."

Garcon felt something like a bee sting, only this stinger as long as a steak knife, and his body became rubber, his skeleton tired of holding his weight, and he fell to shore, barely awake but just enough to see this man take over his boat, motor out towards the lake. The torch at the helm was relit, the boat went north, and Garcon went dark.

——
182

CHAPTER THIRTY-ONE
OF LAMIA GOING TO FIND HER

SUCH A BLACK NIGHT, such sparkling stars, such glory at the end of these last hours I was living.

This was the night everything changed.

The last bit of ash in my veins, the best of them all, the most majestic high, giving me the confidence to take this boat on this lake whose very water was like flames to my skin.

I didn't care. God is good, whatever god it is that was left.

No, I am that God that is left. I am a god and I've come to fetch one of my children. Same way I knew which way gravity pulled, and which way the wind blows, I knew by instinct where to find the rest of her.

I cut the engine, letting the boat coast over the water. The boat beat against the waves, back and forth. One splash of water rose up over the hull, landed on my forearm with a sizzle, a quick burn, but then it was over.

I was on a lake of lava, a lake of flames, but the air in the middle of the lake was glorious. It was nearly as fresh as when I first came up north, back when it filled my lungs with life. Now this land around this lake was being ruined, surrounded by such soft humans who could never build their own homes, till their own fields, or operate on their own wounded. These people did not deserve to be here. They did not deserve the land, the view of the setting sun, or to breathe this beautiful air. God stretched Heaven over the north, and they bought the land and built their houses here.

I thought again how much I could go door to door and kill them all, but I had only a few hours before midnight hit. The world was cold, and I was leaving it, as long as I fulfilled the wishes of the Well. The suffering would end. Tonight.

I had the limbs safely in my bag. I imagined them moving, and certainly begging and clawing for freedom.

I reached down, pulled the drawstring, and tightened the top.

Now they can't crawl out.

I just needed the girl. All of her, not half. Half was already inside me—in and out of my heart, through my bloodstream. And that soul needed its other part, somewhere in this lake, and it guided me north along the lakeshore.

I knew the rumors were probably true. The water turns the ash to life—but out of the water that life turns back into ashes.

The night air was electric, lively, the universe holding its breath at the moment before it started. I was both captain and crew of this ship, but really my whole life I'd been lost, sailing on a sea of fire. The soldiers of the south, the devils from the ground, that demon son I could not help but love inside my own body.

How many people had I healed? Yet here I was, alone.

How many mothers have I given back their loved ones to? This very country I helped save, returning soldiers to the battlefield. I did what I had to, and sometimes I needed to amputate to save lives, the way God would.

Had I not helped free the Black men and women? Unshackled their chains? Had I not freed so many mothers from their grief, giving them back what God could not? Yet none who offered me thanks.

I scanned the horizon. I was near the lake's center, the deepest part, the silence only interrupted by the rush of the fresh blood pounding in my ears. I knew the rest of her was just below me, same as I could connect finger with thumb.

I held the flame to the water, and soon they gathered. First one, then two, then six, then a dozen. Children swimming, reminded me of tadpoles in a clear pond, scattering about.

My first scoop with the net, I captured a child. A soul of a child, incarnate in the lake, an aqua blue tint to its flesh, and a child's aura that beamed so bright. Never had a prey been so willing to be caught, the small child full of joy to be the one chosen, certain the net was to bring them to their loved ones.

Instead, when I scooped them up out of the water and the air hit them, the child became a little demon in the net, like it had been tossed into fire. It flayed about, flopping in the net with rage, screaming obscenities, a barrage of curses, listing transgressions at those who hurt him with words that sliced up my eardrums. His eyes were popping out of his head, a piercing hate in its vision.

I held the net out until all the water dripped and drained from the young soul, not wanting to get the scorching drops on my own flesh. By the time I flipped the net and dropped the young thing into the boat, its skin had burned to a charcoal black. The flawless flesh, preserved by these waters, was no longer. Like watching them burn alive in the crematorium, only this fire was invisible, as clear as the air.

When the process was over, when the screams faded and the soul burning with rage had flickered out, a pile of ashes remained in its place. The cremains dead and stale, lifeless and soulless. They would be easy to gather into a pile, should I wish, but instead brushed them away.

This was not the ash I was looking for. I needed the Jordan girl.

Torch held over the water, they swam like starving fish to the perfect bait, and I kept scooping.

The more I hauled in with the net, and then returned the flame to the surface, the more that gathered. These children, my children, wanted salvation.

Come gather, I'm here to save you from this cursed existence. A true sleep, a dark dip into the void.

One young boy who was illuminated by the flame as he hovered just below the water seemed different than others, the sweet innocence of an angel, but his shade of skin darker than the rest, like he'd been taken out, burnt, and put back in.

He swam below the boat as if he was familiar with its captain, but upon my gaze, didn't recognize the new owner. I mounted the flame, and with two hands on the net, went to scoop up the mesmerized boy. He should be put to death, this sad thing, this deformed soul.

But wait, what's that?

I paused when I heard something emerge from the water behind me. I turned to see a shadow rapidly approaching, swimming right at me, a torpedo ready to strike.

Boom!

It rammed the side of the boat, *don't fall don't fall don't fall,* my legs braced on either side of the boat. My balance was sent in a whirl. I almost flipped over and fell into the fiery water, but with arms split out to my side, knees bent, I was able to steady myself.

Ah, it is you, my love.

I recognized her hair, long seaweed flowing from the top of her head, but the rest of her body had morphed into something beyond human, swimming just below the surface. She was more lake creature than the wife I came here with a hundred plus years ago. A wife who betrayed me and started this curse.

She stopped in the water, turned to look at me, a face so twisted it must bring madness to most men, but to me, just hurt for the love we once had.

"I waited a century for you to visit these waters. Now that you are here, I will make sure you never leave. I will bring you under the waters. Your flesh will burn. My son will be free from the hell he's trapped in."

She hissed, a snake under the surface, spitting venomous words, and I had no time for the likes of her. I flipped the net over, held it like a spear, and stabbed at her. First a miss left, then a miss right, then before she could submerge, I smacked her in the ribs, the Lance of Longinus in her side. She disappeared back into the lake.

You betrayed me, you get nothing.

I stood with knees braced, waiting for her to come assault the boat again. The boat kept rocking, slower and slower with a soft lull, like a crib, but my wife was not done. She would not be put down that easy, so I waited, standing over the limbs in the boat, still there in the bag. I wondered if the rest of the body missed them. The Jordan girl, half in my veins, half below the boat, and each half certainly missed the other. I felt the girl, still bubbling in my blood, still coursing through my arteries.

The rest of her was so close. I knew it.

With one hand holding the net, the other picked up the torch. The oils that kept the flame alight were burning out. I didn't have much time.

As soon as I put it toward the water, I saw her face.

There she was, the Jewel. I remembered her at the hour of death. I sat bedside, holding her mom's hand, watching the life slip out of her daughter's corpse that already seemed cold and rotting in the hospital bed. The girl looked so fresh in the water, not pale, not sickly, but full of love and light, smiling up at me for a moment.

But then her face turned, as if fearful to keep eye contact, and I noticed she seemed fractured, broken, incomplete. Unlike the other children, who were perfect, she was faulty, deformed. With half of her inside him, she was half a soul.

A soul does crave its other half if it's been torn apart.

I was ready to scoop her up in the net when something else

emerged from the water. Something so much bigger than my wife, and it was making a run for her. All the children scattered; the Jewel did not. Some amalgam of whale and squid and lion and elk. Rather than a fin, those seemed like antlers. Tentacles like a giant squid, jaws like a giant shark.

It wasn't fast enough.

I was still a surgeon, and with the precision strike that would make my medical colleagues proud of my work, I sliced the net through the water, under the girl, and lifted.

The lake creature went swimming by, harmless. Jewel was in my care.

I held the net up like a prize, high into the air where she would burn with rage.

Mission accomplished. Soon, her ashes in his boat, sprinkled in the bag of limbs, and then back to the Well, where they'd all fall to the bottom, and I'd be reborn, curse-free.

Chapter Thirty-Two
<u>Of Jewel in the Water and the Blood</u>

TO HAVE SPIRITUAL roots that tap into those who love me, but now taking root in two places.

Only one of those was not love

Being stuck in this diseased body was like getting cancer treatment all over again, but with a team of evil doctors. Another shunt, another test, another needle puncture, sucking out blood, drip-drip-dripping in chemotherapy chemicals. Swimming within the blood of this vampire who ingested my soul, being feasted on by a hundred tortured others who craved to feed, each taking their turn.

This had to be Hell.

The other part of me was in Heaven, playing and dancing and swimming in the glorious blue water. It's so cold because it's so deep.

And it felt like the two parts of me were getting closer. I could taste it, hear it. Sense it with every bit as I moved within and without.

And when the glow of the light came to this lake that's so dark because it's so deep, I went to the light. *Was it Dad or was it Mom?* Mom was close; Dad was below. Was he safe?

He must be safe. All of us were safe, all of us yearning to be close to the flame—the flame is love, love is light, and light is love.

We were swimming in and out and through each other, feeding on each other's excitement, scrambling to be close to the flame, to feel its glow. Everyone was there. I waited my turn, the water getting splashed around. A net was dipping in, and some of us left the water. *Where do they go?* I got closer to the flame, the heat—*I want the heat.* It glowed like a sun or a mom or a dad awaited. *Everything's going to be perfect real soon.*

But something changed.

The pressure in the lake dropped. The children around me scattered like birds from a wire. But not me. I stayed and looked over.

It was Mishi.

She was coming right at me. It was her, I knew it was. I'd caught glimpses before, gazing down from the pontoon into the deepest part of the lake, seeing a fin flip and then vanish. But one glance at her whole body and I knew it was her. She was bigger than I thought. A massive fish, a submarine, a goddess of some sort. But this time, she wasn't diving deep—she was coming right at me.

She eats imperfect souls, and I'm imperfect. My dad took half and the Lamia took the other half.

Mishi was coming, but I stayed by the light. Getting closer, the creature with antlers on its head, tentacles for a tail, jaws opening wide, and I was about to be consumed.

Still, I remained by the glowing fire. The light of love.

Because Mom is up there, I knew it. I'd been crying out to her, crying from the ashes, crying from the lake. *Dad, tell Mom I'm here...so she knows.*

Mishi was coming but my mom was up there and I decided to wait because I wouldn't let these bully sea creatures with the fangs and tails know I was scared.

But I am scared.

Scared of Mishi, but more scared to miss the loving flame of Mom's heart. Each flicker of orange, each flame of yellow, held everything I'd yearned to be with, so I refused to move even as Mishi closed in on me. Her fangs sharp, her mouth open, ready to swallow me whole and...

I got scooped up into the air! *I am saved!* Mishi scooted right by.

But, wait. Wait...

It burns!

The air burned. The fire of love and warmth was gone and instead I was stuck in a net and all around me the air burned. Hotter than any cremation flame, roasting my skin and my memories and feelings. Bubbling lava erupted, a volcano of anger and rage.

My soul full of anger and rage.

My dad was dead on the bottom like he should be. I wanted to dive back down and make him hurt.

My mom. She killed me. She knew I would die. She traded my life for someone she barely knew.

I wanted to gouge her eyes out so they could never see me.

I wanted my dad to feel my death.

Both of them should feel the nausea of chemotherapy. Doctors should poke *them* with their sharp needles.

Everyone lied to me that the doctors would help.

I feel the rage, layer after layer, getting closer to my core, shedding myself with invisible flames, burning and burning and my heart wailing. Losing my years, going back to before I existed. I was 6, 5, 4, 3, 2 years old again, crying in the back bedroom. My parents came for me then, one or the other or both, and took me into their room but now there was nobody and it hurt my core to cry. Of course they wouldn't come for me now. They never loved me, and I hated them for it.

The flame keeps burning and wouldn't go out as I thrashed inside this net. *I have others to kill. My anger has an appetite that needs quenching.*

But I was trapped and burning.

I wasn't just dying. This wasn't the fire that burned my body, this was a fire that burned my soul. My spirit was lighter fluid, the air was flames, and it roasted me from inside out. I let out one last scream hoping my dad could hear at the cold dark bottom or my mom could hear on the surface and they both felt my pain.

Mom could hear me. I knew she could. She was coming. She was watching.

See what you did to your daughter?

Chapter Thirty-Three
<u>Of Sharon Falling</u>

FALLING, FALLING, FALLING down the Well. Flailing and sinking.
Sharon did not land, she only slowed, when she finally hit water. But
even then, she kept sinking, sinking, sinking.

She fell through the Badlands of South Dakota, fell through
the hills of Cheyenne, the blue mountains of West Virginia, the
memories of Mom and Dad, seen in pictures first, but then they came
alive, damaged parts clawing at her from the sides of the Well, but not
stopping her.

She kept sinking, sinking, trying to reach a bottom, trying to
reach for the sides, but couldn't reach far enough, so she sank. She fell
through his history — this pastor, this doctor, watched him sawing off
limbs. His delight grew with each amputation. Saw him using leeches
that crawled from this very spot to heal others, watched as he injected
ashes into his veins, felt him by her side again at the moment of
Jewel's death, stroking her fingers, salivating over her daughter's
soul.

Falling and sinking, falling and sinking. Through the Earth,
this planet is just the eyeball of a giant, the lake just the blue iris,
sinking through her years, to the date of her birth. Damaged parents
giving her damaged parts. Artist Gramma waiting to carry her along.
Fibroids in her womb, put in by God to stop her from having
damaged children, but the lake washed them away.

"Welcome inside."

The voice came to her, so loud, so direct, and coming from
everywhere: inside her, outside her. She felt and heard the voice in
every atom.

What are you? Who are you?

"I wish to remain nameless. I am the teardrop of this
eyeball. I am the daughter of a creator who weeps for what
was created. I am the morbid, I am the miracle. I made a child,
like you, I bargained for that child, like you. Yet what confuses
me is why did you jump? There was no deal."

Because only a dead body will poison the Well. My body.

"You speak true. If the dead are left to rot, it will poison
this Well, and we could speak from it no more. But I use your

dead parts—they do not rot, they only rise. I *need* your dead parts, to make the new. And that is what I will do. Miracles bloom from morbid soils. You can be with him again, you can be with her again. A sibling to my Mishi. We will all be family."

Sharon's anger was gone. Instead, she felt hollow, tiny, nothing, for she saw through a new lens. An infinite view of the planet, the cosmos. She was but a dead floating cell across the surface of the eyeball of a giant, and that speck could never be lost or gained. It could burn or get wet or fly or fall but could never be lost.

How? How will I be with them?

"At night, you are the Charon of the skiff. By day, you are the mermaid in the seaweed. You will watch over the cribs of the children."

The blood in Sharon's body turned aqua blue, but she kept falling, sinking, falling, sinking. Her organs were being filled with new parts, and she kept falling, sinking. A doll who lost its stuffing, replaced with something magical by its maker. And she kept falling, sinking. Being made anew by this god who swims in the iris of the eyeball, this sea witch who wished to remain nameless, who replaced Sharon's damaged parts as she fell, and sank, and fell.

Or was she rising, ascending?

Rising, ascending. Seeing the joy of faces at art fairs, rising higher, the wrinkles of wisdom on her gramma's face, her weathered hand holding hers, rising and rising. Campfires with Kai surrounded by the laughter of children. Rising higher, swimming with Jewel in these waters, floating in the surface, rising higher, into the orange glow of summer sunsets. Rising higher and higher, until she was on the top and up for air, on to the surface of the water. The stars burned above her, the rich, cold deep waters of Torch Lake under her one leg, her good foot on a skiff.

She was back to the water, but was not the same. Two bloody stumps, but new appendages inside. *Misha, I feel you, I am you. Not good at life, good on a lifeboat, for I* am *the lifeboat,* and somewhere on these cold dark waters that night, the shrill scream of her daughter pierced the black sky. The soul dying, a shooting star. Another scream, louder than the last, her last scream began.

Charon needed to reach her daughter before the scream ended.

Chapter Thirty-Four
<u>Of Lucas Lamia with Jewel in his Net</u>

I HAD HER. With time to spare, I had her.

Flailing in the net, water went splashing a bit and a few drops hit my skin, scorching my flesh into an immediate blister—but nothing compared to how the girl's soul was burning from the inside. The child wailed from the pain, screaming with rage. The lakeside homes could surely see this spectacle if they looked, and could hear it the way sound traveled over water.

The scream started to fade. The flame was nearly out. The oil has gone dry. My curse is almost over. Just take this ship back to shore, drop the requested materials down the Well, and I'd be reborn.

I felt a presence, a ship approaching, the subtle crash of a wake from one boat to another.

A shadow stood tall, it came a bit closer, and then I saw her. A woman standing on a canoe, one arm holding a pole, presumably pushing off the bottom—*but how can that be?* It's too deep.

For a split second, I thought it was my wife, who had become something else since betraying me. But no, she could never fully leave the water.

I held out the torch, and there she was. A bloody mess.

The hideous figure, lit up by the flames like a witch burned at the stake, blood soaking her body. Some dried, some fresh, the stub of an arm, the stub of her leg, caked with blood, but seemingly cauterized. Each stub was twitching and turning in its socket, as if looking for their lost parts, as if they came here for them.

I took a glance to make sure—yes, the limbs were still safely in my boat, tied in the bag, drawstring still tight.

She stood on just one leg. From the stump of her other was a fin, an oar guiding the boat, which seemed not just a boat, but the lake come alive, giving her passage, a mist surrounding it. Closer still, and I could see that the blood caked on her body wasn't red but instead streaks of blue, indigo, and purple—the shimmer of a Torch Lake sunset.

"You hear that scream?" I called out to the mother. The voice of the girl burning within the net, on fire from invisible flames. "Good that you're here, but now what? You refused my help. I offered you what no other Power could. I offered you more than any god."

"You are no God. You are but a slave. A slave, and now you're but a storage vessel. You've brought a legion of lost souls, and the lake wants them back. *We* want her back."

"That chance is gone. Her soul is burning and her ashes will soon be mine, my curse will soon be gone, and you'll regret not..."

I suddenly couldn't talk, couldn't think, for the girl's scream hit a pitch so high out the mouth of that little demon in my net that I thought my ears would bust. I thought the lake would turn to glass, and then the glass would shatter, the stars in the sky would rain down.

But the ashes were soon to be mine and then...

A battle cry belch, a howl from the dismembered mother. She was right up against me then, close enough an oar could reach, her gaze full of madness. Eyes made of diamonds and just as sharp and cutting.

She moved her stump, the shoulder twisting as if an invisible arm was attached and she was ready to strike.

And a limb did appear from where her arm once was.

I heard it snap, felt it in the air, the whip-crack of her newly grown tentacle snapping at me. The same monstrous appendage that rose from the Well 150 years before, rubbery flesh whipping and wrapping around my neck. It tightened immediately. Like a demon, she had grown this tentacle from her amputated stump, or it was granted by the Devil himself.

My larynx crunched, a crackling sound as it choked my neck, shutting off my wind. No more air going in and out, no more words.

What monstrous devil has she become?

With my one free hand I tried to wrench it off of me, but my grip wasn't enough, my hand losing feeling, losing strength. It was no longer mine to command.

No. No.

I dropped the net, I had no choice, and winced at the *splash* when the Jordan girl fell back into the lake.

With both hands I grasped at the tentacle wrapped around my neck. It was all muscle, a writhing snake, tightening by degrees. The more I clawed, the more it squeezed.

Then it lifted me up into the air, first above the boat, then like a crane, the tentacles slid me over the water. My legs dangled and kicked like a man in the gallows.

And like a pig about to be roasted.

For she dipped me inside.

She dipped my feet, my ankles, my calves, up to my knees in the water. My flesh sizzled, a pot of acid melting my skin like wax. My wind was blocked, screams couldn't leave my throat so they stayed in my soul.

Drop me in, drop me in now, but she was torturing me.

The souls I collected, all of them, gathered together like a mob trying to leave a building set for demolition, rushing to escape out of my body into the water.

My last breath gone, my body dying, my soul to be burned and no more — but then the Jordan girl appeared in the water. She was a warped color, a different shade, but a soul alive in the lake. When the mutant mother saw, she unwrapped her grip, and she dove into the lake with a splash.

I was free.

My legs and arms flailed, the water to my chest, my throat broken, my body blistery and black. With one desperate lunge, I grabbed the side of the boat. First one hand, then two, pulling the top half of my body out of the water.

I was going to live! Deformed, cursed, monstrous, my body amputated from the waist down, all except the bones, *and God the pain I need some morphine*, but I might survive, if I could just yank myself on to the boat.

A splash in the water behind me, another arm around my neck, strong, slimy, slippery arms, but human.

"I've got you. It took 150 years, but I told you I would get you. Your God has no place here."

She'd grown strong. She'd become one with these waters, and I was pulled back into the lake of fire by my wife, Lilith.

This time I could scream, a banshee wail that ended when my whole body submerged. I fought to reach the surface again to pull my half-body free, fueled by the urgency of pain, but her hands found the top of my head, pushing me deeper below the surface with all her weight. The lake of flames made a bonfire out of my body, boiling my organs, bone resisting as long as it could until the marrow itself began to melt and the tendons and cartilage all disintegrated. No remains

left.
      The Well did not remove my curse and end my misery; the lake did.
      It was always the lake.

CHAPTER THIRTY-FIVE
OF LILITH LAMIA AND HER SON

LILITH WAS INTIMATELY familiar with its forty miles of shorelines. She swam in each shallow through a century of changing seasons. She'd lived on the bottom during winters when the surface was ice, and during summers nipped at the ankles of those drinking beer and throwing frisbees at the sandbar. For over a hundred years she's been living in these waters, serving the Goddess of the Teardrop, wishing she could leave the lake and hunt down the man whose body held her son captive. She tried to walk out of the water many times, but as soon as her last bit of flesh left the lake, the pain demanded a return to water. Involuntary as an eye blink. She had no choice but to remain.

So she stayed in the lake, waiting all these years for this moment.

She had wrapped her arms around Lamia as if her very essence depended on the grip. She pulled him underwater, his legs getting amputated by the burning of the water before his whole body gave way. As she dunked him under and his body and soul decayed and deteriorated into nothing, the explosion of children who'd been ingested by this vampire were given new life.

None more important than Benjamin.

Last time she saw her son was when he woke from his sickness and opened the front door to greet the morning sun. She'd thought she was punishing her husband when she'd injected the ashes into his veins, sure her son's soul was in Heaven and not in that dust. But instead, she had placed her son in the Hell of his father's heart.

Her son was now reborn from the bitterness of his father's blood to the waters of this lake-blue heaven. After all the hurt and pain, now was the redemption, the eternal glow of love and family. Lilith embraced Benjamin in these waters, feeling whole for once, and they swam together in the cold Torch Lake together. A family of souls, a lake of blue, the iris of the eyeball, the joy in the teardrop.

CHAPTER THIRTY-SIX
OF CHARON AND JEWEL

CHARON DOVE INTO the lake after her child, a different mother than the one before. She could reach her child with her new limbs, she could protect her child with these new parts, and she could send love from her heart without fear. For once, no fear of the lake taking her, because the lake had them both.

Jewel became full when the separated parts of her soul united. The half that was released from Lamia's corpse found its mate, and now the child's soul glowed in the water.

Momma, you're here.

I'm here, and we never need to leave.

Because the lake has so much of us we can never get it all out?

The lake has all of us now, and we will never want out.

They laughed and spun and swam to the surface and dove to the bottom and played tag with the whitefish.

There's a Jewel in the lake, it lives in the depths in the dark of night, but when the sun's flame shines down, the jewel rises to the surface in a brilliant display, dancing and sparkling and twinkling. Sharon was the mother of Jewel, the sister of Mishi, the protector of the children, and the hero in the seaweed.

Chapter Thirty-Seven
Of Kai at the Bottom

THE CHAIN WAS WRAPPED around his legs, and the anchor was lodged into the bottom of the lake. His heart was no longer beating, his blood gone cold. There was nowhere to go, so he clung on to the carcass, trapped in the deep, cold water, and all alone. The ominous beast swam in circles around his corpse, keeping him trapped, playing with its meal.

If he could find a way out, would Mishi even let him? No, the thing meant to devour him, body and soul alike, circling and circling and circling his corpse.

Each circle, Mishi came a touch closer. So close that Kai felt a whisker, a tentacle, saw the details of the elk horns, saw the locks of the majestic mane in the darkness, the fins, the tail, that of a dragon. The beast seemed to constantly mutate, never just one. It defied sense.

Do I scare you?

The words of Mishi came to him, the question unanswered, until she spoke again after one more circle.

Are you frightened?

Another circle of his body, wrapping around Kai the way an anaconda might. Closer and tighter. Closer and tighter.

You tell my story to scare the children, but do not share that I keep a sea of perfect souls.

"My daughter is one. I want to be with her."

I know her. She is here and now whole. I know you. I remember your scent by the fire as I listened to the stories. You are not the first human to be stuck here.

"Will I be stuck in this spot forever?"

That depends. Shall you serve the lake, will you be the lake?

The words Mishi spoke were not heard by his ears, but came into his soul.

Will you serve the lake? Will you be the water?

"I was always the lake, always the water."

But not always the water. Can you be the water?

"I will be the water. I will be nothing else."

Mishi swam away from him then, dashing off, disappearing into the dark, and he was left alone.

What did this mean? Did I answer correctly?

No, it was not the right answer, it was the wrong answer, because then the creature rushed at him, no longer circling, but a straight shot right at him, the long tail propelling the behemoth. The fins guiding it, the mouth opening, a shark's jaw ready to eat the corpse whole and consume his soul with it.

Kai prepared to become one with the beast's belly for eternity, his entire essence trapped in that one moment, staring into the mouth the way those Frenchmen must have, the way Dylan had. So close to Mishi he could smell her, the scent of centuries, the essence of this lake pressed into a diamond, the dead parts from across this planet. One sharp fang ready to slice into his skin.

It ripped into his head and he braced for pain, yet it did not hurt. The sharp fang stabbed into his skull and punctured through the flat of his forehead, but then stopped.

And released. The fang punctured, but the jaw did not close.

He was not eaten whole, and Mishi was gone. She left his corpse with a puncture in his skull, a hole in his head.

Be like water, flow like water.

He was like water, he flowed like water, and he slipped out of his carcass then. His spirit escaped through the puncture in his skull the way a swimmer might wiggle out of a wetsuit.

An explosion of joy followed. He was the water, he was the lake, and the lake was indeed alive, and soon he was moving within the deep waters. No need to see in the darkness—he could feel every drop, and every drop could feel him. He was the blood cell of one larger being–a being full of love and acceptance that wrapped its appendages around his soul. His soul set free in this aquatic universe full of grandeur, no longer burdened by earthly weight, but an enchanted domain full of merfolk and sea sprites, Mishi beasts and playful children.

He ascended from the lake's bottom, away from the center, traveling north along the shoreline to where the campfires summoned the children and songs filled the air. Where the Polar Bear Club jumped in on cold mornings, where Sandy the cook made perfect toast, where Mishi once nipped a boy named Dylan and pulled him under.

And there he saw the two beautiful creatures. His daughter, the perfect soul, and his love, the other half of his own soul. Sharon was in the meeting spot as she promised. She had traveled and traveled and journeyed away like she wanted and returned reborn. Her damaged parts were gone and she was fully equipped for eternity in the lake.

They swam deeper into the waters to live as a family of souls, inside a lake of blue, together forever. The iris of the eyeball, the joy in the teardrop.

Kai was the water in the lake, and Jewel was his sparkle. Sharon was the mermaid in the weeds, and the Charon of the ferry, protecting them all. She offered parents who were believers a ride to the spot on the magical waters to sprinkle their ashes. Where children could rest in the cribs and play under the moonlit waters.

The lake is cold, the truth is deep, and you have to earn the right to hear such secrets, for the lake speaks most honestly to those willing to drown.

Epilogue:

Campfire flames rose into the sky, glowing in the lakeside darkness. The sun had set nearly an hour before, and a faint orange stripe still lined the horizon. The lake itself was quiet and calm as if it, too, wanted to hear the campfire story.

The storyteller, Paxton Transou, lead camp counselor and spiritual sorcerer, carried a crooked stick as he circled the fire. His deep eye sockets were all shadows in the glow of the flame.

"My friends, some think it was named Torch Lake because of its shape, but we know differently. It was from the first humans who lived on this lake for hundreds of years, who summoned the creatures of the lake by holding their torches to the water — water that is full of such riches and beings our mortal minds can barely fathom."

Paxton paused, scanning the crowd of counselors and campers.

"Rather than tell this tale of old, I'd like to pass it on to our newest counselor, who was also a camper here but came back to the lake, the way many do."

Dylan Mattison got up from his seat on the bench and stood by the fire. Paxton handed the staff off to Dylan, and then took a seat to listen. Dylan's voice lacked the confidence of his master's, but it had grown in girth and depth since the first time he sat around this fire, fifteen years before.

"I will tell you the tale of the woman of this lake," said Dylan. "Some call her the Charon of the Skiff and tell of how she patrols these waters during dark nights. Others say she's a hero in the seaweed, protecting the children resting in the wooden cribs beneath the water. These were built by the first humans, the first mothers, and they remain in this lake still. You may doubt me now, but when we show you these very cribs on the lake bottom, you'll believe.

"And please believe me when I say she saved my life, and now she lives in this lake with her family, protecting us, protecting the families, forever in these waters that she has wed to. Please respect the lake. Be quiet at night, for no hero in this lake can stop the larger behemoth who lives below. Some say this creature is the product of a water witch who..."

Dylan told the story of Mishi, and rumors of a sea witch who made her children from dead parts and could snatch up a child in the dark of night. So stay away from the beach at night, and do not make noise.

He told the tale as only one who knows the truths of Torch Lake could

#

The next day, soon after the sun rose, a mile south down Torch Lake Drive and up a hill a quarter mile to the east, a family was working on the new land they purchased. The rotted-out wood of the previous home had been piled high, ready for summer bonfires.

Mom was chainsawing limbs in half—she loved using her power tools and wished she had more chances like this. Dad was wearing big canvas gloves, chopping at tree stumps.

"We're gonna have a big deck where we can look out over the lake and watch the sun set," the dad said as he worked.

They were so excited, and if the contractors worked hard enough through the summer, with Mom and Dad's help, they could move here by October.

"Daddy, there's a well. You see that? A well," said the man's daughter.

"Tiff, just stay away from the chainsaw. That could hurt someone."

Dad wasn't ready to listen, he was huffing and sweating and chopping. Mom was busy too, so Tiffany wandered over to the well on her own. She carried a stick on the way, dragging it on the ground. Up close, the stones were shiny, like gems, and she started walking around them in circles.

If only I had money to make a wish. She reached into her pocket to see, knowing already she'd spent it all buying candy at Butch's, didn't even have a penny left.

No money to throw in, she decided to make the wish anyway, saying it quietly, like a prayer only God could hear. She kept walking in circles, and before she took two more steps, she heard the whisper of a mysterious mother, coming from deep in the earth.

"Wish it again," the voice said.

She stood still, not moving. She took a glance behind her.

Mom and Dad were still busy, still happy.

"Wish it again. Say it out loud. Wish it into the Well. It's okay. Wish it into the Well."

"All of it?" she asked.

"All of it," said the voice.

This was scary. Good scary or bad scary, she wasn't sure, but her heart was pounding after hearing this voice from the ground.

She took another look at her dad, his back hunched over, his bicep bulging from swinging the ax. Her mom swinging that sharp chainsaw that could hurt someone, so stay away.

Tiffany thought for a moment about that one wish she'd been thinking of, a wish she'd had for such a long time but had never told anyone, and probably never would.

This was her chance.

And she wished it into the Well.

The End

<u>About the Author</u>

Mark Matthews is a graduate of the University of Michigan and a licensed professional counselor. He is the author of On the Lips of Children, All Smoke Rises, Milk-Blood, and The Hobgoblin of Little Minds. He is also the editor of (and contributor to) a trio of 'addiction horror' anthologies: Lullabies for Suffering, Orphans of Bliss, and Garden of Fiends. In June of 2021, he was nominated for a Shirley Jackson Award. His newest work, Kali's Web, is coming from Crystal Lake Entertainment in 2025. Reach him at WickedRunPress@Gmail

<u>Acknowledgments</u>

Want to thank my parents for gracing me with all the time spent at Torch Lake. The lake is alive, the lake gives life, and it holds so many family memories. Thank you to all of those who are fighting to Keep Torch Lake Blue. Want to thank Dave Foley of Camp Hayo-Went-Ha for the background on legends of the lake.

For helping me shape this book, I want to thank Danni Vinson, Beth Durham, and Julie Hutchings. For all your support now and through the years, thanks to John FD Taff, Charlene Cochrane, Christa Carmen, Mo Moshaty, Kealan Patrick Burke, Emily Vinci and Becky Spratford. Thank you to Clay McLeod Chapman, Laurel Hightower, Sofia Ajram, Amber Reu, Rai Wilde, T Wood, Austin Gragg, Jason Parent, Paula Beauchamp, Paul Goblirsch.

Thanks to Ben Baldwin for the amazing cover art.

For your work on the Horror Writers Association Mental Health Initiative, thanks to Lauren Daniels, Lee Murray, and Dave Jeffery.

For those I've forgotten to mention, and will remember shortly after this publishes, expect a thanks in private.

And finally, thanks to my family: Lisa, Will, and Jade, for watching me drown under my laptop to write this novel. If you've read this far, I now hope you know what I mean when I say: "yes, most of them die, but it's the happiest ending of any story I've written."

Also from Mark Matthews

ON THE LIPS OF CHILDREN
"A sprint down a path of high adrenaline terror. A must read."
— *Bracken MacLeod, author of Stranded*

MILK-BLOOD
"An urban legend in the making. You will not be disappointed."
— *Bookie-Monster.com*

ALL SMOKE RISES
"Intense, imaginative, and empathic. Matthews is a damn good
writer, and make no mistake, he *will* hurt you."
— *Jack Ketchum, author of The Girl Next Door*

THE HOBGOBLIN OF LITTLE MINDS
"This impeccably well-wrought fable proves what many of us have
known for quite some time: Mark Matthews is the reigning king of
modern psychological horror."
— *Kealan Patrick Burke, author of Sour Candy*

www.ingramcontent.com/pod-product-compliance
Lightning Source LLC
Chambersburg PA
CBHW011037190726
48290CB00011B/2882